To the Brink

To the Brink

FIRST FORCE SERIES

CINDY MCDONALD

ISBN: 0991368061
ISBN 13: 9780991368068
Library of Congress Control Number: 2016912265
McWriter Books, Hookstown, PA

Acknowledgements

There are many people I wish to thank who had a hand in the publishing and pre-publishing process of *To the Brink*. My dear friend and confidant, Linda Taylor, who always reads my manuscripts before they go to my editor—thank you for all of those wonderful "suggestions" of yours—I don't know what I'd do without them! I wish to thank my wonderful publishing manager, good friend, and fellow author, Lauren Carr, for her constant support and insightful editorial reviews of all my books. I'd like to thank my editor, Jolene Paternoster, and the creative genius behind this fabulous cover, Dawne Dominique. Last but certainly never least; I want to thank my husband, Saint Bill, your love and support always takes my breath away—you are my everything.

Cover design: Dawne Dominique/DusktilDawne Designs

Cover Model: Christian James

Cover Photographer: Eric Battershell Photography/

Editorial Review: Lauren Carr

Editor: Jolene Paternoster

TO THE BRINK
FIRST FORCE SERIES

One

Tess McMillan had no doubts that there was a private corner in hell reserved for the likes of Ballard Crafton. As if she were a trapped animal, she crouched in a dark corner of the rented cabin. *Damn him.* She hoped that he was feeling the burn at that very moment.

She'd spent most of her adult life with Ballard. She'd been with him since she was seventeen. He'd been her mentor. He'd been her lover, and for the last five years of his life, she had been his wife. That's right, she had been *his* wife—but he hadn't necessarily been *her* husband. He'd been her husband because of a legal contract, not because of a traditional courtship, an engagement, or sappy wedding vows muttered through tears and a veil. No, theirs had been an arrangement based on possession—on his need to possess, period. Ballard had insisted that she keep her maiden name and pose as his personal assistant so that the women whom he pursued with his good looks and alluring charm would be none the wiser to his marital status.

He was wealthy and powerful and audacious. No bones about it—people feared Ballard Crafton. They did exactly as he told them to do—as did she. However, Tess was more cautious than fearful of him. Oh yes, she'd fallen victim to his temper. She'd learned her lesson the hard way. She'd taken her beating and had used it as a survival mechanism rather than a tool of destruction. He'd paid for the plastic surgery to rebuild what he'd damaged, and she'd licked her wounds and quickly readjusted her view of the man. She'd known what he was about. She'd learned how to work around him. She'd become quite astute at the dance.

But Ballard was dead, and she had to deal with the problems that the man had left behind. Quite frankly, they were problems that she'd let him leave behind. Her bad.

The blue Altima parked outside of the cabin was a rental—it was the third rental in as many weeks. She'd left her Mercedes at the airport to make it look like she'd taken a flight, but instead she'd gone to the rental desk for a Camry. She'd picked up a Dodge Durango in New York City and had exchanged it for the Altima in Lancaster, Pennsylvania.

In the wee hours of the morning, she'd switched license plates with the cozy honeymooning couple in the cabin across the way. They'd pulled out the day before, unaware of the rental tags on their Suburban. As far as anyone knew, she was a camper from Oklahoma.

She'd been hiding out in the state park for two days, staying out of sight, keeping the lights off at night, and vigilantly watching all of the vehicles coming and going from the camp area. She'd had very little sleep. It was pure adrenaline that was keeping her upright.

Hiding in the shadows, she held her breath while she watched the black SUV. It slowly rolled along the narrow gravel road that wound through the cabins nestled beneath the tall, wispy pine trees swaying in the light April breeze. The vehicle's headlights filtered through the thin cotton curtains and washed over her face. Tess dipped farther into the corner, pointing the barrel of the .45-caliber semiautomatic pistol toward the floor.

Yeah, there they were—the two men who'd been dogging her night and day for the past four weeks. She checked her watch. It was three thirty in the morning. The boys weren't getting much sleep either. She was certain that they were August's goons. Augustine Crafton was Ballard's younger brother.

She knew what August wanted.

She knew what he wanted it for.

She knew that most likely, he was capable of atrocious things, like Ballard had been.

And she knew what he would do to her to get what he desired.

She didn't know August personally, but she was pretty damned certain that he was as bad as Ballard when money was involved.

Little more than a year ago, she'd made a vow to herself and to First Force operative Grant Ketchum and his wife, Silja that she would destroy the damned serum that had been created in Ballard's laboratory. The serum, which was known as XM-11, had been designed to turn average soldiers into unstoppable beasts.

The Russian government had funded the program when the United States had had no stomach for testing the serum on human beings, at least not for another several years. Moreover, the Russians had been more than delighted to provide Ballard with test subjects—hardened criminals from their prisons. Poor bastards—there had been more deaths than steps toward progress. Still, the serum had shown promise in some areas, and so the testing had continued until Ballard's laboratory had gone up in smoke, courtesy of the international security team First Force. Tess had finally been set free, and upon returning to the United States, she'd reunited with her parents, whom she hadn't seen in seventeen years.

Tess was a wealthy woman. As Ballard's widow, she'd inherited his estate. She'd bought a beautiful town house near her parents' home in Albany, New York, and she'd thought her life would settle down. And it had—until four weeks ago.

Four weeks ago, she'd had the unnerving feeling that she was being watched—followed. Her home felt curiously violated by noises that she'd never noticed before. Suddenly she was haunted by shadows passing the windows and by rattles and bumps that woke her in the night. A black SUV drove past her house during the day, during the evening, and in the wee hours of the morning. Two large, brooding men hiding behind dark aviator sunglasses occupied the vehicle. It didn't take her long to put two and two together and to come up with August Crafton.

Upon moving into the town house, she built her own security system. She'd been in charge of the security systems in all of Ballard's homes. She was good—damned good. They wouldn't be able to penetrate it. She found herself chuckling at August's hired guns—the schmucks. She'd thought that Mr. Greedy

Moneybags would hire the very best, yet they failed to break in. Nevertheless, she slept with the .45 at her bedside. She slept lightly, but she managed to sleep. Still, she worried. She fretted over whether they would attack her parents, so to protect them, she fled the comfort and security of her lair and led August's hired guns away from Albany.

Tess cursed herself for not keeping her promise. She should have burned the notes that the Russians believed had been destroyed when the laboratory had blown up, killing Ballard. Yet something made her hold on to them and protect them. And she knew that the very thing she was protecting could very well be her undoing.

Why?

What made her hold on?

More importantly, what made August believe that she had the information?

Perhaps she deserved what was happening or what was about to happen.

The vehicle drove slowly past the cabin. Stealthily, she slid to the other side of the window and pinched back the curtain to see if they would continue down the road, turn around, or get out of the vehicle to search the area on foot. She had to get out. It was time to find another place to hide. Actually, it was time to find some help—some serious help. She couldn't keep up this pace for much longer. Exhaustion would take its toll on her soon enough.

Tess pulled a business card from the studded hip pocket of her black-leather jeans. Thoughtfully, she flipped it through her slender fingers. Grant had given her the card. She remembered his saying, "If you ever need help, give us a call." There was no doubt about it. She needed help…desperately.

She was certain that August's thugs had continued down the road—that they hadn't made her. Good. She was packed. She'd never unpacked. She'd known that she might have to leave at a moment's notice and that she might have to leave everything behind. Not that she'd brought that much with her—just one suitcase. Even while on the run, there was simply no excuse for not having personal-hygiene products, hair-care products, cosmetics, and several well-chosen changes of clothes. She'd left her cell phone at home. She was well aware that she could be tracked through it, but she'd brought her iPad along—not that it was doing her much good, as there was no Wi-Fi service in the damned cabin. She'd driven down to the ranger's station earlier that morning, and the ranger on duty had let her use the Wi-Fi to check her e-mail. Afterward she'd left the iPad in the trunk of the car so that she wouldn't have to worry about snatching it up if she had to leave in a rush. It looked like that had been a wise decision.

After setting the safety, Tess laid the .45 on the bed. She twisted her long blond hair on top of her head, pulled on a ball cap, and then grabbed the suitcase. Before opening the door, she stuffed the gun into the waistband of her jeans and scanned the area for the SUV or for any movement nearby.

Satisfied with the quiet surrounding her campsite, she scurried to the car, tossed the suitcase into the trunk, and jumped into the driver's seat. Slowly, so as to not attract any attention, she pulled away from the cabin to drive down the dark, secluded road that led out of the camp and to the main highway. So far, so good—there was no sign of the black SUV.

By her calculations, she was about an hour or so away from the First Force Headquarters in Harverton, Pennsylvania. Her lips curled at the irony. She was seeking out the very black ops group that had been her husband's demise.

Her fingers wrapped more tightly around the steering wheel at the memory of Ballard's obsession with yet another talented woman with flawless beauty, the prima ballerina Silja Ramsay, who had become Silja Ketchum—Grant's wife. If it hadn't been for the quick work of the well-trained First Force, the ballerina would have become Ballard's personal possession—or she would have been maimed beyond function, like the others who'd refused to fall submissive to his every whim, and enslaved indefinitely.

It was quite possible that if it hadn't been for First Force, the Russians would have come into possession of the most powerful, unstoppable military in the world. Ballard and his team of scientists would have perfected the serum, and the Russians would have had their armies poised to conquer anyone they desired to conquer—yes, even the good ole United States of America.

Her thoughts were broken by a pair of headlights flashing in the rearview mirror. Her eyes flicked to the rearview mirror to see how closely they were following her. *Don't panic. They don't know this vehicle.* Then again, they hadn't known the Camry or the Durango, yet they'd found her and almost managed to take her.

She rolled the Altima to a stop at the entrance to the main road. Looking in the mirror, she could see that the headlights did indeed belong to the black SUV that had passed her cabin not twenty minutes before.

Help was an hour or so down the road. She didn't want to set them off and make them chase her, so she pressed lightly on the accelerator and eased onto the

9

two-lane road. She didn't have to check the mirror. Their headlights illuminated the cab of the car. Yep, they were following her. *Steady now.* Tess turned on the radio; it was set to a country music station. Not a fan. She fumbled with the buttons until she found something more to her liking. She was careful to keep the vehicle's speed to approximately five miles per hour over the speed limit. She didn't want to appear panicked or suspicious. She wanted to appear to be just an everyday driver from Oklahoma getting an early start on the long trip home.

The GPS on the dashboard indicated that within a mile or so, she'd have a decision to make: she'd have to get on the interstate or continue down the road she was then driving on. The interstate was a faster, more direct route to Harverton, but she was certain that the surly female voice of the GPS system could, with some complaint, help her muddle her way on the longer, more winding two-lane road. The Altima's headlights shone on a sign announcing that the interstate connection was coming up soon.

"Entrance to the freeway in point five miles," Ms. GPS said.

Tess had to wonder whether not getting on the interstate would be a red flag that would encourage August's patsies to follow her. Then again, if she did get on the interstate and they decided to pass her, would they get a good glimpse at her?

A bell sounded, and then Ms. GPS said, "Take the entrance to the freeway on your right."

There it was, just as the GPS had said—the ramp to the interstate was coming up fast on the right. Tess's eyes flitted to the rearview mirror. The SUV had its turn signal on. It was decision time.

Keeping steady at fifty miles per hour, she rolled past the ramp without hesitation—without so much as a wary brake light—smoothly and easily. Ms. GPS was instantly annoyed. "Recalculating route," she said. Tess couldn't have cared less. The black SUV drove down the ramp and onto the interstate.

What a relief!

But it was short lived—Ms. GPS was quick to point out Tess's error in judgment. "Please make a U-turn at the next opportunity. Freeway entrance will be on your left in point five miles."

Tess patted the screen. "Aw, c'mon, sweetheart. Surely you can find another route to Harverton, because there's no way in hell that I'm getting on that freeway now." She glanced at the clock lighting the dash with a soft blue hue. "Besides, its four fifteen, and I could really use some coffee. I'm pretty sure I saw a service center up the road on the right when I drove through here the other day.

Coffee—high octane. That's what I need. Oh, and maybe one of those sugary honey buns that they sell in the roadside stores. The sugar and caffeine should give me the boost I need."

"Recalculating route."

Tess smiled. "That's what I like—a team player."

*   *   *

Because her assailants were well down the interstate by then, Tess spent a considerable amount of time relaxing in the service center. She visited the ladies' room. She'd really hated the primitive bathroom at the state park. The cabin she'd been held up in for the past few days didn't have a toilet, so she'd used the portable facility. *Gross.*

She took her time, sitting at a table, nursing her coffee, and slowly savoring the honey bun she'd purchased while she checked her e-mail on her iPad. Her mom had sent a note to let her know that all was well and that they'd been collecting her mail and keeping an eye on the town house. She clicked on the popular social network Facebook. Of course, none of the operatives from First Force had a page, but she'd discovered that Silja Ketchum had a page for her dance academy in Harverton. It was a charming little school in the quaint little town, and it looked like the school was doing very well—like there were more and more students with each passing month.

Her page featured lots of photos of little girls wearing brightly colored tutus and doing arabesques and older teens in black leotards and pink tights standing at the ballet barre. However, the photo that interested Tess was the one of Silja and her husband, Grant, at their wedding. Most likely, the handsome operative was unaware that his bride had posted the picture. If he'd known, he probably would have made her remove it, but he hadn't—yet. Tess took advantage of Mrs. Ketchum's poor judgment. She copied and pasted the photo to her documents. With a press of a button, Tess moved on to Google Maps to check out the aerial view of the vicinity that she was traveling to. It was surprisingly rural.

By five thirty, a steady stream of people were wandering in and out of the shop, buying coffee on their way to work or putting gas in their vehicles, which she too needed to do before starting out toward Harverton.

After sitting for almost an hour, she decided that it was time to be on her way. She felt comfortable taking the interstate. She knew that at that point, August's goons would be far ahead of her. She put gas in the Altima and then pulled out of the lot.

Ms. GPS said, "Entrance to the freeway on the left in point five miles."

Yes, ma'am. Tess wasn't about to disobey her orders and then have to listen to her irritated tone instructing her to turn around or saying that she had to "recalculate the route." *The little obsessive-compulsive robot-bitch.*

She let the window down just a bit to fill the car with fresh spring air. She felt the need to steady her frayed nerves as she steered the car onto the ramp that led onto the interstate. She checked her side mirrors for oncoming traffic, and then as she was getting ready to merge onto the road, she saw the black SUV pulling onto the interstate right behind her.

Shit!

Shit!

Shit!

They were back! Her stomach clenched. Her head felt instantly hot under the cap. She tugged it off and tossed it onto the backseat. Well, she had to give it to the boys—if nothing else, they were damned good at tracking her. Somehow they'd realized that she had indeed been at the state park, and somehow they'd realized that she'd circled around. It didn't really matter what they'd realized or how they'd come to their conclusions; they were on her tail, and she had to lose them!

Tess jammed the accelerator down hard, pushing the car to eighty miles per hour as she steered in and out of traffic. The boys were more than happy to pursue her. While she maneuvered through the vehicles quickly, she tried to manage her speed and the vehicle as safely as possible. She didn't want to kill anyone—she just wanted to escape. As for August's henchmen, they had their eyes on the prize and had an attitude of "to hell with the safety of others."

"You are traveling ten miles over the speed limit," Ms. GPS said, scolding her.

Tess wasn't listening. She was busy keeping one eye on the road and the other on the rearview mirror and the black SUV that had just sideswiped a red car. Its brakes screaming, the car swerved off to the side of the road. The other cars driving down the interstate began to slow down and change lanes to get out of the path of the SUV.

"Exit on the right in one mile," Ms. GPS said.

The beads of sweat that had formed on Tess's brow were then dripping in streams down her temples. She had hit eighty-five miles per hour while still managing to weave through the cars without hitting anyone.

How, she simply didn't know. It had to have been dumb luck.

"Exit on the right in point five miles," Ms. GPS calmly said.

How could she be so calm? Tess knew damned well that the GPS system was aware of her ridiculous speed. She whizzed right past the exit.

"Recalculating route."

Tess could sense the eye roll that was surely taking place inside that blasted computer. The SUV had just closely passed yet another poor sap and was then in her lane, about three car lengths behind her. Panicked drivers were abandoning the road, pulling off to the side, driving into the grassy center median, and whipping up ramps that they hadn't necessarily intended to use. And then the sound of sirens filled the morning air. Red, blue, and white lights raced down the interstate behind them. One of the drivers must've dialed 9-1-1—most likely the one who'd been sideswiped. One police cruiser pulled alongside the SUV, and one pulled behind it, signaling for the driver to pull over.

Tess immediately slowed the Altima down—first to eighty miles per hour and then to seventy-five, sixty, and fifty-five until she thankfully rolled to a stop on the side of the road under an overpass. In her rearview, she could see two police cruisers pulling up alongside the stopped SUV. Officers jumped out, their guns drawn, and demanded that the boys keep their hands up and exit the vehicle as they approached.

Relieved, exhausted, and mostly terrified, Tess laid her head on the steering wheel, trying to catch her breath as she waited to be arrested.

Well, at least she'd be safe in a jail cell.

She'd have time to rest and to figure out her next step while in the jail cell.

The only women in jail cells were either hookers or women who'd attempted to murder their husbands.

Yeah, she could find solace enough to sleep among that crowd.

"Are you all right, ma'am?" an officer asked through her partially open window.

Tess jerked her head up. Was she all right? Did he just ask her if she was all right? She couldn't believe it! But she knew one thing for certain: of course she wasn't all right! Those men had been chasing her, and no, that wasn't a lie. Indeed, they had been chasing her. How could they possibly deny it? What could they possibly say in their defense—other than that she had in her possession a serum that could turn an average man into RoboCop?

Really?

Wouldn't the officers have a good laugh at that one? Even if the police decided to search her personal effects for such a ridiculous item or for anything that could be considered suspicious, they'd never find it. Oh no, she was as stealthy as her deity, James Bond. The flash drive that held the serum was safely hidden—007 would have been proud of the gadgets that she'd employed.

She didn't have to fake the shaking of her hands. Her hands really were shaking as she skimmed them through her long blond mane, brushing the errant strands away from her flushed face. She finally let out the breath that she'd been holding since the car chase had started.

After swallowing hard, she managed to say, "Yes, Officer. I'm all right…now. They were following me and have been following me for several hours. I don't know who they are or what they want." She cupped her hand over her mouth. "I was terrified that they wanted to get me somewhere secluded and…and—"

"It's okay, ma'am. You're safe now. That might have very well been their intention. Are you willing to file charges?" the officer asked

Wow! How lucky could she get? She'd file charges, and they'd be detained long enough for her to get away—perhaps all the way to Harverton. August would have bail money, of course, but that would take hours. The wheels of justice turn ever so slowly, and in this case, that would be to her favor. She had to fight the smile that threatened to surface on her lips.

"I certainly am," Tess said. "Women should be safe to drive along the road without a bunch of thugs harassing them. I won't have to be in the same room as them, will I?"

"Absolutely not, Ms.—"

"Tessa Lee McMillan." She rummaged through her red-leather Gucci handbag for her driver's license. Handing it through the window, she said, "I'm so thankful that you came along when you did. Who knows what could've happened. They sideswiped that poor man in the red car several miles back."

"Yes, Ms. McMillan, he's the one who called us."

"I hope he's okay."

"He seems to be fine," the officer said.

Ms. GPS said, "Recalculating route."

Two

"Woo-hoo!" Lil Haliday danced through the foyer of the grand Georgian mansion. The early-morning sunshine glistened through the beveled glass window encased in the heavy mahogany door, sending a rainbow of prisms over the marble floor and around the tall Chinese palace vases situated around the perimeter of the foyer. Lil loved the foyer on sunny mornings filled with bright light sweeping over the walls, the floor, and the ceiling, which was so high above her head that it seemed to almost reach the heavens. This sunny morning was special.

She stopped to take note of the pile of luggage stacked beside the door. She slipped the Cinderella backpack from her shoulders and added it to the mound. She couldn't believe it. This was the day. They were leaving for Disney World in Orlando, Florida!

It had been such a wonderful year—her fifth year. She'd gone to kindergarten. Dr. Rayne Lee and her daddy, Jack Haliday, had gotten married, which had made Dr. Rayne Mommy Rayne. That made Lil so very happy, but the best part was that Mommy Rayne was expecting a baby boy in July.

Joy filled her heart. She danced and twirled among the thousands of glimmering, shimmering prisms, watching them wash over her white eyelet sundress as she moved, her curls bouncing about her head. Soon she found that she wasn't alone. Patrizia came in from the kitchen to join in the rejoicing.

Pat had been part of Lil's wonderful year. Her mother, Bibiana Vasquez, whom Lil had dubbed "Bebe," and Pat had come from Peru to live at the First Force Headquarters along with Lil's family. Bebe and Pat lived in the apartment over the garage across the driveway.

Mommy Rayne had hired Bebe as a housekeeper and a medical assistant. Mommy Rayne, or Doc Haliday, as the team called her, was the head medic for First Force. With the baby coming, she needed help with the upkeep of the mansion and with the medical emergencies of her clients and the members of First Force, Uncle Walt's international security firm made up of former military special operatives. First Force rescued people in trouble and worked off the grid for the government from time to time as well.

Since moving into the Georgian mansion, the First Force Headquarters, Pat and Lil had grown very close—they were like sisters, and yes, their relationship included bickering. Fortunately, the squabbling was short lived. Bebe or Rayne would intervene by placing one girl in time-out in one part of the house while the other would serve time in another. The length of the time-out would depend on how loud the quarrel had been, but they would quickly make up and play again. Pat was three years Lil's senior. That didn't seem to affect the friendship. Pat was just as happy as Lil was to have a playmate.

And they were going to Disney World! Yippee! They would finally get to meet all of their favorite Disney characters. Lil couldn't wait to meet Cinderella and Sleeping Beauty. Oh, and Tinker Bell, too. Pat was more interested in Elsa and Anna, and she wouldn't have minded meeting Kristoff if the opportunity presented itself. Round and round the foyer they danced, doused in luminous prisms and the anticipation of a whole week in the magical kingdom of Disney.

Former US Navy SEAL Jack Haliday and ex-marine Grant Ketchum came into the foyer to gather the luggage so that they could pack it into the vehicles. It was almost time to leave for the airport.

"They're not too wound up," Jack said to his pregnant wife, who was in the kitchen, as he and Grant began juggling the luggage.

Grant and his wife, Silja, had decided to join the group going to Orlando, as they hadn't had an opportunity to go on a proper honeymoon. Although they'd been married for almost a year, they thought a trip to the Sunshine State might be a good chance to get some much-needed time away and time together. Despite Lil's and Pat's cajoling, they were skipping the Disney portion of the trip and heading straight for sun and sandy beaches.

"We'll catch up with you for dinner and evening activities," Silja had promised the girls. "Isn't that right, Grant?"

"I guess…if we're not too *busy*," he'd said with a quick pump of his brows. Silja had jabbed him good in the rib with her elbow.

"Busy doing what?" Lil asked.

"Um, looking for seashells," Grant said, lying.

"That sounds like fun! I hope you find a starfish," Lil said.

"Me too," Grant said, lying again. Silja tossed him a withering smile.

The trip was set, and against Walt Wabash's own rules and possibly his better judgment, a good chunk of team First Force was leaving town on vacation: Jack Haliday; Dr. Rayne Haliday; Grant Ketchum; and the head of the company, Walt Wabash himself. Bebe Vasquez and Lil's grandmother, Dale Thomas, were also traveling to Orlando.

"I think this'll be a better, more secure system than the iris-recognition program we currently have in place at the entrance of the headquarters," Clark Rhodes said to Walt as they made their way out of Walt's office after one last briefing before he left town.

Clark, an ex-FBI agent, was First Force's computer guru. He looked over all of the security systems, organized the team's missions, and then watched over the missions while they were in play.

"I agree," Walt said. "Let's have it installed."

"Dan wants to upgrade his system at his ranch, too. I'll order both systems this afternoon. It'll probably be a week or so before they install ours, which will be a good thing—I wouldn't want you all to come home from vacation and not be able to get through the gate," Clark said, laughing.

"That's for sure. It's bad enough that I'll be struggling to not worry about what's going on while I'm away," Walt said.

"Don't worry about anything, Walt," Dan Garrison, a former US marshal, said to his boss as he came up behind the pair on his way into the foyer to help with the luggage. "There're five First Force operatives within an hour of headquarters. If anything comes up, we'll be able to handle it. We've got it all worked out. We'll each take a couple of days to man headquarters. I'm taking the first shift. I'll be here all day today and tomorrow. Little is always in and out anyway, tinkering with the helicopter or mowing or working on something, so someone will always be around."

"Yeah, Clark told me the plan, and you guys are the best there is," Walt said. "I just haven't been on vacation in fifteen years or so. When you work for the CIA, vacation isn't something you get a lot of. I guess I'm just not comfortable with the idea of relaxing."

Dan snorted. "I'm not getting the impression that there'll be a whole lotta relaxing happening on this vacation. They did tell you that you're going to Disney World, *right*?"

Shaking his head, Walt chuckled at the foolish notion that he would be taking it easy. He'd retired from the CIA some years ago to start First Force. There hadn't been much relaxing going on in his life since. He'd thought that on this vacation, there'd be time for lounging around a pool and sipping margaritas with Dale. *Well, so much for that.*

"Are you sure Greta won't be too much trouble?" Silja asked as she made her way from the kitchen and cuddled her calico cat in her arms.

"C'mon, how much trouble could two cats be?" Dan asked, knowing that the team was responsible not only for manning headquarters and handling any mission that cropped up but also—and more importantly—for taking care of Lil's kitten, Tickles, and Silja's cat, Greta, too.

"You'd be amazed. Everything you need for the cats is in the pantry off of the kitchen," Rayne said while handing him the kitty-litter scoop on her way toward the door. Tall and slender and radiant in her pregnancy, she'd only put on about ten pounds in the past six months. She wasn't wearing maternity clothes as of yet. Still, a baby bump was starting to poke out a bit.

After giving Greta one last loving squeeze, Silja tucked the cat into Dan's arms. He let out a sneeze. A tear escaped from his right eye and dripped down his cheek. "God bless you!" she said, resting a hand on his arm. "I hope you're not allergic to cats."

"I...I...don't...th—*achoo*! *Achoo*! Think so!"

After setting Greta and the scoop on the floor, Dan grabbed for a tissue from the box on a nearby decorative table. He wiped his nose, fetched another, and wiped his suddenly watering eyes. Taking in a cleansing breath, he said, "I never was before—that I know of, anyway."

"There are some antihistamines in the supply room in the medical unit," Rayne said to him from the doorway. "They're on the third shelf of the first shelving unit. That's where I keep all the over-the-counter meds. You'll find ibuprofen, acetaminophen, naproxen, basic aspirin, cough syrups, muscle creams, and sore throat spray too."

"*Achoo*! I'm good. *Achoo*!" He grabbed another handful of tissues from the box.

"Of course you are. All badass operatives can manage anything without meds," Rayne mumbled to herself as she stepped away from the door. She joined Lil and Pat, who were then clambering into the second SUV of the two lined up in the driveway, ready to haul everyone and their stuff to the airport.

Tossing him an apologetic wave, Silja followed the doc out the door to supervise the loading of the luggage. Dale, Bebe, and Stewart Little, the team's pilot, were already gathered around the second vehicle, handing off suitcases and carry-on bags to Jack. Jack was lifting them up and handing them to Grant, who was stacking them as tightly as possible.

"We're gonna take up most of the cargo space on the plane. The other passengers are gonna have to leave their stuff behind," Grant said. "You ladies sure don't pack light. Sil, all you need is a carry-on bag with some skimpy bikinis and some skimpier negligees."

Her eyes became wide with embarrassment, and her face turned bright red.

"She's gonna kill you one of these days, dude," Jack said.

"Nah, she *loves* me too much," Grant said. At that, Silja crinkled her face and pointed a warning finger at him. He tossed her an ornery grin. Jack shoved another suitcase into his chest.

Finally the luggage had been stuffed into the cargo areas of the two SUVs. Walt, Dale, Bebe, Silja, and Grant would travel in the first vehicle, and Jack and Rayne would follow with the girls in the second.

"We'd better get moving," Jack said. "We've got a lot of people to get through security."

"Hold up a minute," Stewart Little said. He opened the back door of Jack's SUV to hand each of the girls several gift cards. "Here ya go…some Disney Dollars to spend. Have a good time, and for God's sake, don't get lost. I don't want the team to have to fly down to Orlando to find your sorry butts." He sounded more like a grizzly bear roaring than a man bearing gifts.

"Thank you, Little Big Man," Lil said before squealing in delight. "Little Big Man" was the name

Lil had given the big team member, whose last name was Little. He was as cantankerous as thunder snow in January, yet somehow those little girls were able to look beyond the harshness that inhabited his core and to find the love that he kept so well hidden.

"Gracias," Pat said with a smile on her lips and in her voice.

Each girl gave him a kiss on his cheek. He scolded them. "Now quit fussin'. They're just some lousy gift cards. Put your seat belts on—Haliday's drivin'," he said as he closed the door and moved to walk away.

Rolling his eyes, Jack said, "Is it just me, or is he getting harder to love?"

"This was very kind, Señor Little," Bebe said as he passed her on his way to his pickup, which was parked behind the SUVs.

"It was nothin'. Have a good time," the man of few words said while holding the door to the vehicle open for her and helping her inside. And then with his head bowed and his eyes focused on his feet, he hurried away. Rayne and Silja exchanged knowing grins before slipping into their assigned vehicles. They were amused by the flush washing over Little's cheeks.

Walt slid in behind the steering wheel of the vehicle. Checking her watch, Dale said, "Believe it or not, we're right on schedule. By the time we get to the airport, we'll have a little more than two hours to park, check the luggage, and get through security, which is the recommended amount of time." She let go of a sigh of relief as she sat back against the seat, closing her eyes. Around a smile, she added, "So we're good to go."

Walt glanced at the attractive middle-aged brunette in the passenger's seat and then over his shoulder at the cab of his SUV and the one behind it. In the two vehicles, there were nine passengers. He had no clue how many suitcases. Two hours? He wasn't so sure. He was thinking they might need three or four.

Turning back, he pushed the gearshift into drive and said, "Forward ho!" And then the vehicle rolled toward the wrought-iron gate that guarded First Force Headquarters, and the gate slowly opened.

* * *

Holding the cluster of tissues to his nose, Dan waved good-bye to the vacationers and watched Little and Clark follow them out of the estate in their vehicles. He was then alone in the mansion. Well, not really—when he turned he found Tickles and Greta sitting in the middle of the foyer and staring up at him. They were his responsibility for two days. How hard could that be? His eyes flicked to the scoop he'd abandoned on the floor. Okay…There was no time like the present to find out what would be involved in their care. Hey, he lived on a ranch. He had cats—barn cats he didn't have to clean up after. They did their business wherever. It seemed to him that that was a way better arrangement.

As he made his way across the foyer toward the kitchen, he became overly aware of the echoes of his footsteps through the large, empty space. Funny—he'd never noticed the sound before. Then again, he'd never been alone in the mansion before. The enormous house probably made a lot of noises—creaks and bumps and shifting sounds. Old houses were like that. Jack and Rayne probably didn't notice the sounds either—not with all of the racket that Lil and Pat made.

He was about to cross the threshold into the kitchen when *achoo*! He sniffed and wheezed and turned to find the cats right on his heels, gazing up at him. Geez, were they going to following him everywhere he went?

After all of that sneezing and wheezing, he went straight to the sink to wash his hands in hot water. He spied a dish towel hanging on the stove's handle. How long had it been hanging there? Had it been used to dry anything, or was it fresh? He went through the drawers until he found the one that held the clean dish towels and opted for one of those.

Quickly, he grabbed the pile of tissues he'd laid on the counter. *Achoo*! *Grr*. He washed his hands again and took another fresh towel from the drawer.

He looked down. There they were—the cats were staring up at him. Was it feeding time? Or was that what it was like to have house cats—constant surveillance? After tossing the tissues into the kitchen bin, he grabbed more from yet another box on the counter. It seemed that Doc Haliday kept a lot of tissue boxes about—maybe it was just part of being a doctor— which was turning out to be a good thing for him at the moment.

Okay, like it or not, it was time to check out the kitty-litter thing. Doc had said that everything was in the pantry off of the kitchen. The cats followed him through the open doorway and into a small room with white cabinetry, a washer, a dryer, an ironing board, a laundry tub, and the litter box, which was stationed in the far corner of the room next to the door that led outside. A colorful cloth tube filled with plastic bags hung on the doorknob.

Armed with the scoop in his right hand, he pulled a bag from the tube with his left.

He was ready.

How bad could it be?

There was no odor.

He lifted the lid.

His upper lip curled with derision. Holding his breath, he scooped out the cat dung and dumped it into a plastic bag. Swiftly, he replaced the lid, yanked the door open, and pitched the bag into a flip-top trash bin on the stoop outside the door. After slamming the door closed, he rushed across the pantry, dancing around and over the cats, and to the kitchen sink to wash his hands.

Achoo!

Achoo!

Achoo!

"Where are those damned antihistamines?" His hands all soapy under the hot water, he looked down. There they were, Tickles and Greta, gawking at him once again. "Don't you have some mice to kill or something? Go away! Shoo!" He stomped his foot on the floor. They were unaffected by his antics. Greta lifted a paw and bathed it with her tongue, and Tickles's tail slowly snaked its way around her legs. The fluffy tabby was perfectly happy to sit and watch him wheeze and water and swell up.

On his way to the stairs that led down to the medical unit and the gym, he paused at the gilded oval mirror perched above the claw-foot table in the foyer. There was a smudge on the glass, so he took one of the clean tissues and wiped it away. That's when he noticed his red, puffy eyes. They were swollen and watery, and his nose was red and runny. Shit, maybe he was allergic to cats—at least in close quarters. His cats were out in the fresh air or in the barn. Perhaps his allergy wasn't severe enough for them to affect him out in the open, but in a closed-up house—*bam*!

Doc had been right. He would need some antihistamines if he was going to survive the rest of the day and return to the mansion bright and early the next morning. Sniffling, he opened the door to go downstairs and realized that he was being followed. He turned, and with his foot, he blocked the felines entrance to the stairs.

"No way! You stay up here. I bet Doc doesn't allow you down there anyway, ya little stalkers," he said, closing the door behind him and turning on the light that woke up the medical unit's hallway.

He breathed in the cool, clean, no-cats-allowed air as he descended the stairs. Again the echo of his footsteps through the wide white corridor seemed more intrusive than he remembered. He passed the dark gym, which was outfitted with the latest machines, weights, and so on. Farther down and off to the left was the door that led to a small but well-equipped surgery and then to the three patient rooms, which were always at the ready. A gurney with crisp, clean white sheets covered with a slip of plastic to keep them pristine sat along the wall near the wide doorway at the end of the unit. Finally he reached the supply room door just before where the gurney was parked.

Doc kept her supply room immaculate. There was a place for everything—and everything was most certainly in its place. Just as she had told him he would, he found the over-the-counter medications on the third shelf of the first shelving unit. He had to marvel at her perfect setup. All of the bottles were facing out, and the labels were easy to read—she was a woman after his own heart.

He grabbed the antihistamines, opened the packet, fumbled with the foil until he managed to retrieve two pink tablets from it, and then downed them before replacing the package with its front label forward, as he'd found it on the shelf.

Wiping his eyes, he sank into a chair situated right inside the door and leaned his head back against the wall. The coolness of the basement's wall felt good on his swollen face. He had to wonder whether the medicine would be enough. Perhaps he should trap the cats in a totally different section of the house, away from where he'd be hanging out. He'd have to move the litter box, too. Not a pleasant thought but maybe a very necessary action.

It was amazing. He could breathe in this space. Maybe it was the cool air, or maybe it was the cleanliness of the air—and the fact that there weren't any cats. It couldn't have been the antihistamines. He'd only taken them moments ago—they certainly didn't work that fast. Feeling a little better, he decided to remain in the supply room for a little while, at least until the meds took hold.

He closed his watery, swollen eyes, letting the cool, damp air woo him into a relaxed, calm state.

Three

Whoever said it must've had to file charges at some point in their life. The wheels of justice really do turn slowly—miserably slowly. Tess spent three hours in the police station filing those damned charges against August's hoodlums. At least then she knew who the hoodlums were: one was Leo Talbot, and the police told her that the other was a Russian man named Vlad Guseva.

The names meant nothing to her. They were not names that Ballard had ever mentioned. Most likely he hadn't known Talbot—he was probably part of August's security. It was the Russian man who concerned her. What was his connection to Ballard? Of course, it must have had something to do with the serum, but she was well acquainted with everyone who had anything to do with the project: the scientists who worked in the lab, the engineers, and the office personnel employed by Crafton Laboratories in the United States and in

Russia. As Ballard's personal assistant, she'd dined with or sat in on meetings with every political figure who had anything to do with the project.

Vlad Guseva.

Vlad Guseva.

She searched and searched her mind for any recollection of the name.

Nothing.

Who was Vlad Guseva?

Had the Russian government teamed up with August to hunt her down?

The questions made her stomach coil into tight knots.

Indeed, the police did some checking on Tessa Lee McMillan. They were curious as to why the tags on her car didn't match up with the Altima. Rather, the tags were registered to a Suburban owned by John Cullins from Tulsa, Oklahoma, whom they were unable to contact.

Tess couldn't have been more baffled. The Altima was a rental. She'd paid no attention to the tags when she'd picked it up in Lancaster. Goodness, how could Oklahoma tags possibly have appeared on her rental car? She was a bewildered blonde—for appearances, anyway.

The police officer felt sorry for her after the ordeal she'd been through on the interstate. They found no drugs in her vehicle. She hadn't been drinking and driving. Yes, they did find the iPad, but they had no probable cause to search its files. After all, she was a victim.

The subject of the mysterious tags was dropped. Tess was awarded her personal effects and the Altima, which was sporting the new temporary tags that the rental company had faxed to the police. At last she was sent on her merry way.

Before she walked out the door, the officer said, "Those two will be sitting in that cell until Monday morning. With today being Good Friday, the judges are off, and the courts will be closed until Monday."

Yep, the wheels of justice do turn slowly—especially when there's a holiday involved.

The moment her derriere hit the driver's seat, she opened her purse to make sure that the flash drive that held the notes for the serum was safe. She pulled the faux tube of Hollywood-red lipstick from her cosmetic bag and rolled the lipstick up and up and up until the flash drive surfaced.

She let out a sigh of relief. She considered the lipstick tube a brilliant decoy, yet it wasn't exactly an original idea. Still, the police had taken it for what she'd intended them to take it as: a tube of Hollywood-red lipstick.

With Talbot and Guseva safely stewing in a holding cell, waiting to be arraigned the next week, Tess was back on track to Harverton, Pennsylvania, to seek out Grant Ketchum and his team, First Force. She planned to stop somewhere along the way to trade the Altima for something else. Talbot and Guseva had seen the Altima. It was time for a new ride.

"Turn left onto route eight. Entrance to the interstate will be on your right in one point five miles," Ms. GPS said.

"Okay…on to the first Walmart along the way," Tess said, sighing.

*   *   *

Saliva dribbled out of the side of Dan's mouth. With a sudden snort, he woke up and jerked away from the wall, almost falling from his chair. His eyes snapped around the room wildly, trying to come to grips with his current location. *The supply room.* As he remembered where he was, he sank back into the chair and wiped his chin with his wrist. He'd taken those antihistamines—he glanced at his watch—four hours ago! Holy hell! He'd been sleeping for four hours!

Try as he might, he simply couldn't rush to a standing position. His head was fuzzy with cobwebs from the meds and, most likely, from the effects of his allergic reaction to the cats. Holding on to the wall, he slowly made his way out of the room and into the brightly lit corridor.

Wonder where the little fur balls went, he thought as he made his way toward the stairs that led to the main floor. His hand scrubbed the small of his back. He wanted to make sure that the handgun he usually kept stuffed in the waistband of his jeans hadn't fallen to the floor during his unscheduled nap. His fingers brushed over the handle.

Yep—still there.

As he turned off the lights in the medical unit before climbing the stairs, he found himself wondering what it would be like to have a job that didn't require carrying a piece at all times. Actually, his job didn't require carrying something, but when you've been a US marshal and then an operative for a high-security firm, a gun is almost like an arm or a leg—ya just don't go anywhere without it. You don't go anywhere without your old friend paranoia either. Oh yeah, he's a regular guest at your dinner table, and he's with you when you're watching TV and even when you're in your bed.

Guns and paranoia—what would life be like without his two constant companions? He was almost certain that he would never know.

Then at the top of the stairs, he brushed his fingers over his short military-style haircut. The cobwebs were beginning to fade, yet he knew that the cats were somewhere on the other side of the door that he was about to open. With his luck, the little sadists were probably sitting right beyond the door, waiting for him.

He flicked off the lights for the staircase and turned the doorknob, and when he stepped onto the main floor of the mansion, he was taken aback. His jaw tightened. The cobwebs instantly cleared. Quickly and agilely, he yanked the gun from his waistband and trained it on a beautiful blond woman standing just beyond the door.

Her hands went up. Her blue eyes widened. "I'm… I'm looking for Grant Ketchum," she said.

"He's not here. How did you get in here?" Dan asked, keeping the gun level with her chest.

"You have an iris-recognition security system. That's so yesterday. It's very easy to breach. I'm Tess McMillan, and you would be?"

"What do you want with Grant?" Dan's tone was concise; his gun, steady.

"I need help. Grant told me that if I ever needed help, I could come to First Force."

"Did he say that you could breach the security system? Who's with you?"

"I'm alone. I assure you that no one is here but me." Her eyes rotated to the floor. "And those cats."

Damn!

Sheer terror made him look to his right. No bad guy he'd ever faced had made him feel as helpless and as vulnerable as those freakin' felines did! And there they were, padding across the marble until they came to Dan's legs. Purring as smoothly as a sports car, they circled and caressed his legs with their furry little bodies as if to say, "There you are, Dan. We've missed you. Can we make you feel any more miserable?"

Taking in the man's watering eyes and red nose, the blonde asked, "Are you okay?" Slowly, she lowered her arms to plant her hands on her hips. "Since you won't tell me your name, I think I'll just call you Grumpy."

"What time is it?" Dan wondered out loud.

"Time for some antihistamines would be my guess," Tess said.

"Been there, done that bullshit," Dan said.

He couldn't believe how fast the effect of a cat allergy could take complete control of him. His eyes began to water. He could feel his face swelling.

Achoo!

Achoo!

Achoo!

Tess ducked, worried that he would pull the trigger by accident while sneezing and wheezing. When he finally stopped and grabbed some tissues from the box on a nearby table, she relaxed a bit.

"I take that back. Maybe I should call you Sneezy."

Dan stuffed the gun back into his waistband, relieved that he hadn't turned the safety off—he could have shot her. Wiping his nose, he said, "Never mind what you should call me. What kind of trouble are you in that you need First Force? I thought we took care of Ballard Crafton's problems a year ago."

"So you know who I am?"

"I remember your name. If I remember correctly—*achoo*!" He stumbled to the side, almost falling over Greta. *Achoo*! The calico tossed him an angry glance but held her spot without wavering. Blinking his watering eyes and sniffling, he continued. "You were Crafton's wife slash personal assistant. You were mixed up in that hot mess with Crafton's lab in Russia. Is that...is that...wh—*achoo*! *Achoo*! *Achoo*!"

"Is that what this is about? It's related to *that* hot mess, yes," she said. "Look, Sneezy, it's obvious that you're struggling with the cats' presence. Is there somewhere else we could talk?"

Dan dived for the basement door. Yanking it open with a *whoosh*, he said, "You read my mind. Down… st—*achoo*! Don't—*achoo*! Let—*achoo*! *Achoo*—"

"Don't let the cats downstairs? Gotcha," she said, slipping past Dan and down the stairs.

Dan followed her, slamming the door behind them. He flicked on the light so that neither would take a tumble down the stairs—and to make sure that they wouldn't be followed by those hairy little allergens.

The cool air instantly felt good on his burning face. He needed more antihistamines, but he didn't want to be in a blurred state or unconscious, for that matter. This was Ballard Crafton's woman, and although he'd been involved in the rescue operation of Grant's wife, Silja, from Crafton's subjugation, he hadn't had any direct contact with the man or with this woman. He was well aware of what Crafton had been capable of. He knew that Crafton had been working on some kind of serum that turned men into machines, but the serum had been destroyed—right?

So what was it that Tess McMillan was capable of?

What did she want from Grant or from First Force?

There was no doubt in his mind that it had something to do with Crafton and his former operations in Russia, but what?

When they reached the lower level, he turned on the lights to illuminate the medical unit. Wiping his nose, he leaned against the wall. "Gimme a minute."

"Sure." Tess wandered along the corridor, peeking into the rooms. She opened the door that led to the small surgery. Her brows rose. "Your operation seems to have it all, including a well-equipped medical unit." She opened the door to the gym. "Oh, and a very impressive gym, too. Not bad, Sneezy."

"But not a foolproof security system, evident— *achoo*! Ugh!"

Tess snorted. "Don't be too hard on your program. I'm an expert in security systems, and I know how to get around just about every one of them. The iris-recognition program is one of my favorites to breach—it's kind of fun. It's almost like doing a little craft—not that I'm into that sort of thing."

Dan sank into the bench positioned against the wall across from the surgery. Rubbing his itchy eyes, he asked, "What's that supposed to mean?"

Smiling, she sat at the other end of the bench, dug through her purse for a handful of tissues, and then tucked the purse next to her. Looking at her askance, he accepted her tissues, which were almost like a peace offering. "I came across Silja's dance academy's page on Facebook. She had a picture of her and Grant at their wedding on it. She looked gorgeous. Her gown was absolutely perfect for her shape and complexion—"

"Anyway—"

She cleared her throat. "*Anyway*, the photo was a professional shot done by a very good photographer, so it was high quality and had many pixels—very high quality. I copied it to my documents, and then on the way here, I stopped at a Walmart and had the photo enlarged so that I would have a good replica of Grant's irises. I cut his eyes from the photo with a scalpel, carefully attached them to marbles, and voilà! I held them up to the scanner in front of my eyes, the gate swung open, and here I am."

As Dan tried to concentrate on her explanation, his smoldering eyes narrowed. She continued. "Rather new yet simple hacking techniques are busting through security systems. For example, many high-profile celebs are having problems with their fingerprints being lifted from photographs, which makes it easy to breach many fingerprint-security programs. Celebs are being encouraged to do less waving on the red carpet. Your irises are very close to the surface of your eye—easy to reproduce—but your retina is deeper in the eye. I would recommend changing from an iris-recognition system to a retina-recognition system—if you don't mind my saying."

Closing his eyes, Dan laid his head against the wall. "Okay, you're real sharp. I'm impressed. So why are you here? What's the problem that a smarty-pants like you can't handle?"

Tess laid an elbow on the back of the bench and cradled her cheek in her hand. "Well, it seems that I'm not as smart as all that. You see, I have Ballard's notes containing the ingredients for the XM-11 serum. It's an injection that transforms a basic human into a superhuman, hence the name, XM—X-Men. The eleven stands for the year that Ballard began working on the serum. I told Grant that I would destroy the notes. I told myself a million times that I should. But for some reason, some really stupid, unknown reason, I didn't."

"And?"

"And now Ballard's brother Augustine Crafton wants them. He's got two very large, very mean-looking thugs following me."

Dan sat straight up. "Did they follow you here?"

"No."

"How can you be sure?"

"Because I left them sitting in a jail cell waiting to be arraigned sometime on Monday. I know their names: Leo Talbot and a Russian man named Vlad Guseva. No, I don't know who they are. Only that they're August's thugs. Ballard was a total jerk-ass. I don't know August well, but for all I know, he could make his big brother look like a Christmas elf."

"Where're these notes?"

"They're safe," she said. Dan glanced at her purse. She smiled. "I'm a smarty-pants, remember? Do you actually think I'd keep something that important in my purse?"

"Down your bra?"

Tilting her head to the side and tossing him a baleful look, she asked, "Seriously?"

"By the way, thinking back, Grant said that he didn't have much trouble breaking in to Ballard's house in Russia. He said he got in through a sliding glass door. So how do you explain that security snafu, smarty-pants?"

She shrugged. "Nobody's perfect."

* * *

Dan decided that they would spend the rest of the day down in the cat-free zone of the medical unit. His head was slowly clearing. His eyes were burning a little less. He was feeling a bit better. The only real detriment to being below ground level was that the cell service was dicey.

He tried to call Clark several times to give him the names of the two men who'd been chasing Tess so that he could gather intel on them and on Ballard's brother, Augustine. The connection was poor, so he opted to leave the mansion and go to his ranch, which was about ten miles away, and contact Clark from there.

"The upstairs is locked up, so we'll just exit from down here," Dan said, leading Tess toward the large door at the end of the hall. Dan pressed a button on the wall.

"Don't want to face your furry little adversaries upstairs?"

"Damned straight."

"Mind if we take my vehicle?" she asked. "It's got all my stuff in the trunk."

"Not a problem. Let's go."

They made their way out to the lower driveway, where Dan's pickup was parked. He stopped to make sure it was locked, and then they traveled up the drive to the front of the house, where Tess had parked her fresh rental, a silver Cadillac CTS Vsport.

"Nice ride," Dan said.

"It's a rental—my fourth. I picked it up in Somerset County."

He had to give her credit—she was keeping the bad guys guessing. Then again, Ballard Crafton had not been a saint. She'd most certainly learned a great deal from the man, so was Tess McMillan one of the good guys? He couldn't be sure. Still, as they made their way along, he urged her to keep a swift pace with his left hand on the small of her back and scanned the fenced-in perimeter of the grounds for anyone lurking about, keeping his right hand on the Glock stuffed into his waistband. His good buddy paranoia was in charge of his every movement.

Tess slipped into the driver's seat, and Dan took the passenger's. When she approached the gate, it was already swinging open. "Take a left out of the drive," Dan said.

They drove along the road in complete silence. Dan watched his mirror for anyone who might have pulled onto the road to follow them. Several cars fell into line, but they turned off at intersections. They would then pick up another, and it too would turn. An air of relief drifted into the car when they realized that no one was showing them any special interest.

"Turn here," Dan said, hitching his chin toward a stone entrance similar to the one at First Force Headquarters. A large metal gate guarded the driveway. A wrought-iron archway hovered over the stone walls flanking the entrance. The curly black-iron overhead twisted into a circle in the center and formed an Old English *g*.

"What's the *g* stand for?" Tess asked.

"Grumpy," Dan said, getting out of the passenger's seat to place his face against the iris-recognition scanners. There was a click, and then the gate gradually rolled open and folded behind the stone wall to their right. Dan jogged around the car to slip back into his seat. Tess steered the Cadillac through the gate, taking note of the thirty-five-second pause before it began to roll back into a closed position.

The winding driveway was lined with white fencing. Inside the fence the springtime grasses were lush and green. As she drove, she saw the most peculiar-looking cows grazing in the distance. Each was black with a wide white swath encircling its midsection. There were dozens of them beyond the fence. She'd never seen cows that looked like that—not that she'd really seen that many cows up close in her thirty-four years.

"What kind of cows are those?"

"Belted Galloways. They originated in Scotland. Very good beef cows," Dan said.

"You raise them?"

"Yep, I grow my own hay and oats, too." He pointed off to the left toward rambling fields, where evidence of new growth was staunchly pushing up from the ground. He continued. "It's lots of work, but it's work that's good for the soul."

As they rounded the bend, a cedar-and-log house came into view. The front was partially contructed in river stone and had a high-pitched roof and a porch that ran the length of the house. The home was nestled among old maple trees that had budded, and the buds were patiently waiting for the perfect sunny day to burst into fat green leaves.

Seemingly out of nowhere, a dog came running alongside the car, barking joyfully. Nervous that the exuberant pooch would bolt in front of her, Tess slowed the Cadillac. Her eyes flicked to Dan, who was wearing a wide grin. The fuzzy fellow must've been Grumpy's friend.

She rolled the car to a stop in front of the house. The dog seemed to instinctively know that his master was in the passenger's seat. When Dan opened the door, the dog was dancing about, waiting for him.

"Your ranch is beautiful," Tess said, flipping her purse over her shoulder and stepping out of the car into the light evening breeze.

"I like it here," he said, waving her toward the front porch.

The black, white, and tan border collie's tail wagged feverishly. One ear stood up at attention while the other drooped a bit at the tip. His mouth partially open, he looked like he was wearing a welcoming grin. Still,

Tess was wary. Ballard hadn't allowed pets. She hadn't had any pets growing up either, unless she counted goldfish—but are they really pets? They don't make any sound. They don't cuddle up to you like cats do—or at least like people always say their cats do. Goldfish just swim around a bowl with their mouths doing that funny pumping thing. The nice thing about her goldfish was that they never got in her space, which was what the dog was doing at that moment. Another positive for goldfish—they're odorless, unlike dogs, which smell like…dogs.

"That's Boo," Dan said before being asked.

"Boo?"

"Yeah, Boo. He wants you to pet him," Dan said. Tess remained statuesque with her arms crossed under her breasts and stared at Boo with her upper lip curled as though he were an extraterrestrial life-form. "He's friendly. He won't bite. Go ahead…Pet him on the head," Dan said.

Tess's eyes rotated from Boo to Dan and then back to Boo. Hesitantly, she lowered her hand toward the dog's head and gave him a swift tap between his eyes. As a thank-you-very-much gesture, Boo sat down, offering her his paw. The right side of Dan's mouth lifted; he was clearly proud of Boo's manners.

Taking a short step backward, Tess asked, "Now what?"

"Seriously? Were you born in a barn? Shake his hand." He could see that Tess hadn't been quite sure of what to make of petting or tapping the dog's head, and the idea of shaking the dog's hand seemed beyond her compliance. "Aw, c'mon. It's taking every one of his four IQ points to pull this off. Cut him a break— shake his hand."

She let out a beleaguered sigh and shrugged, and then she took the dog's paw in her hand and gave it a quick wobble.

Looking quite pleased, Dan squatted down next to Boo, wrapped his arms around him, scrubbed his fingers over the dog's chest, and said, "Good boy, Boo."

"Why do you call him Boo?" she asked.

"I got him on Halloween ten years ago. He was the runt of the litter." Lifting the dog's face so that she could see him better, Dan continued. "It just goes with his personality. Look at him…He looks like a Boo to me."

"Oh yeah…I see it now," Tess dryly said.

Standing, he asked, "You don't like dogs?"

"I don't know anything about dogs."

"You never had a dog growing up?"

"Goldfish."

Dan let out a haughty snort. "You were deprived."

"Because I didn't have a dog? I don't think so," she said, matching his haughty tone.

Planting his hands on his hips and cocking his head to one side, he drank her in. Hot damn, she was a sight. He really hadn't paid that much attention to her looks until that moment. After all, his eyes had been swollen and weeping, and his breathing had been all but halted. But then he saw her. Then he noticed the perfect curves, the dewy skin, and the golden-blond tresses tumbling about her shoulders. Her blue eyes would've matched a sapphire sky on a sultry summer afternoon. Oh yeah, he saw her.

No, she hadn't been deprived, and she most definitely hadn't been born in a barn. Rather, she'd been brought up with privilege and deprived of the true pleasures in life—the simple ones that kids remember all their days, like having their faces licked by puppies and chasing kittens through a hayloft. Hell's bells, he doubted that the poor little rich girl had ever seen, smelled, or touched a bale of hay. She'd probably never been anywhere near a barn, for that matter.

"Well, I guess we should go in," Dan said while unlocking the door. Boo waited impatiently for the door to open, and the moment it swung inward, he hurried through it.

"He's allowed in the house?" Tess asked, openly appalled by the mere thought.

"He's my roommate."

"No wife? No live-in girlfriend?"

"Nope."

The blonde rolled her eyes. "And *I'm* the one who's deprived?"

With a grand sweep of his hand, Dan invited her to step into his home. Just one stride inside, Tess came to a standstill. The interior of the cedar-and-log house was as breathtaking as the outside—maybe even more so.

The sprawling open area was covered in oak hardwood floors. The floors' rich tones gleamed as if someone had just polished them. The walls were made of smooth- planked logs that climbed to a tall cedar cathedral ceiling lined with huge knotty logs. Off to the right stood a stone fireplace with a boldly curved hearth bigger than any she'd ever seen. Mounted above the mantel were three Canadian geese that appeared to be in flight. It was as if they were soaring right out of the masonry.

Dark-chocolate leather couches surrounded the fireplace, in front of which an imposing bearskin rug lay over the floor. The bear's massive limbs stretched out, and his head was perched on his chin.

Tess's eyes were drawn to the expansive kitchen fit for any gourmet cook. A generous bar constructed of stones with polished-oak counter tops hovered above a lengthy granite work space. Setting the boundaries of the kitchen, the bar corralled the cabinetry and the stainless-steel appliances. A huge island set smack-dab in the middle provided even more space for cooking and prepping, and there was a stainless-steel sink at the end of it. The large stove was incased in a stone archway with a short chimney above it. The head of a majestic twelve-point buck was mounted on the chimney.

Paintings of wildlife and running horses placed just so dotted the walls, and a stained-glass chandelier dangled over the island. Baskets sat here and there atop the cabinets, and decorative platters and bowls sat along the bar. The leather-topped barstools had been positioned just so, with the exactly even amount of space between them. The chairs around the oak puritan-style table had been aligned as if someone had taken pains to measure them out, and a chandelier made of horns cradling faux candles hung over the table. Beyond the line of four glass doors just past the table, a large deck looked over a good-sized lake.

Decorative American Indian throw rugs had been positioned, not tossed, about the floor. Tess turned her head to take in the massive oak staircase and its chunky oak banisters, which curved around the fireplace and climbed to the second floor. She marveled at the call to detail in the entire space. How could there not have been a woman involved in the design of the home? Furthermore, it was spotless. One could've eaten dinner off of the perfectly polished floor!

Ballard had owned many beautiful homes. She was no stranger to fine decor and furnishings. But Ballard's tastes had been more elegant—more discerning. His homes had been filled with expensive works of art and vintage vases filled with the fresh-cut arrangements that had been delivered on a daily basis. This home was masculine in a cozy, comforting manner. To her own surprise, she liked it. She liked the rustic charm that coaxed her to sit down, put her feet up, and relax.

She couldn't believe that the dog was welcome to wander about the home, and yet not a single dog hair could be spotted on the floor. But Boo wasn't wandering about the house—he was standing about four feet away wagging his tail, shuffling from paw to paw, and seemingly welcoming Tess into his domain.

"It's absolutely…Gorgeous," she said, unaware that anything had tumbled from her lips.

"It's home," Dan said, closing the door and locking it. "Make yourself comfortable."

"There's no TV," Tess said as she approached the living room to take it all in. After all, all men had a TV, usually a big, big TV so that they could watch football and baseball and March Madness and *SportsCenter* twenty-four-seven.

Dan made his way around the couch to a long cabinet next to the fireplace. He pressed a button. A huge flat-screen TV slowly emerged from within. "There ya go. Here's the remote—watch whatever you want," he said, handing her the device before heading for the kitchen.

Boo jumped up onto the couch and nestled into the cushions as if to say, "*SportsCenter* is on channel twelve. Can ya get me a beer, honey?" But Tess's attention was drawn to something else. Sitting on the end table was a framed photograph of an attractive redhead.

After setting her purse on the couch, Tess turned on the lamp and picked up the photo. The woman looking back at her through the glass had short, curly tresses framing a lovely face sprinkled with tiny freckles. The emerald-green cable-knit sweater that she was wearing accentuated her pixie-green eyes. Her smile was bright and full of laughter. So Grumpy did have a wife or a girlfriend. *Big surprise.* Men are all alike—liars and users.

Tess looked down at Boo, who was looking up at her. His ears were then relaxed back against his head, and he slapped his tail against the leather once. He knew who the woman was. She held the frame up for Dan to see and asked, "Who's this? Your *sister*?"

He'd been popping open a beer, but he stilled. "I've got a phone call to make. There's food in the fridge. You're welcome to whatever I've got." With that, he took a swig of the beer and then swept through the living room, removed the photo from her hand, and carried it with him up the staircase.

She'd hit a nerve. A big exposed nerve. She wasn't exactly sure why, but remorse spilled into her heart.

Four

After pulling his cell from his hip pocket, Dan sat on the edge of his bed and dialed Clark Rhodes. He'd tried to explain the situation with Tess McMillan earlier, but the connection in the lower level of the mansion had been poor. He wasn't sure if Clark had gotten any of the information at all.

"Rhodes here."

"Clark, we've got a situation," Dan said.

"Already? Walt's only been gone about twelve hours."

Dan let out a careworn sigh. "Yeah, well, guess who I've got at my ranch? Tess McMillan."

"I'm listening."

Dan detailed the circumstances surrounding Tess and the two thugs who'd been chasing her. He informed Clark that the notes for Ballard Crafton's serum still very much existed and that yes, Tess had possession of them.

He continued to explain the situation. "Tess believes that Crafton's younger brother, Augustine, hired Talbot and Guseva to track her down. She's pretty good at giving them the slip, but they keep tracking her down fairly quickly. She can't figure out how they're finding her."

"Does she have a cell phone on her?" Clark asked.

"I haven't seen her with one. But who knows what she's got in that big purse of hers."

"If she does, you know what to do with it. More importantly, you've got to get her to surrender the notes."

"She's not real trusting," Dan said.

"Get her to trust you—anyway that you can. In other words, be *supernice* to her, Garrison."

"What? I know how to make nice with women," Dan said, knowing that he was more than a little rusty where the softer sex were involved.

"All I'm sayin' is gain her trust—get the notes. I'll start researching on my end. Keep her at the ranch. I'll go to headquarters and work from there."

Dan couldn't deny that relief washed over him upon hearing that he wouldn't have to return to the mansion in the morning. "Will do. Thanks, Clark."

"I'll be in touch." With that, the line went dead.

He laid the photograph facedown on the night-stand, letting his hand linger on the back of it before retracting it and rubbing it over the nape of his neck.

"I'm sorry," Tess said from the doorway.

Dan turned to see the blonde leaning against the jamb. She flashed him a sweet smile with her plump, freshly glossed lips. The woman was beautiful; she also looked done-in. She had slung her red purse over her shoulder, and she was holding an iPad case in her right hand and clutching the handle of a small roll-along suitcase in the other. She'd ventured outside to get her things from the car.

"Sorry for what?"

"I don't think the woman in the photo is your sister. If I've upset you…I'm sorry."

Her eyes held a look of sincerity that he really hadn't expected from Crafton's woman. He was kind of taken aback by it—kind of. "No worries. We've got more important things to take care of. You told me that Talbot and Guseva track you down pretty easily."

"Yes, they seem to."

"Have you got a cell phone in that big purse?"

Tossing him a baleful look, she said, "Let's review: I'm a smarty-pants—emphasis on the word 'smarty.' My cell phone is at my house in Albany, New York.

Why? Because I'm not that stupid. I'm well aware that I could be tracked that way."

"Okay…If I've offended you, I'm sorry," Dan said, pushing himself up from the mattress. He went to a dresser and retrieved a phone from the top drawer. Extending it out to her, he said, "Here ya go. This is a burner phone. It's untraceable. My number and the number of Clark Rhodes, First Force's director, are preprogrammed into it." Half smiling, he added, "You've had a rough day. You look beat. You should turn in early."

"I'm exhausted. I'd love to take a hot shower if that would be okay."

"I'll show you the room you're staying in, and then I'll show you where the bath is."

With a svelte smile on his lips, Dan gently maneuvered the suitcase from her hand. Letting him be the gentleman that she suspected he was, Tess relinquished the case to him and smiled. She followed him down the hallway.

All of the doors along the hall were constructed like old-fashioned crossbuck barn doors. They were on rollers rather than dangling from hinges.

Instead of round doorknobs, they had twisted metal pulls. Very cool.

"So you're not going to tell me where Grant is?"

"He's unavailable," Dan said over his shoulder.

"I see. He's on some covert mission rescuing a gorgeous damsel in distress, right?"

With a chuckle in his voice, Dan said, "Not exactly. He's away with his wife for some much-needed R and R."

"No problems, I hope."

"Don't think so." Dan pointed to a door. "That's the room where you can stay. It's toward the back of the house, which is a safer bet. Next door down is the main bath."

He turned on the light in the bathroom. Tess stepped in. Her jaw dropped. The hardwood floors flowed throughout the house. The bathroom was surrounded by floor-to-ceiling windows that looked out over an easy slope behind the house to a wide lake that yawned across a field. The sky was giving way to the cloak of night, and the sun was lowering ever so slowly, leaving feathery swaths of purple and pink above the herd of grazing Belted Galloways.

A stacked-stone fireplace stood in the corner of the room. A sunken whirlpool tub lay just below the hearth. Even though no flames cracked or danced inside the firebox, she could almost feel the warmth of an imaginary fire and the bubbling of steaming water. She looked up and found a huge skylight over the tub.

Votive cups filled with candles dotted the massive mantel, and some sat among the stones. Deliberately placed just outside the tub, three big, fluffy white towels rolled tightly in long tubes were stacked in a pyramid.

"Each room is more impressive than the last. I can't decide if you're gay or if you have a superacute case of OCD."

Dan crossed his arms over his massive chest. "*Nice...*Women are all the same. If you'd come into my house and found stacks of dirty laundry and piles of dishes in the sink, you would've accused me of being a slob. But since the house is well kept, I'm either gay or obsessive!"

Tess couldn't stifle the chuckle that bubbled to the surface. He was big. His broad shoulders narrowed into chiseled abs that melted into lean hips. He sported a very trim military hairstyle. His jaw was square and strong. She doubted that he was gay—there was too much testosterone bouncing off of the man, and she remembered his reaction to the photograph—but she pushed his buttons anyway. Matching his crossed arm stance, she said, "So... Which is it? Gay or OCD?"

Shaking his head and letting out a defeated breath, he said, "I'll admit I'm a little obsessive, but in my defense, there's a lotta charm to being neat, organized, and neurotic."

"I agree, Grumpy. Your house has a rustic charm that I absolutely love. I can't wait to see what the bedroom looks like. But…Don't you have a shower?" Tess asked, her eyes searching the room.

"Sure. Walk around to the other side of the fireplace."

Tess made her way to the opposite side of the fireplace and found a shower stall constructed of the same stacked-stone design. The stall was big enough for at least four people. Flat stones stuck out of the walls, forming natural shelves for soap and shampoo. Just outside the half wall that barricaded the water in the shower was a warming rack with more fluffy towels hanging perfectly straight. To the far left was a double-sink vanity with mirrors encased in wrought-iron frames above it.

"First Force must pay very well," Tess said.

"Hazard pay. We're compensated quite a bit for putting our lives on the line. I'm not always sure the pay is worth the risk. Enjoy your shower. I'll put your suitcase in your room. May I take the iPad too?"

Tess raised an eyebrow. The right side of her lips curled. Handing him the case, she said, "Feel free to snoop, Grumpy. The notes aren't on the iPad, but you're welcome to read the e-mails from my mom if you'd like."

The right side of his mouth lifted. Taking the case from her hand, he said, "It's Dan. My name's Dan Garrison." With that, he turned to make his way out of the room with the suitcase and the iPad. He stopped when he reached the pile of towels lying next to the tub. Bending down, he reached under the towels, retrieved a handgun, and then left the room, closing the door behind him.

"Well, aren't you an interesting piece of work, Dan Garrison," Tess said to herself. She laid her purse in a corner, wondering why he hadn't asked to take it away.

* * *

Tess lingered in the warm spray, letting the water and the heat wash over her and melt away the day's edge. She wasn't exactly sure what the next day or week would bring. The simple fact was that August was not going to stop searching for her unless she surrendered the flash drive to him. Seeking out First Force hadn't been an exercise in poor judgment. She simply wasn't sure where it would get her. But she had to admit that the accommodations at Dan Garrison's ranch were very comfortable—and out of harm's way. But what could First Force do for her? It would only be a matter of time until they too would ask her to yield the notes.

She was in a Catch-22 situation: She could give up the flash drive to August, who would undoubtedly use it to build some kind of personal army, but at least he'd leave her alone to live her life…maybe. Or she could give it to First Force, who would most likely destroy it…maybe. She couldn't be sure. There was no doubt that First Force was the lesser of the two evils, but where did it all leave her?

Dipping her face into the soothing rush of water, she remembered how impervious August had been to the news of his brother's death. She had only met August a handful of times during her relationship with Ballard.

Certainly, Ballard Crafton had been a man who knew what he wanted, and he'd known exactly how to get what he wanted. But she didn't consider him to be as unfeeling or as unmoved as his younger sibling. Augustine Crafton had about as much benevolence as a bucket of rocks. She thought back to the conversation they'd had shortly after Ballard had died.

"Thank you for calling me, Ms. McMillan. I truly appreciate all the years of loyal service that you gave to my brother. He was quite fond of you," he'd said.

She'd been flabbergasted that Ballard had never informed him of their marriage. August had still been under the impression that she'd merely been his personal assistant. It had made her blood boil.

"I'm sure that Ballard had a will."

Her lips curled in satisfaction over knowing what that pompous ass did not: she was the beneficiary of Ballard's fortune. She'd seen to that for sure.

"Yes, Mr. Crafton. Ballard had a will. He was a very generous man, and he rewarded loyalty. I'm pleased to tell you that I'm the sole beneficiary of his estate."

He didn't have to say a word. She could feel the animosity permeating through the telephone. She could hear the hitch of anger in the quickening of his breath. She continued. "I'm well aware of your love for fine art. Ballard would be pleased if he knew that I shipped some of the most valuable pieces to you in his memory. Furthermore, I made a generous donation to the Novikov Ballet Company. Ballard attended their performances regularly during his time in Russia. I also intend to make equally generous donations to the New York City Metropolitan Opera on behalf of singer Lucinda DeRolf and to the Boston Pops Orchestra in the name of concert pianist Yung Lo Ming."

His silence was like a hot acid drip. Oh yeah, he was acquainted with Lucinda DeRolf and Yung Lo Ming. He knew that they were two women whom Ballard had loved and demanded submission from—and that when they'd refused, he'd destroyed them. And what did August get from the conversation?

"Why the ballet company?" he said in an almost civil tone.

"There was a ballerina whom Ballard was enamored with, Silja Ramsay—"

"I don't want to know!" he said. And then after gathering a controlled breath, he asked, "What of Ballard's work? What happened to the project that he was so involved with?"

Ah, he was getting to the crux of his intentions. Sure, August loved fine paintings and vintage Ming vases, but to have the notes concerning Ballard's serum would've been to have the world by the proverbial ass. Problem was, he wasn't going to get what he wanted. Not from her. The second problem was that like his brother, August didn't understand or recognize the feeling of wanting something.

"I'm sorry. His work was destroyed in the blast. Everything in the building was. Nothing could be salvaged, I'm afraid," she said while caressing the flash drive with the tip of her finger.

As she recalled, the conversation had been cut short after that statement. She'd exchanged a few e-mails with August to make arrangements for several well-chosen paintings and most of the vases to be shipped to his home in Connecticut, but she hadn't heard from him since he'd received his inheritance—until Talbot and Guseva had started coming around. She still couldn't figure out what had made him decide that she'd lied to him. How and when had he realized that she did in fact possess the XM-11 serum?

After stepping from the shower, she wrapped her long blond hair in one of the warm towels and dried herself with another. She felt refreshed and clean but still drained and ready for a good night's sleep. Suddenly, she was sorry that she'd let Dan take her suitcase to her room—she didn't have any clean clothes to change into. She took the towel that she'd dried her body with, wrapped it around herself, peeked out the door to make sure that she was alone, and then hurried across the wood floor to her room.

"Sleep well, Tess," Dan yelled up the stairs.

The man was not only obsessive but also could evidently hear a pin drop. "Did you enjoy the e-mails?" she asked.

She heard him chuckle, and then she heard the TV click on and the drone of the *SportsCenter* commentator. Her eyes flicked to her suitcase and to the case that held her iPad, which was lying on the bed—the very big bed that seemed to grow right out of the floor and all the way to the ceiling. The four squared-off poles at each corner were connected to the floor and to the ceiling. White sheers gently draped from one pole to the next. The bedspread was a soft blue. There were piles of fat throw pillows along the headboard. There was nothing particularly ornate about the room, yet it held a calming country allure. She felt drawn to the room, which was lit only by the moon's pearly light filtering through the window. Turning on the lamp would have only ruined the surreal effect that nature was having on her at the moment.

Obviously, exhaustion was playing tricks on her thoughts. She was a city girl—born and raised. The wide-open spaces and simplistic life were for the likes of country folk. She couldn't imagine an existence surrounded by all of that peace and tranquility—surely it would become darn right mind-numbing. Then again, her mind had almost become numb over the past weeks with chaos, commotion, and turmoil. A little peace and tranquility would be a welcome change.

Accepting the quietude that Dan Garrison's home offered her, Tess slipped into the last pair of fresh panties in her suitcase and then into a silk nightgown, brushed out her hair, and climbed into the bed. She felt secure between the cool, soft sheets. She could sleep that night in the knowledge that no one knew her whereabouts.

Talbot and Guseva were neatly tucked in a cell, and August was no doubt marinating in a stew of agitation.

Yes, she would sleep well that night. She had to let go of the angst about what the coming tomorrows would hold.

* * *

Stamford, Connecticut

August Crafton pitched his cell phone across the room. Instant fury flushed his cheeks as he brushed the petite brunette aside and crawled over the tall, busty redhead before planting his feet on the floor with a loud *thud*.

"You all done, Aggie?" the brunette asked, tucking her breasts into the cups of her sheer pink bra.

The handsome millionaire tied the sash of his black satin robe. Running a frustrated hand through his chestnut hair, he said, "No, I wasn't, but I have business to attend to. You girls may go to your rooms. I'll call for you later." The girls gathered their bits of lingerie and crawled out of the king-sized bed to make their way toward the bedroom door. "Tell Vatonia to come freshen my bed, please."

"Anything you say, Aggie," the brunette said, blowing him a kiss before easing the door closed.

After she closed the door, he clenched his hands into fists at his side at the news that his attorney had just divulged to him: Talbot and Guseva had been arrested. *Incompetents!* August hurried to the French Regency desk nestled in the curve of the massive bow window. Blue and gold taffeta drapes framed the window and the desk. One of his brother's Ming vases stood next to the desk. A dragon curled majestically around the creamy-white porcelain. It had been one of Ballard's favorites, and it had been given to August.

He dropped into the chair and quickly opened his laptop. His fingers raced over the keys, and then with a breath of dismay and disappointment, he slammed it closed.

"Damn her! She's not on. She hasn't logged on to her freaking computer since early this morning at the filling station." He massaged his temples in aggravation. Over the past weeks, he'd been able to track her every move through her computer. He'd hired a high-priced hacker who'd installed a GPS program that detected everywhere her URL went. August had captured her URL while exchanging e-mails with her. She'd been most generous in giving him vases and artwork from his brother's estate. The hacker had made good use of the information August had gleaned.

When Tess logged on to her computer, the GPS informed August of her location. Not only did he know where she was but also he could see her through the tiny camera at the top of her computer, the one used for Skype sessions.

He envied his brother, who'd had a beautiful assistant to serve him for seventeen years. He had no doubt that Ballard had rolled her many times. Tess McMillan was completely unaware that she was being watched. Sometimes she would turn off her computer, leaving it in an upright position. It didn't matter if it was off. He couldn't track her, but he could still see her.

Oftentimes he'd watch her strip. Her body was flawless. Her breasts were firm and round and full. He imagined her in his bed, pleasing him, while he clutched her long blond tresses tightly in his fist. He wanted to taste her lips. He wanted to feel the wetness of her sex and to run his hands over her pebble-like nipples.

Tess McMillan was as intelligent as she was beautiful, and that was just as much of a turn-on as watching her strip. As angry as it made him that she'd managed to slip past Talbot and Guseva, it also made him horny as hell for her. He would give her anything she wanted if she gave herself to him. He would let her live if she simply submitted Ballard's serum to him. Yet the chase for Tess had continued for three weeks.

She was logging on to the computer less often. He was growing weary of it. His impatience was escalating by the day.

Until recently he really hadn't given much consideration to the fact that Tess might have taken possession of Ballard's notes—especially since she'd been so generous with some of his most prized possessions after his untimely death. She'd told him that everything Ballard had been working on had been lost in the explosion. He'd had every reason to believe her. What would she have gained from keeping the serum to herself? None of the scientists from Ballard's employ had reported that she'd contacted them with the intention of resurrecting the XM-11 project.

He'd decided that Tess was biding her time after a woman named Jingjing Choo had contacted him little more than two months ago.

Jingjing was a Chinese scientist who had worked in Ballard's laboratory in Russia. She'd convinced him that Ballard never would have kept all of his information in one place.

"Tess McMillan was Ballard's right arm," Jingjing said during their initial conversation. "He entrusted everything to her. He would have kept copies of his notes in the safe in his home. I'm sure of that. And Tess would have had access to that safe."

"You would know how to reconstruct the formula if we could retrieve it from Tess?" August asked.

"I could do that and more, Mr. Crafton. I was the head scientist on the project. I was also working on my own project on the side. When I showed Ballard the progress I was making, he assigned me a laboratory of my own so that I could continue my work in complete privacy while I oversaw the XM-11 project," Jingjing said.

"And what did your project entail?"

"When perfected, Ballard's serum should give the subjects superhuman strength and agility. But because none of the subjects we tested it on survived the initial injections, we didn't have the opportunity to find out whether the subjects could carry out directives. The formula I was working on would've added mind-control elements to the XM-11 serum, making the subjects not only strong but also able to be controlled by their master."

"Did Tess know about your project?"

"She knew that I was working on something special, but Ballard assured me that it was top secret—a secret that he hadn't shared with anyone, including Tess McMillan," Jingjing said.

"Why wasn't your project destroyed in the explosion?"

A deep, devious chuckle seeped through the phone. "I kept my notes with me at all times—even when I left with Vlad to get married during the weekend of the explosion. Only my laboratory was destroyed—not my notebook."

It didn't take August long to reconsider his assessment of Tess. He made arrangements for Jingjing and her husband, Vlad Guseva, to come to the United States. He had a laboratory built in the basement of his home so that Jingjing could continue her work. No, the basement lab wasn't as posh or as extensive as the one his brother had provided for the brilliant scientist back in Russia. He was absolutely sure of that. The walls were formed of cement blocks, and the ceiling was open, exposing the floor beams above, the plumbing, and the ductwork of the house. In his defense, he'd had little time to prepare for Jingjing's arrival—only two weeks. But the area had been thoroughly cleaned, and she was provided with everything she needed and had mentioned on the detailed list she'd sent in advance.

August had partnered Vlad, a former security guard in Ballard's laboratory in Russia, with his own security head, Leo Talbot, to nab Tess McMillan, but it was to no avail. Because of their epic failure to detain Ballard's former assistant, he hadn't a clue of Tess's whereabouts. He would have to wait for her to log on to her computer—if she hadn't already realized that they were tracking her through it. Talbot and Jingjing's husband wouldn't be given many more chances. August was growing weary of the chase. He wanted the serum so that they could test it, perfect it, and then market it to the highest bidder. There were billions to be made.

As August drew near to the door that led downstairs, the sound of classical music filtered through it. When he opened the door, the sound was so blaring that it almost knocked him backward. A concerto—Vivaldi, he believed. While he enjoyed classical music, he never felt the need to play it so vociferously. Shaking it off as a mad scientist's quirk, he made his way downstairs and found Jingjing in the laboratory hunched over a table making notes as a golden liquid simmered over a Bunsen burner.

The woman impressed August like no other ever had. She worked tirelessly. She rose early in the morning and worked late into the night. August's housemaid, Vatonia, delivered meals to the lab and reported that the scientist barely touched her food. In fact, he hadn't seen her in two days, maybe three.

Jingjing was short and reed thin. Her long, silky indigo hair fell to her petite waist. Her face was wide and flat; her lips were slim and usually drawn in concentration. She was a woman of few words and even less patience.

August walked across the laboratory, watching her tiny fingers manipulate the pencil over the notebook as she glanced through a pair of safety glasses at the liquid then coming to a boil. Completely engaged in her work, she was unaware of his presence, and her sleek Siamese cat, Shan, was sitting near the computer as if to supervise the scientist's progress.

Switching off the CD player, August said, "I'm sorry to interrupt you."

Jingjing's head jerked up. Her narrow eyes trained on the black satin robe pulled tautly around his body. "Are we not getting dressed today, Mr. Crafton?" She stroked the cat's ears and then went back to her notebook, dismissing him as a pesky intrusion.

"It's nearly ten o'clock at night, Jingjing. You should consider getting some rest."

"Who could sleep with your neighbor's dog constantly yapping?"

"I'm assuming that that's why the music was blaring?" Jingjing scowled. He continued. "Mrs. Bennett's poodle is an annoyance, but still, you should try to rest."

"Mine is not a life of leisure, Mr. Crafton. As you can see, I have a project in progress."

"Of course. I thought you might like to know that your husband is in jail. My attorney called with the news only moments ago."

With that, her eyebrows rose slightly. Turning the page of her notebook, she managed to say, "Vlad has not been very helpful. I will have to have a talk with him. When will he be back?"

"I'll travel with my attorney to his arraignment on Monday. Would you like to come along?"

She pitched her pencil into the crease of the notebook. Malevolence filled her tone. "I am very close to a breakthrough, but I need the serum, and I need a test subject. So I need Vlad to do as he is told, and quickly—*very* quickly. He's making me angry, and anger is a waste of time. Traveling to wherever Vlad is incarcerated would be too."

August scratched a spot just below his ear and scrunched his face. "You don't act like a woman who's madly in love. You're not even making excuses for your husband."

Her narrow eyes heated. "My father is old-school Chinese. He was very unhappy that I hadn't married. He bitched about it constantly. So to please him, I made a choice. I married."

"Seriously? You also don't strike me as someone who does what others want you to do. I'm surprised."

"My father is very wealthy, and I will be too upon his death—if I at least attempt to please him. He preferred that I marry a Chinese man. I preferred to marry someone I could control. He wasn't overjoyed, but I did as he asked. As for love—it is a useless emotion. That being said, I love Vlad more when he's doing what he's been told to do. We should consider hiring someone else—someone more aggressive. One of Ballard's men. I have his contact information." August grimaced. She could see that he didn't appreciate the offer. She changed directions. "But for now, tell me… Who will be my test subject when the time comes?"

"I'm sure we'll find someone—perhaps Vlad."

Unamused, she stared at him over her glasses for a moment, stroked Shan's ears, and then picked up her pencil, dismissing him once again.

Five

Wincing, Tess turned over in the bed and buried her face in the pillow to hide from the sun's rays blasting through the windows. The bed felt so warm and comfy. It was easy to forget that she was a woman on the run, a woman in possession of a formula that could possibly change the way soldiers fight—the way wars are won.

She opened one eye to peek at the clock on the nightstand. It was nine thirty in the morning. What? Jerking upward to get a better view of the clock, she couldn't believe that she'd slept so late, but indeed, she'd read the clock correctly: it was nine thirty in the morning. She flopped back down on the pillow. Oh well, she must've needed the sleep. The good Lord knew she'd been completely exhausted when she'd laid her head down the last night. She barely remembered crawling into the bed.

Draping her arm over her eyes, she decided to rest for a little while longer before facing the day. Dan hadn't come knocking on the door demanding that she rise and shine. The house was quiet. She listened. Birds were singing outside, and then she heard a dog barking...Boo. The dog's bark brought her to her elbows so that she could listen a bit more closely. The bark wasn't alarming. There was no growl or snarl mixed in with the baying—it sounded playful, so Tess tossed the blankets aside and went to the window to see what the noise was all about.

She pinched back the curtain, and she was in awe of the morning and of how beautiful Dan's ranch was in the light of day. Below her window the sun gleamed over a patchwork of golden dandelions, deep-purple violets, and wide swaths of blue forget-me-nots. The flowers spotted the lush green grass that tumbled over the easy slope and toward the edge of the lake. A monstrous weeping willow resided right at the water's edge. Its sinewy branches dipped into the tarn while those funny-looking black and white cows grazed in the distance.

She had to lean just a bit to see Dan tossing a stick for Boo to fetch. The dog seemed to be enjoying the game. He would run and jump up high to grasp the wood in his teeth and then return it to his master so that he could pitch it again.

A boy and his dog, Tess thought, and she couldn't help but smile at the same time. She noted how imposing Dan looked with the square-rimmed cowboy hat on his head—he was darn right yummy.

They weren't making their way toward the house. Rather, they seemed to be heading toward the large barn beyond where the cows were eating. Her hand found its way to the nape of her neck. It was stiff—stress. Assuming that Dan was off to do "chores," she figured that she had time to relieve her stress. She took note of the cedar crossbuck doors that closed off a closet across the room. When she slid the doors aside, lights automatically illuminated the interior of the closet and revealed three racks of pressed dress shirts.

Dan's eye for detail was once again apparent. The shirts were hanging precisely three inches apart on black hangers—all facing the same direction. Pristine white shirts were on the top level. The second level held blue and gray shirts, and on the third level was one lone tangerine shirt. Below the racks was a built-in dresser. Sitting atop it were three Stetson cowboy hats in a row—a silver one, a black one, and a brown one. The front rim of each hat was squared almost as though someone had taken an iron to it, much like the one Dan was wearing. She opened the top drawer and found assorted ties folded neatly in order: solid ties, striped ties, polka-dot ties—there were very few polka-dot ties—and a holiday tie decorated with lines of tiny ornate Christmas trees.

After stepping out of her nightgown, she carefully folded it and laid it on the bed, and then she pulled a gray shirt from the second rack and draped it over her body. It wasn't her usual workout attire, but it would have to do, as in her hurry to leave her home she hadn't packed any yoga pants.

After making the bed, putting her nightgown neatly in her suitcase, and getting washed up, Tess made her way downstairs. The bearskin rug seemed like the perfect spot on which to stretch away her worries. It was Saturday morning. August wouldn't be able aid Talbot and Guseva until Monday. She had time to consider her options.

* * *

Dan had always been an early riser. Up by 6:00 a.m. He and Boo had waited and waited for Tess to make an appearance in the kitchen, but by 9:05 a.m., he'd decided that he'd waited long enough. He was already late to feed the cows and to take care of his chores. He wasn't particularly surprised that she was sleeping in. The woman had looked dead on her feet the night before when they'd said their good-nights.

He had peeked in on her before going downstairs to make sure that she was okay. Her blond tresses had been splayed out over the pillow. She'd been as beautiful as any model they'd use in a mattress promotion. He'd paused at the door to watch her sleep. As he'd closed the door quickly but quietly, he'd been happy that she was resting so comfortably.

Dan hurried through the barn work so that she wouldn't wake to an empty house. Boo ran ahead through the tall grasses toward the house when the work was done. He figured the dog had a plan, and he was fairly sure what that plan was.

Quietly, Dan stepped through the kitchen door, listening closely for any sound of Tess. One step inside, and he had a full view of the living room. He stilled. Boo looked up at him, his paws dangling over the edge of the couch and his tail wagging, slapping the leather. It was as Dan had suspected—he'd beaten him into the house through the kitchen doggy door.

Yep, he'd found Tess. There she was on the bearskin rug in a low, tight kneeling position. She was facedown with her arms resting at her sides. Her long golden hair was pulled back into a loose ponytail that snaked down her spine, but what made him stare—what brought him to a complete pause—was the fact that she was wearing nothing more than a pair of lacy lavender bikini panties and a matching lacy bra.

Deliberately being quiet, he eased the door closed and dropped his hat on the hook inside the door as he stared. He was defenseless. He couldn't help himself. The stunning blonde who had showed up unannounced at headquarters after breaking through the security system was then in an incredibly sexy, incredibly vulnerable position on his bearskin rug—and she was making his man parts stand straight up in a salute.

What the hell is she doing?

Then as quick as you please, she pushed herself up until her sweet, tight little bottom was in the air, and she was in some kind of upside-down, totally kinky, totally erotic position—in his opinion, anyway. Man, oh, man, he needed to shake this off—like, instantly. He wasn't exactly sure how he was gonna manage to hide the solid column pushing against the zipper of his jeans.

He hurried across the kitchen as if he hadn't noticed her and then made sure that he was positioned behind the island. Boo jumped from the couch to greet him, alerting Tess to the fact that he was close at hand. *Traitor.* Seemingly impervious to his presence, she moved smoothly into another position, only that time he was looking at her full, beautiful breasts pushing up from the skimpy bra.

"Good morning," she said, unerringly holding a lunging position, her arms stretched out as she breathed in deeply and then exhaled slowly and measuredly from deep in her belly.

"Good morning," he said, patting Boo on the head, careful to hold his position behind the counter and to hide his lower half. "What're you doing?"

"Yoga."

Nodding as if he were familiar with the concept, he crossed his arms over his chest. "Mind if I ask if you always do yoga in your…um—"

"Bra and panties? No. I usually do yoga in yoga pants and a sports bra, but I didn't pack any, and I didn't have anything on hand that would stretch or bend with my body, so I opted for this," she said as casually as if she were giving him directions into town. Then she lay on her back. The bear's wispy fur tickled the contours of her body. She grabbed her right leg and extended it toward the ceiling.

Dan's stomach contracted. He stammered. "I'll… I'll make some coffee."

"Done. It should be ready—nice and hot," Tess said, switching legs.

Yeah...It was hot—way too hot. "Thanks" was all he could manage to say. Keeping his back toward the fireplace, the bearskin rug, and the smokin'-hot yoga Yoda, he made a nimble move to the counter where the coffeemaker sat, and for the first time ever, he wished that his floor plan were a little less open.

While pouring coffee into his mug, he noticed the hushed hum of music flowing through the downstairs. It was coming from his flat screen, and the volume was turned down very low. She'd put on some music channel that played that weird meditation-relaxation mumbo jumbo.

It was hard to not watch her. He tried to busy himself in the kitchen by pouring half-and-half into his coffee, stirring it, drinking it, and watching her. The watching was simply beyond his control. He went to the cupboard to set a mug out for her in case she wanted some coffee after she was done.

Finally she sat in a pose that he recognized as a yoga position—he saw it on TV programs and in commercials all the time. She was sitting cross-legged with her head up, her eyes closed, and the backs of her hands resting on her knees. Her ponytail was gently lying over her shoulders, hovering between her round breasts, and moving up and down as she breathed.

Boo seemed every bit as rapt in the sight as he was. The dog had returned to his perch on the couch and was resting his head on his paws and watching Tess's every move up close. Dan was darn right envious.

Her eyes fluttered open. Her lips curled, but Dan didn't get the impression that she was smiling at him or the dog—she seemed to be smiling because of an inner peace. That was good, he supposed.

Tess grabbed the shirt that was lying on the floor near the rug and shrugged into it. As she draped it over her shoulders and began buttoning it, Dan recognized it as one of his dress shirts. Boo's tail wagged, slapping the leather. Tess smiled at him. She didn't touch him, which he was begging her to do, yet Dan felt the smile was a measured improvement from the day before.

She made her way to the kitchen, failing to turn off the eerie music, fetched the mug from the counter, and then poured herself a cup of fresh morning java. Her long, shapely legs dangled below the hem of his shirt. That ponytail was tucked beneath the fabric and between her breasts.

"Nice shirt," he said while peeking at her over the rim of his mug.

"I found it hanging in the closet along with all of the other perfectly pressed, perfectly lined-up dress shirts all hanging in order according to color: whites, blues, grays, and, oh, there was one lone tangerine—I really liked that one," Tess said, lifting the cup to her full, plump lips.

His eyes were mesmerized by her lips as she spoke. She wasn't wearing any makeup, and God love her, she didn't need any.

Before she drank, she said, "Namaste."

Dan cocked his head to one side. "What?"

"Namaste—you're supposed to say it back to me," she said, peering over the top of her cup with those sensual blue eyes that were completely knocking him off balance.

"What does it mean?"

She chuckled. "Were you born in a barn? It means 'I respect you. I bow to you.' We say it at the end of each yoga class, but I don't have a class to say it to, so I'm saying it you. Namaste."

The left side of Dan's lip kicked up. Bowing his head, he said, "Namaste." He had to admit that she was a sight in his shirt—and whether he liked it or not, he was enjoying the sight very much. "It's a beautiful day. I was thinking we could go for a ride and have a picnic," he said.

"Go for a ride? A ride on what?" she asked over her cup.

"My motorcycle. Nothing clears your head like a nice easy ride on a Harley, and I pack a pretty mean picnic lunch, too," Dan said.

"A motorcycle? I've never been on one."

"Seriously? Case closed—you've been deprived."

She tossed him a baleful look. "No pets and no motorcycles. How did I ever survive?"

"I have no idea. Crafton was a wealthy man. I can't believe he didn't have a motorcycle."

She snorted. "Motorcycles weren't Ballard's style. He was more of a limo man."

"He wasn't much fun, then."

"No argument there. Okay, I've had my morning stretch and my morning coffee. I guess I'm up for an adventure in motorcycle riding. I'll let you pack your mean picnic basket while I go upstairs and put on some clothes."

"Sounds like a plan," he said.

After taking the last gulp of her coffee, Tess set the cup in the sink and then made her way across the living room. She tossed him a smile before she began to climb the stairs.

Dan made no move to finish his coffee or to begin packing the basket. He simply leaned a hip against the counter to watch her retreat—to watch the gentle sway of her hips beneath the shirt, the way she flipped her silky hair over her shoulder, and the way her fingers caressed the banister. And yes, even the way she tenderly placed each foot on each step as she climbed turned him on.

Once she was out of sight, he shook his head to shake off the stir that was brewing somewhere deep in his gut. He hadn't felt that rouse in a long time—he'd almost forgotten what it felt like.

Whoa.

He shouldn't have been feeling anything at all. Tess McMillan was a client—a mission, for crying out loud. He needed to get his head in the game.

Objective number one was to gain her trust.

Objective number two was to get the notes about the serum.

Period.

That was the score.

There hadn't been any mention of feeling warm and fuzzy toward the sexy blonde in the directives.

Get your head screwed on straight, Garrison.

* * *

The selection of clean clothes in her suitcase had dwindled down to almost nada. Tess pulled on a pair of jeans and the last clean cami she had left, and she decided to wear Dan's shirt tied at her waist—not her usual sleek look, but it would have to do for the day. She dug through her purse to retrieve the .45. She stuffed it into the back of her pants. Yeah,

Talbot and Guseva were in jail, but that didn't mean that August hadn't found other resources.

After placing the purse back on the dresser, she turned to leave the room, and then she hesitated at the doorway. Turning, she went back to the dresser to dig through the purse again. She retrieved the faux lipstick tube that concealed the flash drive with Ballard's formula for the supersoldier serum on it. Returning to the closet, Tess slid the door open, pulled open the drawer where Dan's ties lay, and folded the tube inside the second striped tie—a purple and gray one.

After Tess came back downstairs with an armful of laundry, which Dan was happy to allow her to throw into the washing machine, they gathered up the basket and an old blanket. Dan retrieved the straw cowboy hat from the hook and dropped it on his head before they made their way outside with Boo on their heels.

It was unusually warm for mid-April. Tess breathed in the fresh air. The dewy grass soaked the hem of her jeans and brushed over her shoes, leaving wispy wet marks as they meandered across the field toward the lake. Boo danced all around Dan, coaxing him to throw him a stick. Once they were within twenty feet of the lake, Dan obliged his old buddy. He found a nice-sized stick and hurled it into the lake. Boo took off running.

He dived into the lake and swam to claim the stick in his jaws. After making a wide, sweeping circle in the water and swimming back to shore, he shook off the wetness from his fur and then trotted toward them with the stick. He dropped it at Tess's feet and then sat down, waiting for her to respond.

"What does he want?" Tess asked.

"He wants you to throw the stick back into the lake," Dan said. He could see that she was baffled by the concept. She wanted to toss it, but she just wasn't sure. He encouraged her. "Go ahead. Toss it for him. You'll be his hero."

Tess bent down to grab the stick. Boo flinched in anticipation of the toss. Wary of the dog's sudden movement, she pulled back.

Dan snorted. "It's okay—he's just excited that you're gonna play with him. Go ahead, and pick it up. He won't bite you or jump on you."

Keeping an eye on the dog, she picked up the stick and chucked it into the lake. Boo whirled around to dart down the short slope and then leaped into the water. Tess chuckled and clapped her hands at the dog's antics—and at his simple joy over fetching a stick for a human being. Much to her surprise, she was actually starting to become fond of Boo. Much to her surprise, she was beginning to understand the bond between people and dogs. Hey, dogs are so much more fun than goldfish. Maybe Dan had had a point—maybe she had been a bit deprived while growing up, or at least very sheltered.

Boo returned to shore, shook off the water from his fur, and brought the stick to Tess's feet again. Smiling, she bent down to pat the top of his dry head. "Good boy, Boo."

"Hmm, I think I've just been replaced," Dan said. Tess laughed. It sounded good. He continued. "C'mon, he'd fetch that stick all day if we wanted him to, but we've got a picnic to get to. I keep my motorcycles in the garage attached to the barn."

"Will he be coming?" Tess asked, still petting the dog's head. Boo leaned into the love.

"No, Boo doesn't leave the ranch. He might follow us to the gate, but then he'll go back to the house or the barn or the porch. He's got plenty of options."

"He certainly does," she said. He had far more than she'd ever had with her parents or with Ballard.

Urging Tess forward, Dan reached out his hand to her, and without pause, she took it. They continued across the field under big sky with Boo bounding after them. Finally they arrived at a large barn. Dan pushed the tall barn door aside and stepped inside, but Tess didn't follow him.

She had noticed a lone Belted Galloway in a corral just beyond the barn. The other cows were in the distance. Wondering why that cow was isolated, she decided to get a closer look at the creature and at the wide white swath around its belly. So instead of following Dan, she made her way toward the corral.

The overly large cow lifted his head from the stack of hay that he'd been munching to watch her approach.

Boo barked.

Tess arrived at the corral.

The cow walked toward her.

Boo growled and barked again, beating his front paws against the ground.

Tess stepped up on the first rung of the metal corral to get a closer look.

The cow started to trot toward her.

Tess stepped up on the second rung.

Suddenly, strong arms wrapped around her and pulled her from the fence. "Whoa, Amos!" Dan yelled.

The cow came to a sliding halt. Tess found herself enveloped in Dan's arms.

"I'm sorry," he said. "I shoulda warned you that that's the bull. He can be very aggressive, as many bulls are—especially with breeding season coming up. Please stay away from this corral. I don't want you to get hurt."

She was up close and personal with Dan Garrison. Looking into his brown eyes filled with concern, she thought that he was like her knight in shining armor. Okay, how hokey was that? But seriously, that's what it felt like.

On the other hand, perhaps he wasn't her knight. Perhaps he was the hooded executioner stationed at the guillotine. Her time spent with Ballard had been seventeen years' worth of "WTF?" Seventeen years of having to stand aside and watch his sick infatuations with and fetishes with other women.

Okay, to be fair, Ballard might have pulled or yanked her away from the pen—but he wouldn't have vehemently swept her up into his arms to protect her like this man had just done. Then again, they wouldn't have been anywhere near a bull or a cow or a dog, for that matter.

Yeah, Dan Garrison was looking a lot like her next big mistake, yet somehow she was feeling good about it all—astonishingly good.

After several moments, Dan became aware that he was still holding her. He also became aware of the gun tucked into the back of her jeans. His arm was brushing up against it. She wasn't so trusting, but he couldn't really blame her. Gently, he set her feet to the ground. "Sorry."

After clearing her throat, she said, "I should've realized that it wasn't a good idea. Boo was barking and growling."

"Yeah, he's a bit protective. He knows the dangers on the ranch."

She patted the dog's head again. "So…The bull's name is Amos?"

"Yep."

She watched the bull mosey back to his pile of hay. "How did you come up with that name?"

"Take a look at—"

"No, let me guess—he just *looks* like an Amos."

"You're catching on, Ms. McMillan."

"Well…I'm not so sure about that."

Again, he took her hand. "C'mon, let's go."

That time Dan made sure that she followed him into the barn. They walked through a large area with tie stalls and past a huge stack of hay bales, and then Dan pushed another big door aside. Barn swallows swooped down just over their heads and flew out the door into the sky. Tess ducked. Dan chortled. When they stepped into the large space, she saw that there were five motorcycles lined up in a straight row. All of the cycles' handlebars were turned to the left. Behind the cycles were metal shelving units that held jugs of motor oil, cans of polish, jugs of wash, and other motor-head paraphernalia—all of which were, of course, in perfect lines with their labels out. Iconic posters of scantily clad women posed with Harley-Davidsons or lying across the hood of a muscle car dotted the walls. Tess chuckled to herself—oh yeah, Dan Garrison was a man in every sense of the word.

Spreading his arms wide, Dan said, "Say hello to the bad boys."

Tess was in awe of the shiny motorcycles. They were simply beautiful. She'd never been so close to a motorcycle. She walked down the line, admiring each one of them.

"Why so many?" she asked.

Dan was clearly confused by her question. "What do you mean?"

"Well, you can ride only one at a time, right?"

"Yeah…Why do women have so many shoes? You can wear only one pair at a time, right?"

Tess rolled her eyes. "Shoes aren't nearly as expensive as these 'bad boys.' But your point is noted. So which one will we be riding?"

Crossing his arms over his chest, he said, "Take your pick. I like them all."

Smiling, Tess looked down the line. They were all different and yet very alike. They were all Harley-Davidsons except for one—its logo said "Indian" in script lettering. The bike was orange with an Indian's face encased in chrome on the front fender. The face looked like it would illuminate when the headlights were turned on. Even though the cycle was in mint condition, it was obvious that it was an older model than the others in the lineup. The Indian had a character all its own. She thought it was really cool, and she wanted to see that Indian face light up in the darkness.

Pointing to the unique cycle, Tess said, "This one. It looks different from the rest. Why does it have those covers over the tires?"

"Ah, that's a 1977 Indian. It was my dad's bike. Those are fender valances. They're an Indian trademark, so to speak. They provide protection from road spray and from gravel kicking up. Very good choice— I'm impressed." Dan opened the box that was attached to the back fender of the bike and placed the picnic basket and blanket inside it. "I had this box added to the bike about ten years ago. All of my bikes have one in case I want to take something along—like this picnic basket."

"How very resourceful of you," Tess said, teasing him.

Tossing her a wink, he pushed open a large door at the other end of the garage, and then he went to a shelf and fetched an orange Indian helmet from it.

After eyeing several others on the shelf and Tess, he chose another. He placed his cowboy hat on the shelf and the helmet on his head, and then he fastened it. He lowered a blue helmet over Tess's head and took great pains to make sure that it was fastened correctly.

"Let's go," he said, smiling into her baby blues.

Tess was filled with anticipation of the ride, the picnic, and what the rest of the day would hold.

Six

Wow! Tess had never felt as invigorated as she did on the back of the motorcycle. At first she wrapped her arms around Dan's torso so tightly that she wondered if the poor man would suffocate. As the miles passed, an unfamiliar sense of freedom swept over her. She felt like a kid on a roller coaster. She felt the urge to raise her arms over her head and to touch the wind whipping through her fingers as the coaster roared down the death-defying drop. Woo-hoo!

Dogs, cows, log cabins, rolling green fields, and then a motorcycle. It seemed like a new world—a world that she'd never known existed—was opening up before her eyes, and she liked it. Much to her absolute shock, she loved it!

They rode along curvy back roads and down sweeping thoroughfares. The sunshine beamed through the trees' sparse, leafy canopies, forming sinewy shadows over the blacktop. It was almost like traveling through a tunnel. The tall grasses that grew near the edge of the road swayed as they passed. They rode for about an hour before Dan rolled the motorcycle into a clearing along a winding creek and stopped.

Twisting in his seat to face her, he said, "Well? How'd ya like it?"

She couldn't lie. She was aware that the grin on her face was stretching up to her eyes. It was an unstoppable grin. Tess freely confessed her thoughts on the ride. "It was wonderful! I loved it!"

"Good," Dan said, tugging the helmet from his head. He swung his leg over to the ground and then offered her a hand to help her dismount. He assisted her with the removal of her helmet. Her blond hair was askew from the wind and the pressure of the helmet. Dan fed his urge to run his fingers through it and to lift the hair from her scalp. Like silk, it glided through his fingers. She seemed totally at ease with him and with her surroundings. Good.

Not once did Tess even feel for the gun that he knew was hidden behind her back. While he set the helmets aside and began to unpack the picnic, she made her way creekside to peer into the crystal water rushing over the rocks. He watched her kneel down to dip her fingers into the quick, shallow current, and then she sat down in the grass and gathered her knees to her chest to watch the water flow past her. He could make out the outline of the gun beneath his shirt on her back.

Suddenly she tensed and cupped her hand over her mouth. Dan flinched forward, reaching for the Glock that he had tucked away, but then she turned toward him, pointing across the stream at a doe with twin fawns. Tess was absolutely mesmerized as she watched the doe guide her babes downstream to cross it a safe distance away from the humans on the bank.

Stealthily, Tess rose to her feet, grabbed a nearby tree, and peered around it to watch the trio continue down the creek until they disappeared into the thicket. Dan felt a tug of pity for her. It was becoming more and more apparent to him that she'd experienced very little of what nature had to offer. She'd been kept under tight wraps. Although she was worldly in other facets of life, the fresh air, the open spaces of his ranch, Boo, and the cows—the things that he took for granted every day—were all unfamiliar territory for Tess. He realized that there was a lot that he wanted to show her—if she'd let him and if fate would cooperate.

When the deer were gone from sight, she turned to him, smiling. It was a smile of sheer discovery—it tugged at his very fiber. He fumbled for the simple question on his mind. "Hungry?"

"Starving. I don't think I've eaten since yesterday morning."

He was instantly filled with remorse. "I'm...I'm so sorry. I should've offered you something to eat last night. I never thought—"

"Don't worry about it. I probably wouldn't have eaten anyway. I was too tired and way too stressed," she said, trying to ease his guilt.

"Still, I feel bad."

She touched his arm. "Let's eat now."

They set straight to laying out the big blanket that Dan had brought along and to unpacking the basket filled with picnic goodies, including a bottle of Chardonnay, a box of pita crackers, and a small block of blue cheese to pair with the oaky flavor of the wine. He'd also packed chicken salad on croissants and a small peach pie. She was truly impressed. Dan Garrison hadn't been exaggerating—he really did pack a mean picnic lunch.

Tess took a sip of the Chardonnay and closed her eyes, savoring the oaky taste that was entertaining her palate. "Mm...How did you know Chardonnay was one of my favorites?"

"Just a good guess." Dan placed a bit of cheese on a cracker and lifted it to her lips. She let him slip it into her mouth. He enjoyed watching her chew. He enjoyed watching her lips curl around the wine glass. He wanted to taste her lips freshly saturated in Chardonnay. He wanted to lay her back on the blanket and to hold her against his body.

Slowly she opened her eyes, dragging her gaze to meet his. There was a sultry glimmer in those baby blues of hers. Absently, he licked his lips.

"So, Grumpy, where'd ya get the peach pie? I didn't see any baking going on," Tess said.

"Peach pie is my favorite. I usually have some around. Want me to cut you a piece?"

"Thought you'd never ask."

He smiled in reply and then pulled the pie from the basket so that he could cut her a slice. "More wine?"

She held her glass out. "Always."

He poured more wine into her glass, handed her a small plate with a generous portion of pie, and then stretched out on the blanket, leaning back on an elbow with his slice in his other hand. "Up for a little target practice after we eat our dessert?"

She peeked at him askance. Around a mouthful, she managed to say, "Target practice?"

After reaching into the basket, he produced a pile of Styrofoam cups. "Yeah, you can show me how well you handle that .45 you've got stuffed in your pants."

As she chewed, her lips curled. After swallowing, she asked, "And you'll show me how to handle the Glock 19 you're toting?"

She'd noticed. He wasn't surprised. He didn't believe that too much got past Tess McMillan. Was she ultraobservant? Or was her survival mechanisms kicking in? He couldn't be sure. "Sure, it'll be…educational."

"Set 'em up, cowboy. Let's do this," Tess said, pushing herself up from the blanket and brushing her hands together in mock anticipation.

He liked it.

After finding a log in the brush, Dan pulled it into the clearing and then set up six cups atop it. Tess pulled the gun from under the shirt and disengaged the safety. After stepping the proper shooting distance away, Dan did the same with his weapon.

"How many do you want me to shoot?" Tess asked.

"Show me whatcha got."

Wrapping both hands around the .45 caliber, she leveled it at the cups stationed on the logs about fifty feet away. She took in a breath as she pulled the trigger—and the first cup popped off of the log and fell to the ground. Moving her aim, she trained on the next cup. She pulled the trigger, but the bullet hit the log just below cup number two, abrading the wood. Letting out a breath, she moved on to cup number three and pulled the trigger. It jerked, and when it dropped to the ground, there was a huge hole in the middle of it. She demolished cup number four and missed number five, but she had every confidence that number six would meet the ground, and it did. As she lowered the gun, her lips curled in satisfaction.

"Four out of six—not too shabby."

"I was pleased. Your turn, Grumpy."

He set up six more cups and then returned to his spot next to Tess. Planting his feet firmly under his hips, he lifted the Glock 19 and took aim.

"What? No blindfold?" Tess asked.

The edges of his mouth kicked upward—the woman had sass. "I'm saving that for another time."

"Dang."

The gun exploded. The first cup pitched into the air and fell to the ground, and then the second and the third did the same. The fourth split in half and fell on each side of the log, and the fifth and the sixth cups quickly met their demise in much the same manner. Dan lifted the gun to his mouth to blow on the end of the barrel as though he were on an old Western TV show. He winked.

Tess laughed. "Very good marksmanship, Marshal Dillon."

"Unfortunately, I get a lot of practice," Dan said while stuffing the Glock back into its hiding place.

"There're lots of bad guys out there?"

"I'm afraid there are."

Falling quiet, Tess turned and made her way back to the blanket. After kneeling down, she set the .45 off to the side, poured more wine into their glasses, and made herself comfortable as she held Dan's glass up in an invitation for him to join her.

He stretched out next to her. Before taking a sip of the wine, Dan asked, "Who taught you to shoot?"

"I told you—I took care of the security for Ballard. I've taken quite a few shooting classes over the years. Ballard liked that I carried heat and that I knew how to defend myself or *him*, if need be. I took a couple of shots at Grant when he came to sneak Silja out of Ballard's house."

"You missed," he said.

"Good thing," she said.

The silence stretched between them as they measured each other's eyes. Finally, Tess lifted her glass to her mouth, took a sip, and licked her lips slowly and easily.

"I gotta agree with Crafton—a woman who can handle a gun is a turn-on." With that, he leaned in and did what he'd been longing to do since he'd seen her sleeping early that morning—or was it since he'd walked in on her yoga workout? Or maybe it was since the moment she'd showed up at headquarters? It didn't matter. He pressed his lips to hers. When he felt her react, when he felt her lean in to the kiss, he deepened the kiss and caressed her cheek and her neck with the backs of his fingers.

She tasted good.

She tasted of the wine and the fresh air and the afternoon filled with promise.

Tess wrapped her fingers around his neck and pulled him on top of her body. Dan found himself exactly where he'd wanted to be and where he wasn't supposed to be, but he wasn't sure that he gave a flyin' flip. Her skin heated beneath his caress, and the ache and the throb and the swell of his erection pushed against his jeans. No need to hide his primal urge that time. He knew she was well aware of the hard-on pressing against her hip. She rotated her hip to feel it, to encourage it, even though he didn't need a whole helluva lot of persuasion.

His lips moved down her throat to her chest while his hands found their way to her breasts. They felt through the fabric of her cami and fumbled to move it aside so that he could caress her skin and her nipples into stiff peaks and finally run his tongue over them. Just then she yanked the cami and the shirt from her body to offer him both breasts, naked and hard and yearning for his mouth. He didn't disappoint. Dan swept his hungry tongue over her nipples, took the left one between his teeth, and sucked it until she sighed with pleasure.

Tess's fingers groped the snap on his jeans and then freed his erection. He lifted his hips to assist her in peeling his jeans off of them. "I hope you don't mind, but I really want you, Grumpy."

"No…By all means, be my guest, gorgeous."

He lay on the blanket admiring the view while she stood, topless, to shimmy out of her jeans. After tossing them aside, she straddled him unashamedly, letting him take in her nakedness and watching his erection grow harder and harder by the moment, knowing that he ached for her, for only her, and that no other woman was in his thoughts or the object of his desire.

She squatted over him, her sex hovering just above his rock-hard penis. "So what's your pleasure, Mr. Garrison? Have you got a pair of handcuffs in that box, or do you want to spank me with a switch from one of these trees?"

His eyes popping open, Dan stilled on the blanket. It took him a second to take in what she'd just suggested, and then anger rose in his throat like bile. He grabbed her wrists and looked into her suddenly uneasy eyes. "What the hell? Is that what that asshole used to do to you? Is that what lovemaking is for you?" He watched her expression turn from a sultry one to one of shock. "That's not how I make love, Tess. I'm a man. I'm the kind of man who doesn't need to punish a woman with a spanking before sex, and I'm not a sick jerk who feels the need to handcuff a woman to make her helpless. I want to make love to you, and if that's never happened to you before, let me show you how it's done right now."

A nanosecond later, he flipped her down onto the blanket. Then he was straddling her. Then he was watching her breathing accelerate. His big, calloused hands became like velvet as he slipped them through her long tresses to lift her head upward so that he could press his lips to hers. "Lovemaking is gentle and kind and sometimes quick but always loving," he whispered as his lips caressed her jaw and her throat and then moved down her chest to her breasts.

Delicately, his tongue stroked her nipples as he eased inside her and slowly pumped his hips, waiting for her hips to join in the rhythm. She sighed and wrapped her legs around him, joining the cadence of the lovemaking. She grabbed his face and lifted it up, and then she kissed him long and hard and with the passion that he realized she'd been denied. The passion that he had every intention of reminding her existed.

The passion that she deserved. He would give it to her. That's right, she could have the kind of love that she'd been robbed of, and he would give it to her freely for as long as she wanted it.

Her body arched beneath his. This was the moment—the moment he'd looked forward to. The moment she would reach her climax. "C'mon, Tess, enjoy it. 'Cause I'm right there with you, baby. I'm...right... there...with...you." With that, he scaled the top of his desire. He held her yet tighter, pressing deeper into the kiss, and held her until her body became liquid and his felt boneless.

She opened her eyes and smiled.

Yeah, that was the look.

He'd put that look in her eyes.

His cell phone rang.

They stilled, exchanging amused glances.

It rang again.

"Damn...I gotta answer that."

"Well, at least their timing isn't all that bad."

"That's a matter of opinion." Rolling away from her body, Dan swallowed hard and reached into his hip pocket. After clearing his throat, he answered his phone. "Garrison."

After a pause, Clark asked, "You okay, Garrison?"

"Um...yeah...sure. Why?"

"You sound out of breath."

Dan snorted. "No. What've ya got?"

"Can you bring Ms. McMillan to headquarters? I've got some questions for her."

"Sure, we'll drop by in a bit."

"Trust, not sex, Dan." With that, the line went dead.

It was more than trust, and it was more than sex—way more. He was invested in the woman—and that was exactly the way he wanted it. Dan shoved the phone back into the pocket.

"Trouble?" Tess asked.

"No, Clark wants us to stop by the mansion. He says he's got some questions."

"Ah, I was hoping for another motorcycle ride."

Dan smiled. He ran his finger across her jaw. He could see himself giving the woman damned near anything she wanted. "No hurry. We'll take the long way."

* * *

Tess's head lay against his shoulders when Dan rolled the Indian to a stop at the gates of First Force Headquarters. It felt good to have a woman's arms wrapped around him again. He'd almost forgotten how good it was to have someone holding on while he drove along with nowhere in particular to go.

Turning the bike off, he twisted in his seat. "Should I put my face to the screen, or do you want to use your hocus-pocus marbles to open the gate?"

Tess chuckled. "Sorry, I left my marbles at the ranch."

"Lost your marbles, have ya?"

"Oh, you're a regular comedian, aren't you?"

"I'll be here all week, ladies and gentlemen." He placed his face on the chin rest to allow the scanner to read his irises. There was a click, and then the gate slowly folded open. Dan started the bike, pushed off, and drove toward the Georgian mansion.

* * *

Tess's stomach tightened. What kind of questions would Dan's boss have for her? What kind of a man was he? Would Clark Rhodes be an overbearing bully, demanding quick answers to tough questions? Would this be a hostile interrogation situation? Would Dan be her knight in shining armor, or would he allow his boss to intimidate the hell out of her? She didn't believe that for a moment. Dan had made love to her. It hadn't been sex. He had given her everything—everything that Ballard had never been able to give her. No, Dan wouldn't abandon her.

Still, her afternoon of picnics and motorcycle rides and carefree lovemaking in the grass was over. It was time to find out what kind of ally or enemy First Force was going to be.

When they stepped through the door, a man who she assumed was Clark Rhodes was crossing the foyer with a cup of coffee in hand. He wasn't at all what Tess had expected. He was tall and thin. His dark hair caressed the collar of his polo shirt and swept across the top of the rims of his dark-colored square-shaped glasses. He was sporting a pair of tan loose-fitting cargo shorts and flip-flops.

Clark Rhodes wasn't the muscle-bound beast she'd envisioned. Whew! On the other hand, appearances can be very deceiving. Maybe the man was a real monster when he wanted answers. Her stomach wasn't letting go of the bundle of knots just yet.

Dan broke through Tess's silent deliberations. "Clark, this is Tess McMillan."

The dark-haired man smiled at her and offered her his hand. When she placed hers in his, she felt a firm but friendly greeting. Looking into his eyes, she could see strength and resolve.

"Good to meet you, Tess. Please, let's go into the office. I have some information and some things you may be able to clear up for us. Who knows? I may be able to clear up a few things for you, too."

She followed Dan and Clark into the large office. The walls were dotted with computer screens and security cams constantly sweeping the exterior of the estate. Clark directed her to a wingback chair near a large desk and then perched on a corner of the desk, allowing his leg to drape over the edge of it.

"Can I offer you some coffee? It's fresh," Clark said.

"That would be great."

"Dan…Could you do the honors?"

Dan's spine stiffened. "Where're the cats?"

Clark's brows fell into a V. "I dunno. Walt doesn't allow the cats in his office."

"Why?"

"Too much hair," Clark said with a shrug.

Tess let the chuckle that was lodged in her throat bubble up. "Never mind. I really don't need any coffee. I'll have some later, when you're better armed."

After closing the door to the office, Dan sank into a chair. Clark tossed him a questioning glance.

Turning his attention to the subject at hand, Clark asked Tess, "Do you know a Chinese woman named Jingjing Choo?"

"Yes, she was the head scientist on the XM-11 project."

"How well did you know her?"

"We weren't exactly BFFs. Why are you asking about Jingjing?"

"She wasn't among the people killed when Crafton Labs blew up. Seems she went to Moscow that weekend to marry one of the security guards from the laboratory, Vlad Guseva. Lucky them," Clark said. "Since this woman was a scientist for Crafton Labs, I think you just found your connection to the Russian man. Both Choo and Guseva came to the United States about two months ago. They flew into Bradley International Airport in Windsor Locks, Connecticut."

"August Crafton, Ballard's brother, lives in Stamford," Tess said. Her teeth bit down on the inside of her lip as she sank into the chair. "It's hard for me to picture Jingjing as a married woman. I truly believe she is the original ice princess. In any case, she was working solo on another project. Ballard even gave her a private laboratory. She had no assistants. It was top secret. They were going to start testing whatever she was working on in addition to the XM as soon as they could get at least one of the test subjects to survive the XM injection."

"So you and Jingjing didn't get along because Crafton never told you what she was working on?" Dan asked.

"I wasn't happy about it. Ballard told me everything, but this was his little secret with Jingjing. I was left out of the loop. Jingjing is a bit of a bitch—that's really the reason she and I didn't get along." She lifted a shoulder. "I dunno. Maybe she was going to be the next flavor of the month if Silja Ramsay didn't work out—although she wasn't exactly Ballard's type."

"Meaning?" Clark asked.

Tess let out a weary breath. "Of course, she's very intelligent, but she lacks the beauty that Ballard lusted after." Her eyes searched the floor, not really seeing it. "No, on second thought, it must have been strictly business between them. Jingjing has great brains, a great body, and fabulous hair, but in the looks department, she would've fallen way below the bar for Ballard's discerning tastes."

"So it had to be the whole package?" Dan asked.

Tess rolled her eyes. "Puh-leaze, just when I thought the man couldn't get any more shallow, he'd let a little more water drain from the tub."

"So you don't think they had an intimate relationship?" Clark asked.

"No, like I said, she simply isn't good-looking enough. Ballard didn't bed just anyone."

"Whoa." Dan put up his hand. "How could you say that? We know for a fact that Crafton participated in the auctions for sex with the dancers in the ballet company that Silja danced with in Russia."

"That's true," Tess said. "But those women were very talented, and there wasn't a homely one in the group. They were all beautiful, and because they were all ballerinas, like Silja, having sex with one of them would help him fantasize about the ballerina he couldn't have. Although I don't know how that really applies to the situation at hand."

"And August?" Clark asked. "Is he as sick of a bastard as his older brother?"

"I've only met August once or twice. Ballard didn't speak of him very often, and when he did, it was in generalities. I really don't know much about him."

"Well, I'll tell you what I know," Clark said. "Augustine Crafton is ten years younger than Ballard. When the boys' father, Princeton Crafton, died eleven years ago, Ballard opted to buy Augustine out of the research laboratory his father had built and made millions with. Ballard paid his brother forty-five million dollars to walk away. Augustine was accustomed to playing the part of the millionaire playboy, and he still is. He's never been married. No children. I guess my questions are, what does he intend to do with the XM-11 if he gets his hands on it? How does he know that you have it? And most importantly, where is it?"

There it was. First Force wanted to know where she had the serum hidden. Tess wasn't sure the first two questions were really important to Mr. Rhodes. Leaning back in the chair, she wondered what the next step would be if she refused to divulge the location of the serum.

She glanced to her left. Dan was sitting with his right leg crossed over his left. His arms were dangling over the arms of the chair. He was watching his foot rotate in a small circle. He must've felt her heavy gaze on him. He glanced askance at her.

Her eyes snapped to Clark, who was still seated on the desk. He was studying her with his left eyebrow arched. It was plain to see that he was waiting for an answer—an answer she wasn't absolutely sure she was ready to give.

"The serum is safe, I assure you. I suppose my question is, what do you intend to do with the serum if I give it to you?"

Clark took a sip of his coffee, slipped from the desk, and then made his way around so that he could ease into the chair. "What do you want us to do with it, Ms. McMillan? You searched us out. You wanted our help. So what is it that you want? Protection? A new identity? We're certainly capable of providing such services. That said, you are in possession of a powerful weapon—a weapon that you were supposed to destroy a year ago. So I guess before I agree to anything, I feel a responsibility to know what *your* intentions for the XM-11 are."

"That's fair enough. I was a fool to not go through with my plans to destroy Ballard's notes. I regret my stupidity, but there's nothing I can do about that now. I do not have nor have I ever had any intention of marketing the serum. I want it to be destroyed as originally planned, but how or when, I simply don't know—especially with August on my heels."

"So you feel your life would be in danger if August found you and you *didn't* have the serum?"

"Definitely."

"Would you feel just as threatened if he found you with the serum in your possession?"

Thoughtfully, Tess brushed an errant wisp of hair behind her ear. "Yes, I believe I would."

"Damned if you do, and damned if you don't." Clark snorted.

"Damned straight."

"Do you feel safe at Dan's ranch?"

"I do."

"Good. We can provide you with asylum until you make a firm decision about how and when the serum should be destroyed. I'd prefer that that decision be made within the week. Like you, I believe Dan's place is as secure as the mansion, so we'll keep things as they are. If you decide to go into an identity-protection program, you'll have to give up all contact with family and friends. That's a tough decision for anyone, but I would think it would be even more difficult for you, Ms. McMillan."

"You mean because I've just recently reunited with my parents? You're very good at gathering personal information, Mr. Rhodes."

"Yes, I am, Ms. McMillan—that's why they pay me the big bucks. So let me reiterate: If you choose to go into a witness-protection program, you won't be able to contact your family again—ever."

"I understand. I have a lot to think about."

"And very little time to do so," Clark said.

Seven

Stamford, Connecticut, Sunday Morning

August was taken aback when he found Vatonia climbing the stairs with a large breakfast tray on her shoulder. The tiny, bent-over African American woman had been in his employ for eleven years. She'd worked for his father for many years before. She was loyal to a fault. She said nothing about the comings and goings of his live-in pleasures over the years, kept the house top-notch clean, and cooked so well that she could've been Wolfgang Puck's mentor. Vatonia was a gem, but that morning, she looked agitated as she schlepped the tray upstairs.

His eyes narrowed. August hadn't requested breakfast in bed for himself or for his girls. Furthermore, it wasn't like Gina or Christine to ask Vatonia for anything. Even though both had lived with him for more than a year, they seemed to be intimidated by the woman. August couldn't imagine why. The girls were courteous to her, and likewise, she to them. Yet he found that they avoided her as much as possible.

Holding tightly to the railing that wound along the curved wall, the old woman of sixty-five paused halfway up the stairs to take in a few breaths. Quickly, August made his way downward to take the tray from her hands.

"Let me take this upstairs for you, Vatonia," he said while scanning the items on the tray. There was enough for two. "Did the girls order breakfast in bed? I certainly didn't."

Huffing between each word and each rising step, Vatonia said, "No…The girls were shooed away from the table this morning by Mrs. Guseva. Seems she wants to talk with you alone, so now I'm traipsing up these steps with a breakfast tray. I didn't realize that I take orders from *that* woman, but she informed me in *no uncertain terms* that I should take breakfast upstairs to Gina and Christine this morning." She added a weary harrumph.

August's brows furrowed as he reached the top floor. "Gina! Christine!"

Within a moment, two doors opened. The young women stuck their heads out of their rooms. "Please take your breakfasts from the tray, and when you're done eating, return the dishes to the kitchen."

"Certainly," Gina, a lovely brunette, said.

"Of course," the redhead, Christine, said. "We're sorry you had to bring them up here, Vatonia. You should have texted us. We would've come down to get them at the bottom of the stairs."

"That's okay, child. You have a nice breakfast now," Vatonia said with a wave of her hand as she started back down the staircase.

"Thank you, girls," August said, and then hesitating, he turned toward Vatonia. "Isn't today Easter? You usually take the holiday off to visit your daughter and her family."

"They decided to go on a cruise while the kids are on their spring break this year."

"Ah, I remember—you suffer terribly from seasickness."

"Mm, it doesn't matter if I wear a patch or take those pills, I'm turning green and prayin' for death within an hour of steppin' on the ship," Vatonia said with a chuckle in her voice.

They stepped through the archway into the dining room, where they found Jingjing sitting at one end of the long table with a cup of coffee in her hand, wearing the surly expression that was present on a daily basis on her face. Shan was perched on her right shoulder.

August managed a pleasant tone. "Good morning, Jingjing. No breakfast?"

"I offered," Vatonia said, raising her hands in surrender. "But all she'd have was a cup of coffee."

"Thank you for speaking for me, Vatonia. How would I have ever communicated otherwise?" Jingjing said in a low and terse voice.

"She's kinda bitchy too, if you're askin' me," Vatonia said under her breath. "And I hate that damned cat," she added while shouldering through the swinging door that led into the kitchen.

August smothered a chuckle as he pulled out his chair and sat down. Slipping the linen napkin over his lap, he asked, "What's so important that we must eat in complete seclusion this morning?"

"There's been a breakthrough with my additive for the XM. I am ready to test the formula on a human. This way, we will know whether my formula has been perfected, and when we get the XM, I can make the proper adjustments, add my formula to it, and then test the modified serum on another subject before we begin to market it."

Just then Vatonia came through the swinging door to deliver August's breakfast. Taking another sip of her coffee, Jingjing sat back deep in her seat. The scientist could sense Vatonia's disapproval for her by the way the woman pursed her lips and raised her brow as she poured the coffee from the fine-china carafe into

August's cup. Shan's deep purr reverberated through the silence.

Vatonia's tone was stiff when she said, "More coffee for you, Ms. Guseva?"

The steam swirling between her almond eyes, Jingjing glowered at her over her cup.

"I think she's good, Vatonia. Thank you," August said. Shrugging, Vatonia returned to the kitchen.

"I don't need you to speak for me, Mr. Crafton. I was attempting to communicate with your servant through telepathy. I'm certain my answer would have penetrated if you had given it more time."

"I think your sour attitude toward Vatonia was communication enough. Now, when do you plan to test the formula?"

"Immediately."

August's eyes widened. "Immediately? But we don't have any subjects for the experiment."

"I beg to differ. We have two perfectly healthy specimens upstairs eating breakfast."

"Gina and Christine? I don't think so. Shouldn't you experiment on test animals first?"

She lifted a shoulder. "I already have—on your neighbor's poodle. It was quite successful. The stupid dog was a menace, barking constantly, but after the injection, she would sit, beg, roll over, and dance for me—without a treat."

August choked on his toast. "Dear God! You *stole* Mrs. Bennett's poodle?"

"The old biddy was thrilled when I returned her. I told her that I found the dog two streets up earlier this morning. She was so happy to have the stupid mutt back that she didn't ask any more questions. I tested my formula. She got a better-behaved dog in return—win, win."

Sitting back, August massaged his forehead with his fingers. "I don't know, Jingjing. I feel there should be more testing on animals—like on all of those lab rats you specifically requested when you arrived two months ago rather than on the neighbors' pets. I must insist that you run your trials on them before testing the formula on humans."

"You are forgetting that we stand to make billions with this formula. I told you, the dog was fine afterward. Human testing may be different, but if so, sacrifices must be made for the good of our cause. Your bimbos would be nothing more than collateral damage. Surely you could replace them quite easily," Jingjing said.

"Let me clue you in—Gina and Christine are both college students. Both are not only beautiful but also intelligent women with bright futures. They're my companions in exchange for college tuition and other perks. On that note, Vatonia has been with my family for many years. She is a valued employee, not a servant."

"How very endearing, Mr. Crafton. I suppose I should be grateful. At least I won't be wasting my formula on brainless specimens, as Ballard was forced to do. The Russians would only provide him with criminals to experiment with. They were uneducated, warped Neanderthals. Ballard was less than pleased with his test subjects."

"I'm not going to let you experiment on Gina or Christine, and I don't think my brother would have either."

Gathering Shan into her arms, Jingjing stood. "I'm not so sure. I'll be in my lab. When you come to your senses, bring one of the *intelligent* young ladies down. We'll see if she will follow any and all directives I give her after an injection."

Jingjing marched out of the room. Her frustrated footsteps could be heard as she stomped down the hallway until she slammed the door that led to the basement.

August pushed his breakfast away.

*　*　*

Vatonia had just rounded the corner, and she heard Christine talking. "I don't know, Aggie. That woman creeps me out. Her cat's creepy too. She's always scowling at everyone, and she never says a word, and I think she's been down here cooking up some kind of zombie stew," she said as August led her down the basement stairs.

Vatonia drew closer to the door to listen to her.

August forced a chuckle. "No…I told you, I hired her to make an injectable formula that will help with muscle definition. If we can perfect it, I can market it to body builders and people who simply want more muscle definition from their workouts."

Carefully, Vatonia eased the door open just a bit to see what was taking place.

Halfway down the stairs, Christine hesitated. "But I think they already have formulas like that. I think you can buy powders to add to smoothies that help with that stuff. My grandfather used to use a powder called More Muscle for his racehorses for that very purpose. If it's available for horses, I'm sure they have it for humans."

"I'm sure they do. But this will be an injection. It will go directly into the bloodstream and, therefore, be more effective more quickly. You work out all the time, Christine. This will boost your muscle mass almost instantly."

"I don't know——"

He took her by the shoulders and looked into her brown eyes, which were filled with reservations.

"Have I ever done anything to harm you?" She shook her head to indicate no. "Have I taken care of all your college bills, provided you with a cool car, and bought you all kinds of fine clothes?"

"Yes, but——"

"You must trust me, Christine. You won't be harmed. I promise. The worst thing that could happen to you would be getting better-defined muscles, right?"

"I suppose——"

"Good, then let's go."

He held her hand more tightly and led her into the basement. Vatonia eased the door open and then slipped into the stairwell.

Jingjing had set up a gurney with clean sheets. When they approached, she managed a svelte smile and gestured for Christine to lie on the gurney. August helped her up. He stilled, glancing at the CD player on the shelf. "Your music—it's playing softly."

Puffing up the pillow, Jingjing said, "Of course. The poodle is quiet now." She touched Christine on the shoulder. "Lie back, and make yourself comfortable. This will only take a few minutes. It won't hurt at all."

After Christine was in position, Jingjing dabbed her veins with a cotton ball soaked in alcohol and then picked up the syringe from the stainless-steel tray on her worktable. With nervous fingers, August stroked Christine's red hair while Jingjing jabbed the needle into her arm, pressed the formula into her system, and then withdrew the needle before covering the tiny prick with a square of gauze.

"Is that all?" Christine asked.

"Almost," Jingjing said. "I'd like you to lie here for a few moments just to make sure that you don't get dizzy. We wouldn't want you to fall going up the stairs and harm yourself."

Before closing her eyes, Christine rolled them in disdain for the scientist. August tossed Jingjing a wary glance. The scientist was stoic as she watched the young woman on the gurney.

Christine opened her eyes. "I'm feeling dizzy and a little woozy."

"That's the formula working. You'll be okay in a moment," Jingjing coolly said.

Christine jerked up to her elbows. "The room is spinning! I'm not feeling good at all!"

Pushing her back, Jingjing said, "Just lie back. It'll pass in a few minutes."

August tensed. His eyes snapped to Jingjing. She waved a careless hand at him and mouthed, "Only another moment."

Vatonia cupped her hand over her mouth. Her stomach twisted into knots as she watched.

Christine's breathing quickened.

Her hands began to shake.

Her body began to shudder and quake uncontrollably.

August tried to steady her so that she wouldn't fall from the gurney. "Jingjing!"

Jingjing stood back with her arms crossed over her flat chest, observing her.

The shaking became so violent that August could barely keep Christine on the gurney. Still, Jingjing was unaffected and steadily jotted notes down in her book.

"What the hell, Jingjing! She's having a convulsion! She's gonna die!"

"Will you calm down? I assure you, it's almost over."

As if Christine had heard her words, her body stilled, her eyes closed, and her breathing returned to normal. The young woman lay completely at peace on the gurney. Her head fell to one side.

August's body stiffened. He whispered, "Is she dead?"

"No. She's unconscious. I will monitor her vital signs until she wakes."

"How long will she be out?"

"It depends on her system. I added a slight sedative to the formula so that the subject will rest for a short time before I begin the experiment. I want to make sure that her vital signs stay steady and that the brain does not swell. Mrs. Bennett's poodle didn't have either of those reactions. When sedated, some people sleep for an hour, and others sleep for several hours. Go upstairs. Don't worry. I will text you when she's conscious." With that, she dismissed him with a wave of her hand. She went straight to taking Christine's vital signs and marking down notes in her book. Shan jumped up on the gurney and padded across the young woman's body.

Pallid, August stood quietly. His gaze rotated from Jingjing to Christine and back. Vatonia remembered Ballard as a fearless individual. August—not so much. If he wanted to become the billionaire he'd always dreamed of being, he too would have to be intrepid—unafraid to make big sacrifices to get where he wanted to be. Vatonia sighed. Unfortunately, it looked as though Christine would pay that price. Unable to watch for another moment more, Vatonia quickly stepped onto the main floor and eased the basement door closed behind her.

* * *

"Please, August. Go," Jingjing said

This was it. This was the first human trial. Hopefully, Jingjing's additive would be successful. Then they would need the XM-11. They would need Tess McMillan. He was considering giving the beautiful blonde the option to replace Christine. If she didn't agree to it, she too would become collateral damage.

All he could do was wait to see how Christine would come through it and what the outcome of the injection would be. Turning, he dragged himself toward the steps.

* * *

Dan's Ranch, Sunday Morning,

Dan rose earlier than usual. It was Easter morning, and although Tess was not a child, he thought it would be fun to have some colored eggs in a bowl on the counter for her. So he jumped out of bed at five in the morning, boiled a dozen eggs, colored them, and set them out.

Opting for a comfortable Easter, he remained in his gray lounging pants and a T-shirt with the word "Army" scrolled in black lettering across the chest. He would wait until Tess got up before heading out to the barn for chores—they could wait.

By seven, he decided to try to wake Tess by cooking up some bacon. Perhaps the smell of bacon cooking in a pan would waft up the stairs and stir her from her slumber. He puttered around the kitchen in his comfy clothes and bare feet, hoping she'd soon make an appearance.

"Up early, as usual," Tess said as she stepped from the staircase. Dan stopped his cooking to drink her in. Whoa, she was a sight in the morning and the afternoon and the evening, too. She was wearing that same gray shirt of his, and damn, he liked seeing the woman in it.

Boo dived from the couch to greet her. She patted the dog on the head. "Good morning, Boo."

"Happy Easter," Dan said.

"Easter? I'd forgotten. I bet it's been seventeen… no…eighteen years since I've celebrated Easter. You know, Easter baskets, eggs, and…Oh, wow! You colored eggs!" Wide eyed, Tess hurried to the counter to admire the bowl filled with brightly colored eggs. "I love hard-boiled eggs, especially on Easter. Thank you, Dan." She quickly made her way around the counter to kiss his cheek.

Dan's heart swelled. It wasn't a diamond necklace or earrings—it was a lousy bowl of hard-boiled eggs—yet the woman was gushing with appreciation. "Are you gonna call your parents? I mean, it is Easter. They'd probably like to hear from you."

"I'll send my mom an e-mail later on. If I call, I'll have to answer a bunch of rapid-fire questions."

"I see. Like, who are you with? What's he like? Does he have a good job? And more importantly, is he handsome beyond belief?"

She giggled. "Something like that. My parents are hard to please—no, let me rephrase that. They are *impossible* to please. They never met Ballard, but I guarantee they would've hated him."

"Can't say that I would blame them," Dan said. Tess snorted. "Would your parents approve of me?"

"Gawd, I hope not. That'd be no fun at all."

"How old are you again?"

"Old enough to not need my parents' approval—that's for damned sure. Have you got any orange juice?"

"Sure, top shelf in the fridge."

Tess blinked when she opened the refrigerator. She shouldn't have been surprised, but she hadn't expected the refrigerator to be as organized as his wardrobe. Clearly, she'd been wrong. The bottles of water were lined up as precisely as soldiers at attention on the lower shelf of the refrigerator door. Likewise, bottles of Honey Brown beer were stationed on the shelf just above the water. The labels were facing outward at a perfect angle so that one could read them without difficulty. Tess's eyes scanned the rest of the contents of the main shelves. The creamers, ketchup, mustard, milk, mayonnaise, and maple syrup—all of the labels were facing outward and were perfectly straight. Smiling, she shook her head.

"They have therapy for this kind of stuff, you know," Tess said over her shoulder.

"What're you talking about?"

"Your perfectly organized refrigerator," she said, plucking the orange juice from the top shelf. "Your incredibly clean house, your clothing hung in perfect symmetry in the closets—yeah, there are doctors who'd love to hear all about *your* potty training."

"My potty training was just fine, but thanks for asking," Dan said, placing a golden-brown pancake onto a neat stack in the middle of a platter.

"Perfect, I'm sure," Tess said.

Setting the spatula aside, Dan cocked his head. "What's so wrong with being organized and neat? Makes life a helluva lot easier—I guarantee it."

Tess snorted. "It's one thing to be organized—hell, I'm superorganized. But it's another to be obsessed, phobic, or fixated on perfection. In other words, to be living with a stick up your ass."

Dan blinked and then blinked again. "I don't have a stick up my ass."

Laughing, Tess tossed her head back. "Oh, Grumpy, that stick is so far up your ass that it would take major surgery to extract it."

He wanted to be angry with her. He wanted to tell her that she didn't know what the hell she was talking about, but the facts were in her favor. Damn it, she was right. He was uptight. He watched her luscious lips moving in laughter—her sparkling eyes smiling, enjoying the moment. He set the platter on the counter and then made haste across the kitchen, took her by the shoulders, and pulled her toward him.

She stopped laughing when her blue eyes met his brown ones. In a quiet, husky voice, Dan said, "Teach me to relax, McMillan. Show me what you know that I don't."

Her sultry baby blues studied him. The curve of her brow raised and then lowered again. "I taught myself how to survive severe stress through relaxation years ago. There's hope for you, Grumpy, if you trust me to show you how."

"So this will require trust?"

"Maybe a little." She shrugged. "But if you can breathe, you can relax."

He took her by the hand and led her toward the living room. "Show me."

"I dunno, are you man enough to do my yoga workout?"

Dan stepped to the middle of the bearskin rug. The corners of his mouth curved upward. "Namaste," he said around the grin.

"All righty, then…Take off your shirt," she said.

He was a little surprised by the request, but he liked the idea. He complied, attempting to toss the T-shirt aside. Tess caught it midair, rolled it up, and then, stepping behind him, draped it around his eyes, making sure that his nose and mouth were exposed as she tied it behind his head.

His constant companion, paranoia, slithered up his spine, but he fought back—after all, he'd made love to this woman just the day before. Just the day before he'd felt something that had eluded him for years—love. Somehow a little voice in his head told paranoia to stand down—and that it was okay and that he could trust her. *You asked for it, Garrison. So shut up, and put up.*

He heard the sound of toenails clicking over the floor and then the sound of the cushions on the couch giving way—Boo had just joined the yoga workout from the comfort of the couch.

Who was envious then?

Tess must've glanced his way.

Dan heard his tail slap the leather once.

She stretched up on her tiptoes and whispered in Dan's ear. "I had a yoga instructor once who had us do our class blindfolded. He said it was a sure way to block out the outside world and all of its distractions. I found it to be quite liberating. You definitely need to lose the distractions, and that includes the dog."

He was fine with Boo leaving the room, but he wasn't sure about the blindfold. After taking in a breath and bracing himself, he said, "Okay."

He heard her bare feet shuffle through the bear's fur. "Come, Boo," she said as she padded across the wood floors. Boo jumped from his perch. His toenails clicked and clacked across the floor. The door opened, and the door closed. Tess padded toward him. He heard several clicks, and then the TV was on, and soft, eerie music was wafting through the room.

Tess gave him instructions. "Stand tall with your feet slightly apart, your shoulders squared, and your chin up, and breathe deeply. This position is called 'standing in mountain.'" He did as he'd been told. She continued. "Good. Now, take some slow, deep belly breaths." She ran her hands across the back of his muscled shoulders.

Closing his eyes behind the blindfold, Dan took in several long, slow breaths.

"Good," Tess said, purring.

Her hands felt like feathers caressing his skin—across his shoulders, down his arms, and through his fingertips. And then when her touch left his body, he instantly missed it—he longed for it to return. He was completely conscious of her movements. He sensed her feet stepping away from the rug. His brows furrowed as he wondered whether she was going to leave the room, but then she stilled, taking his hand in hers. Ah, there it was—her warm, engaging touch.

"Now lie down on the rug with your legs apart, your arms down to the side, and your palms up." She kept ahold of his hand while he lowered his body over the rug. He maneuvered into the position that she'd requested.

Once in place, he tried to relax. He was trying not to allow certain parts of his body to stiffen and extend, but it was hard. Yep, he was worried that it was going to get very hard. The blindfold let nothing else penetrate but the sensual melody of her voice; her slow, steady breathing; and her hushed, catlike movements around him. Finally he felt her body close to his. He sensed her kneeling next to him. He could actually feel the heat from her body.

Her soothing voice hovered over him. "We're breathing. When you inhale, your abdomen rises, and when you exhale, your abdomen falls." Her fingers splayed out wide, she laid her hand lightly over his navel. The warmth permeated from her palm out through her fingers, heating their tips. And then in that easy voice that was seducing the hell out of him, she said, "Inhale, abdomen up. Exhale, abdomen down. Feeling okay?"

Not really.

Oh, he was enjoying the seductive tone and the feel of her hand over his abs, but he wasn't really relaxing. Actually, he was feeling more and more tense and worrying that things would get beyond his control—that body parts would betray him by swelling and sticking out of the lounging pants. There would be nowhere to hide. He was getting to the point where he wasn't so sure that he wanted to hide.

Trying to keep it all together, he managed to say, "Uh-huh."

"Good…Feel the rug beneath you. Feel the soft fur caressing your spine, your shoulders, and your neck. Feel the energy of your breathing."

That's when Dan heard the flapping sound in the kitchen, the toenails clicking over the floor toward them, and then Boo's body flopping onto his pillow bed beneath the window. He couldn't dismiss it. It was just too good. Dan's lips curled. A chuckle escaped from them.

"You knew he was gonna do that, didn't you?"

"I had a feelin'."

"Smartass."

"Me or the dog?"

"Both."

"We'll take that as a compliment."

"Not surprising. Now you're going to go into 'bridge,'" she said. "Arch your back up while leaving your neck and shoulders on the rug. Ready…lift…good…hold…breathe. Now slowly lower back to the floor. Good…Now bring the bottom of your feet together and lie in 'cobbler.'"

Dan's felt confused about the position she was asking for. Evidentaly, Tess could see his confusion about the position, so she helped him bring his feet together and bend his knees.

"Relax," she said, almost purring as she slipped her hand under the waistband of his pants and briefs to feel the flesh of his arousal. Dan took in a deep breath as she peeled the fabric down to set his erection free. Yeah, this was seduction—pure and simple. She was calling it "yoga," but it was sexual manipulation—and he had no problem letting it go on and on and on.

"I've got to admit that your yoga workout is one helluva aphrodisiac, sweetheart." His hand reached for the blindfold, but Tess grabbed his hand and gently returned it down to his side with its palm up.

"No," she whispered. "I want you to *feel*, not see."

"Oh, but I want to see. I really, *really* want to see," he said, pleading with her.

She chuckled. It came from deep in her throat. It was low and husky and laced with a wickedness that he found sexier and more sensual than any chortle he'd ever heard before. He had to admit that the blindfold provided a stronger sense of touch as her silky hand ran up and down his hard-on until it was replaced by the caress of her moist tongue—liquid fire. His breathing quickened. God, without the sense of sight, he could feel every tiny taste bud on her tongue gliding over him, stroking him, exciting him, and making him want more. She pulled away. He could feel her breath feathering the wet trail she'd left behind on his manhood.

"Namaste," she whispered.

"I love that word."

And there it was again, that low, wicked, beautiful little chuckle. He could've listened to her do that all day long.

"Legs stretched out on the rug," she said. He was quick to obey. He heard her shuffle, and then he felt what he'd been anticipating: the wet, warm feel of her as she eased him into her sex, slowly, steadily pumped her hips, and squeezed tightly around him. His fingers dug into the rug. Tess glided her tongue over his lips, teasing him, and then she pressed hers against his and pushed her tongue into his mouth. He could bear it no more. He was completely at her mercy. He was coming undone. He could feel the pressure of his climax pushing, pushing, and pushing him to the top until the peak of his pleasure exploded. His back arched, and he grunted. Unable to fight off the urge to touch her, he grabbed her by the waist as she rode him to the apex of their desire.

He heard her groan with elation. Oh yeah, she was in the exact same place that he was. He was hoping that they could always go to that place together. Suddenly, she whipped the blindfold from his eyes in time for him to witness her beautiful body arching in euphoria.

Her hair fell like a golden waterfall around her face when she looked down at him, and then after taking a sated breath, she lay beside him, resting her head on his shoulder.

"Now that was relaxing," Dan said. An ornery grin slithered across his lips. "I can feel that stick sliding right out of my tight ass."

Tess buried her face into his chest, laughing so hard that tears began to drip from the sides of her eyes. Damn, it felt good to hear her laughing. It was like music to his soul. It had been so long since he'd heard a woman's laughter in his house. It seemed like it had been forever.

Finally she managed to say, "Well, I'm glad to hear that!"

He pulled her back into his embrace. "C'mon, all kidding aside, do I really come off as a stick-in-the-mud?"

"Did I say that?" Tess asked as if she were innocent of the accusation.

"Yes…Something along those lines, anyway."

"Well, if I did, I apologize."

An errant blond strand fell across her face. Dan swept it away with his finger. She felt good in his arms. It felt good to be inside her, and when she laid her head down on his chest, he wanted nothing more than to lie there indefinitely, running his fingers through her hair and listening to her gentle breaths.

Yeah, he was ready for a relationship.

To hell with missions.

To hell with trepidation.

Fuck you, paranoia!

If Haliday and Ketchum could have a life, so could he. But before they could begin, there were things they would have to know about each other. It was time he told her.

"Her name's Amanda."

Tess lifted her head from his chest. "Who?"

"The woman in the photograph that you asked about on Friday—she's my wife. Amanda."

Tess took in a breath. *So it begins...He's married.* "I thought you said—"

"I'm not. Not anymore. She was murdered ten years ago."

"Oh, Dan...I'm so sorry."

His eyes remained locked on the ceiling fan whirling far above them. "She was a bank teller. I was a US marshal at the time. The bank was robbed on a Friday afternoon. Everything was going smoothly. The robber was just a kid, but the witnesses in the bank said that he was pretty calm. He had two lookouts with him. Amanda was handling everything very professionally and doing exactly as they asked, and then a cop who wanted to cash his paycheck during his lunch break walked into the bank through a door that I guess they didn't realize was there." He swallowed hard, trying to keep his composure in check.

"The kid panicked—thought he'd been had. He shot Amanda in the chest, point blank. By the time the dust settled, Amanda had died, the kid had died, the lookouts had been arrested, and the police officer had been critically wounded."

She caressed his chest with her fingertips. "How awful. I'm assuming that you didn't have any children."

He let out a miserable snort. "Oh, that's the best part. She was seven months pregnant. They tried to save the little boy. He lived for about three days. We buried her with him in her arms." He wiped away a tear. "I'd just gotten Boo a month or so before. To tell you the truth, I think that dog kept me sane. He helped me through it—kept my mind on other things like housebreaking him, training him to round up the cows, and throwing sticks in the lake for him. Yeah, ole Boo and I have been through some stuff together."

Tess glanced across the room. Boo was cuddled up beneath the window, snoring. The sight warmed her heart. She was becoming a convert. Yep, a dog with a wagging tail getting all up in your space was better than a goldfish swimming in a bowl and doing that funny pumping thing with its lips. Hey, you can't shake a goldfish's fin. Yes, one could watch you do yoga from the bowl, but that's not quite as personal or as a friendly as a dog watching from the couch.

"So there really is something to the old saying 'man's best friend,'" she said.

A svelte smile crept across his mouth. "Boo's the best—that's for damned sure."

Tess rolled over to her back. "So have there been other women since Amanda?"

"I'm a widower, not a monk," Dan said. "Truth is, after Amanda's death, I spent a good deal of time drinking, and during that time, I woke up in the morning with a good deal of women in my bed—not to mention with hangovers. I got through that phase of grief right quick. Thank. You. Jesus."

"Good to hear," Tess said, chuckling. "So…No one special in your life since the death of your wife?"

"In my line of work? No. When I leave for a mission, there are no guarantees that I'm coming back, so relationships are a little hard to maintain. I envy Grant and Jack Haliday. Somehow they've found a way to make a go of it. I don't know how, but I'd like to try. What about you? How did you get mixed up with a douchebag like Ballard Crafton?"

"That's *Mr.* Douchebag to the likes of us, Grumpy." They shared a chuckle. She lay still and quiet for a time, watching the curtains lift and flutter in the breeze over

Boo's head and then fall softly against the wall. "I was very young when I met Ballard, and I wasn't in a very good place. I had been in a juvenile-delinquent facility. I'd participated in a convenience store robbery. My parents were horrified. They pretty much disowned me, and I don't blame them."

"You made a mistake. They couldn't forgive you?"

She let out a beleaguered sigh. "Let's just say it wasn't my first rodeo. Anyway, Ballard was spending the summer as an advisor at the facility. He was so handsome and charismatic. That man could've charmed the stripes off of a tigress. He was my counselor, and then he was my lover, and then he was my legal guardian. He taught me right from wrong, and believe me, I learned. He put me through college. He was my world, and I was foolish enough to believe that I was his."

"When did he start adding other women into the mix?"

"I'm pretty sure it was while I was in college. He was always a possessive man, but as the years went by, it grew into an obsessive-possessive thing, and then it just got totally out of control." She sighed. "I'm glad it's all over. I'm glad to be my own person—someone I never knew I could be. It feels good." Tess waved her hand as if to wave any recollection of Ballard away.

"Enough of that. I don't want to think about him anymore. I have a big decision to make. I know that the XM notes have to be destroyed, but how will I escape the repercussions? How can I make this all go away?"

Dan pulled her closer and kissed her forehead. "I won't let anything happen to you, Tess. I'll protect you with my life."

She smiled against his chest. "I feel safe with you and your dog and your ranch and even with that big ole bull in the corral. I trust you and this place. You've never once asked me where the notes for the XM are or tried to steal them from me. Why?"

"That's not what I'm about, Tess. Sure, when you first got here, I was suspicious of your intentions—"

"And now?"

"Well, like you, I had to figure it out. Who is this gorgeous woman who busted through our security system, and what does she want? Now I don't care what you decide to do with that serum. I just want to keep you safe and with me."

"Mission accomplished, Grumpy. Now we—I have to figure out how."

Tipping her chin upward with his forefinger, he looked into her eyes. "We'll figure it out together."

Eight

August couldn't stand the waiting. It had been three hours since he'd left Christine down in the laboratory for Jingjing's impromptu experiment. What the hell was going on down there? Had Christine not come to yet? Had she had a stroke, or had her heart failed, and Jingjing wasn't prepared to tell him?

He glanced down at his Rolex. In fact, it had been three hours and fifteen minutes. He wasn't going to give her much more time. Jingjing needed to produce results or a confession—and soon. Either way, he was on edge.

For the third time in as many hours, August checked his laptop to see if Tess had logged on. Nothing. He slammed down the lid. Dammit, where was she? If Jingjing's experiment had been successful, they would need the XM immediately. Over the past weeks, it had become apparent that Talbot and Guseva weren't enough muscle to bring the woman in. He'd let it drag on because the additive hadn't been ready—and if he was being totally honest, because he hadn't wanted to allow Jingjing to call in any of Ballard's henchmen. Yeah, it was his pride. So be it.

But Jingjing claimed that she'd made a major breakthrough. If her claim turned into an actuality, it would definitely be time for reinforcements. He would make the necessary phone calls after he gleaned the results of the experiment. Just then his phone beeped—he had a text message from Jingjing Choo.

"Success! Come to the laboratory. Bring the other girl. ASAP."

He sucked back a breath. Trepidation coiled through his gut. What did she want with Gina? Her experiment with Christine had been successful, so why did she require another subject? Shit. He'd had enough trouble convincing Christine to go down to the laboratory with him. How would he persuade Gina to do it? He sank onto the edge of his bed.

"Aggie," Gina said from his bedroom door.

August's head snapped up. He shoved the cell phone into his pocket. "Yes, sweetheart."

"Where's Christine? I've been looking for her. She's not in her room."

"She…um…agreed to help Jingjing with an experiment this morning."

Gina blinked. Cocking her head to one side, she said, "Christine went down to the lab with the creepy mad-scientist lady? *Seriously?*"

"Yes, seriously." Standing, August managed to collect his thoughts. "As a matter of fact, I just received a text that the experiment went very well. They want us to come down to see the results," he said as he slipped his arm around her waist, urging her toward the hallway and the staircase.

As they passed Vatonia on the stairs, Gina said, "I can't wait to see the laboratory. Why did she ask Christine, not me, to help with an experiment?"

"I don't know. We'll have to ask her."

* * *

Hugging a fresh set of sheets to her chest, Vatonia watched while August escorted Gina to the main floor, and then she waited until she heard the door open and then click closed.

After taking a wary breath and bracing herself, she set the sheets on the step above her, and then with measured steps, she descended the stairs and stealthily rounded the corner toward the same door.

She wrapped her arthritic fingers around the doorknob and then just as quickly retreated them so that she could gnaw on a fingernail. Leaning in, she listened for movement or voices on the other side of the door. She could hear August's and Gina's hollow footsteps echoing down the wooden steps and their muffled conversation.

When she was certain that they'd gone deeper into the laboratory, she took hold of the knob again and eased the door open.

* * *

By nine o'clock Dan reluctantly left the serenity of Tess's arms and the comfort of the bearskin rug to go do the barn chores. Tess lay on her tummy and cupped her chin in the palms of her hands to watch him as he slipped his pants and T-shirt on, and then he dug deep into a nearby coat closet to find a shoulder holster equipped with a handgun. He strapped the holster on, pulled on his boots, made his way to the back door, dropped a cowboy hat on his head, and, after tossing her a sexy little wink, walked out the door. Boo followed along dutifully.

As she slipped into the gray shirt, Tess had to chuckle to herself about how silly he looked in a pair of lounging pants, combat boots, and a cowboy hat. The man really was uptight—he never went anywhere without a gun. At the moment she could definitely identify with that—the next day Talbot and Guseva would be set free. A shiver of anxiety skittered up her spine. Trying to shake the thought away, she made herself at home on one of the barstools at the kitchen counter. She plucked a brilliant-blue egg from the bowl, rolled it over the counter top with her palm, and then began to peel the shell away until she had a naked, slightly blue hard-boiled egg. She doused it with salt and then bit the top of it off. Holding the remains of the egg in between her forefinger and her thumb, she decided that this Easter egg tasted as good as—no, better than—what she remembered. It had been so long, too long, since she'd indulged in the simple joy of eating a vibrantly colored egg on Easter morning.

After snatching another from the bowl, she slipped from the stool and crossed the living room toward the stairs as she tossed the bright-pink egg from one hand to the other, hoping that Dan would be inclined to take another motorcycle ride. She felt safe with him. She felt—no, she wasn't ready to go there just yet. As she stepped into her room, her eyes fell upon the iPad and the burn phone lying on the desk. Pausing, she set the egg down on the nightstand next to the bed.

She thought she should e-mail her mom to wish her a happy Easter.

She crossed the room toward the device.

She smiled. Yeah, she should tell her mom about the terrific guy she'd met on this trip.

Her fingers brushed over the case as she contemplated the message she would send.

She had a feeling that her dad might just like Dan Garrison—he was a man's man.

Tess sighed. Then again, she really didn't want to spoil her perfectly good mood with a frustrating game of twenty questions. Instead, she shrugged out of the shirt, and without shame, she strutted butt naked down the hallway for a shower. As she passed the sunken hot tub in front of the fireplace, she thought that a sexy romp in bubbling water near a warm fire just might be in order later that evening.

Stepping into the shower, she realized that she was falling hard for Dan Garrison, the ex–US marshal who'd lost his wife, Amanda, so tragically.

Was it too soon for her to take a new lover?

Was it too soon to let someone into her life?

Did she really need another man messing up the independence she'd just discovered—especially one who was plagued with OCD?

Ballard had been obsessive compulsive but in a twisted way. Dan was just overly neat and organized. His lovemaking was manly—no whips or handcuffs, just sizzling flesh sliding over flesh.

Tilting her head back, she let the warm water rush over her body. Damn, he'd felt so good inside her. Her nipples stood at attention under the hot spray. Damn, she was already yearning to be with him again, and damn, she was seriously considering handing over that freaking flash drive so that she could get on with her life—a life that yes, might include Dan Garrison. What a surprise—what a perfectly pleasant surprise.

* * *

Her hands folded in her lap, Christine sat in a folding chair next to Jingjing's worktable. The scientist stood behind her with her hand on her shoulder, sporting a grin that stretched across her usually sour face and almost to her narrow eyes.

Jingjing watched August study Christine and search for signs of brain damage. "Christine, tell Mr. Crafton how you're feeling," she said.

Christine's eyes met August's. Smiling, she said, "I'm feeling very well, thank you."

"Very good," Jingjing said, purring. "Now could you please get me the bottle of water I left on the gurney?"

Christine looked across the room to where the gurney had been parked. Indeed, a plastic bottle of water was sitting near the pillow. "Of course," she said as she rose from her seat to retrieve the water and to give it to Jingjing.

"Very good, but not particularly impressive," August said. "Christine is a kind girl. She would've gotten the water for you out of courtesy even before—" His eyes snapped to Gina, who was obviously baffled by the display and curious about the goings-on in the lab.

"I have no doubt that she would have. Let me show you more. Christine, follow me, please," Jingjing said as she led the woman toward the middle section of her worktable, where a Bunsen burner was sitting. "Christine, please turn on the burner." Christine complied with the instruction. "Turn the flame up to full strength." Christine twisted the dial until the flame rose upward about four inches. A wicked smile slithered across Jingjing's lips. "Now hold your hand over the flame until I tell you to pull it away."

August's jaw dropped open, and Gina gasped and cupped her hand over her mouth as Christine willingly held her hand directly over the flame, which scorched and burned her flesh. Tears ran down Christine's cheeks.

Jingjing explained what was happening. "Unfortunately the formula does not block pain or provide the subject with superhuman strength—it merely forces the subject to obey all instructions given by their commander."

Gina couldn't stand it anymore. She raced over and yanked Christine's hand away from the flame. Christine's face twisted with rage at the fact that her directive had been interrupted. She shoved Gina to the floor and then brought her hand back to the flame.

"Enough, Jingjing! Tell Christine to remove her hand!" August yelled.

Jingjing shrugged. "Very well. Christine, please remove your hand from the flame, and go rinse it in cold water at the sink."

After pushing up from the floor, Gina turned to August. "What the hell have you let her do to Christine? What kind of experiment is she doing down here, and why would you let this *freak* hurt Christine?"

"Calm down, Gina. I'll make sure that Christine's wound is properly tended to," August said.

"You bet your ass you will! I'm taking her to a hospital, and then I'm going to pack us both up and get us the hell out of here!"

Jingjing handed Christine a scalpel. "Kill her, please."

"Wait a minute!" August yelled—but it was too late.

Ninja quick, Christine acted upon the directive, diving at Gina and driving the scalpel into her heart. Gina fell backward to the cement floor. Blood pumped from the wound.

"What the fuck!" August yelled. "What the fuck are you doing? There was no reason to kill her!"

"She wasn't going to cooperate. She wanted to leave, and I'm sure she would've gone directly to the police." She turned toward Christine, who was standing over her friend, oblivious to August's outrage as she waited for another command. "Thank you, Christine. Please wash the scalpel thoroughly with hot water in the sink."

Christine pulled the scalpel from Gina's chest, made her way to the sink, and began washing it under hot water as if she were washing a plate or a cup from Sunday dinner. Jingjing, who was wearing an expression of self-satisfaction, observed her.

August buried his face in his hands. "I'm a businessman, not a murderer! We've killed an innocent girl! I didn't sign on for this!"

"Will you please calm down? You needed to see how potent my formula is. You needed to witness how commanding the mind control is after an injection," Jingjing said.

"I told you that you needed to do more testing on lab animals *before* testing on humans!"

"And I obeyed your wishes." Jingjing reached under her worktable and pulled out a stainless-steel tray with five dead rats on it. Three of the rats had a scalpel stuck into their stomach, and two had been decapitated. As she placed the tray on the tabletop, August's eyes widened. He looked as if he would puke up his lunch at any given moment.

"Why do you think it took me three hours and twenty-five minutes to text you? I was running further trials. I wanted to make sure that Christine would follow all directives without hesitation. She killed these lab rats without as much as a blink of an eye. I think my experiment has been more than a success, don't you, Mr. Crafton? Your brother would have been overjoyed. He wouldn't have had any problem imagining the impact that my formula could have on subjects when mixed with the XM."

Leaning in close to his ear and lowering her voice to a cunning purr, she said, "Listen to me, August... We will have the entire planet by the ass. World leaders will line up to pay us any amount of money for such a powerful weapon."

Running a harried hand through his hair, August said, "I apologize that I'm not as well versed in murder as my brother must have been. That said, the reality is that we don't have the XM at this time. We don't have the world by the ass. So my question is, *now what*? We have a dead girl in the basement. What do we do with her body, and where do we go from here?"

"Come, Mr. Crafton, surely you have staff who can get rid of a body for you after dark. As for where we go from here—that's very obvious. We find Tess McMillan. Only she can give us what we need in order to move forward with our plan. I suggest that when you get my husband and Mr. Talbot out of jail tomorrow, you inform them that we will not tolerate anything less than positive results. *Immediate.* Positive. Results."

August's attention was drawn to the beautiful young redhead washing a bloody scalpel in the sink across the room. Christine had been a sweet girl. But she was willing to do anything, including kill a good friend on Jingjing's command. The entire display had been frighteningly impressive. At no time had Christine behaved or presented herself like a robot. She had come off as completely normal—until the directives had been issued.

Honestly, the only things missing had been a glazed-over expression accompanied by a stoic response—like "Ye-e-e-s, ma-a-a-s-s-s-ter-r-r"—and a zombielike totter toward her victim. No—she'd simply, quickly, and effectively done as she'd been told to do. If Jingjing's mind-control additive had been mixed with the superhuman-strength elements of the XM-11, Christine would've been able to kill two, three, or maybe more people with that one scalpel.

He should've been thrilled. He was most certain that his brother would have been. Yes, he was a multimillionaire, but with the success of the XM and Jingjing's additive, he stood to become a multibillionaire. It was as Jingjing had said—Gina and Christine were collateral damage. He knew he should get over it.

"I need a drink," August said.

With feigned compassion, Jingjing said, "Yes, I'm sure this has been a lot to absorb for one day. Have Vatonia mix you a good stiff one. I'll have Christine clean this mess up with bleach, bag the body, and wait for someone to come to dispose of it later."

"You do that," he said, making his way toward the wooden staircase.

* * *

Cupping her hand over her mouth, Vatonia quickened her steps up the stairs, through the door, and into the kitchen, where she vomited into the sink. She turned on the faucet to wash away the bile and patted her face with cool water.

Hearing the basement door slam, she stiffened. She gripped the sink so tightly that her fingernails turned white. She stood statuesquely, waiting for August to enter the kitchen to demand that stiff drink, but instead, she heard his footsteps over the slate floor in the foyer as he made his way into his study. And then the door to that room slammed.

She let out the breath she'd been holding since she'd crept into the basement stairwell and twisted her shaking hands in her apron, trying to make them still. Despite how prone to seasickness she was, Vatonia was wishing that she'd gone on that Caribbean cruise with her daughter. Hearing Gina's murder had been awful, yet she was grateful that she hadn't actually witnessed it.

What was she to do? Her eyes flicked across the kitchen to the phone on the wall, to the swinging door, and back to the phone. That horrible woman had done something to Christine that had made her obey her command to kill Gina. Poor girl. What would they do with Christine next? It seemed that August was on board with Jingjing's wicked objectives. Would they kill Christine too?

With her head spinning, she kept an eye on the swinging door as she inched toward the phone. She knew she should call the police. She laid her hand on the receiver. What would she tell them? Jingjing already had plans to clean up Gina's remains. If the police came and found nothing, what would that evil woman and August do to her? August was willing to do away with the two beautiful young women who'd lived with him so intimately for the past year, so surely her life would be worth even less to him.

Just then her service cell phone, which she kept in the pocket of her apron, beeped. Flinching, she pulled her hand from the telephone. Relieved, she fell against the wall when she realized it was just a text message from August: "Plz bring me warm cognac & 3 ibuprofen. I'm in my study."

Evidently, he had decided that it was time for that stiff drink. Her hands still quivering, she dabbed her face with her apron. She had to act as if she hadn't heard anything and didn't know anything. After gathering the pain medication from the pantry, she went to the bar in the dining room to gather the cognac and the warmer.

During Vatonia's many years as the Crafton's maid, she'd witnessed countless unscrupulous things but never a murder. August's father, Princeton Crafton, had had his women and his dirty deals, yet to her knowledge, he'd never killed anyone, and certainly not in his own home. She'd never felt threatened by the very household that she served—until that day.

Lord have mercy! What a terrible way to observe Easter—with a murder!

She popped two ibuprofens into her mouth and swallowed hard. Trying to calm her shattered nerves, she concentrated on the simple task of gathering the matches from the drawer in the server. She lit the tea light, poured a bit of Cognac into a snifter, and then gently inserted the snifter into the arms of the warmer. Before placing the gadget on a tray, she dropped three ibuprofens into a tiny crystal dish, and then she lifted the snifter and spit into the golden liquid—for Gina.

God rest that poor child's soul.

Upon entering the study, Vatonia heard August talking into the phone. "Afterward, be at the Paramount Suites no later than eleven tomorrow morning. You'll be briefed with the other two." He looked up, tucked the phone between his chin and his shoulder, took the pills from the dish, tossed them into his mouth, grabbed the snifter from the warmer, and then hitched his chin toward the door, indicating that she should make an immediate exit.

She paused, and as the door clicked closed, she heard him say, "I don't want any more mishaps! You take care of business tonight, and then you make damned sure that this time, when we locate Tess McMillan, she doesn't get away!"

What was going on? Who was this Tess McMillan, and what did she have to do with Jingjing and the laboratory downstairs? Vatonia's chest tightened. She felt trapped inside a nightmare that she couldn't wake up from.

"Vatonia."

The old woman jumped back as she turned, and she found herself face to face with Christine. She took in a breath and tried to respond, but the words would not come out.

"I'm sorry. I didn't mean to scare you," Christine said.

"No…No, you didn't. I just didn't…um…expect to see you," Vatonia said, stammering.

Christine held out a yellow tank top. "Could you please wash this for me? I don't know how to get this stain out," she said as casually as if she were asking for a cup of tea.

Vatonia's jaw dropped. Her eyes widened at the sight of a large bloodstain on the front of the garment, and then she noticed that Christine was standing before her in a pair of jeans and her bra. "That's… That's b-blood. How did you get blood on your shirt, child?"

Christine looked down at the shirt. Vatonia could see her searching her mind for the answer to her question, but she couldn't find it. Finally, the young woman shrugged. "I dunno, but could you soak it or something? It's one of my favorite shirts," she said, extending the shirt out toward the maid.

Vatonia didn't want to touch it. She knew where the blood had come from. It was Gina's blood. Looking down, she noticed that Christine's right hand had been bandaged. Again, she didn't have to ask—she knew exactly what had happened. Christine had held that hand over a flame, allowing it to burn her, until Jingjing had given her permission to remove it from the flame. Vatonia shuddered at the memory. With trembling fingertips, she took the shirt from Christine's hands and held it as far away from her body as possible.

"Thanks," Christine said. With her left hand, she ran her fingers through her hair. "I'm feeling very tired.

Jingjing said I should go to my room and take a nap. I'll see you later."

Vatonia cupped her hand over her mouth, and tears trickled down her face as she watched the young woman slowly make her way to the staircase and, just as slowly, climb it.

What would become of her?

Panic rushed through Vatonia's veins. The blood-stained shirt she was holding in her fingertips was evidence that a murder had taken place on the premises. Did Jingjing know that Christine intended to have the shirt laundered? Would she come looking for it later? She couldn't risk being caught with the shirt in her possession—they would know that she knew that something had happened, and then what? They would kill her for sure!

Her head snapped to the right and then to the left. Trying to stifle the cries that threatened to burst from her throat, she hurried to the kitchen, yanked open a drawer, pulled out a plastic shopping bag, and stuffed the shirt into it. Turning in tiny circles, Vatonia searched the room for a place to hide the bag.

She had to find a good place.

She had to act like nothing was amiss.

She had to calm down.

She'd always known that Princeton's boys were trouble.

She'd known the moment that that scientist had walked into the house that she was no good!

And she was certain of another thing: she was too damned old for this crap!

Vatonia stilled.

Closing her eyes, she whispered, "Help me, Jesus. Help me calm my frazzled nerves. Help me find a place to hide this bag, and please, help me find the strength to get through this mess." She took in several calming breaths. Slowly, she opened her eyes. A smile curled her lips. "Thank you, Jesus," she said as she opened the drawer where she kept her clean dish towels. She placed the bag with the bloodied shirt beneath the neatly stacked towels, and then upon closing the drawer, she said, "No way anyone will look in there—not one of them would know what a dish towel was if I smacked any one of them across the face with it."

Nine

Disturbingly quiet—that was the only way Vatonia could've described the blanket of calm that had fallen over the Crafton mansion. The house was silent, yet it screamed and yelled and kicked with anxiety and despair.

After Christine had retired to her room earlier in the day, she hadn't come out. Vatonia had checked on August several hours before only to find him passed out on the couch in his office. He must've mixed a sleeping aid with his drink. How convenient. He'd found an escape.

Coward.

She'd seen Jingjing climb the stairs with that malevolent little cat in her arms about an hour before. She'd looked quite pleased with her day's achievement. Jingjing never came up from the laboratory that early in the evening. Perhaps the dead body was getting to her—although Vatonia had her doubts. Jingjing was a coldhearted person—she didn't seem to have a heart or a soul at all.

No one came to the dining room for dinner, so she packed the roast, mashed potatoes, and vegetables into containers and put them in the fridge. Taking off her apron to hang it on the hook, Vatonia checked the time: it was nine at night. She was off duty. Exhausted, she let out a beleaguered breath and looked out the window. The dusk-to-dawn lanterns that lined the driveway were slowly blinking on. A soft rain had begun to fall.

How appropriate.

She wondered when the men she'd heard August talking to on the phone would come to claim Gina's body and where they would dispose of it. She shuddered at the thought. She didn't care to witness their arrival. The basement had a service entrance, and they'd most likely been instructed to use it, so she turned off the kitchen lights and made her way upstairs to her private suite. Her feet seemed to weigh fifty pounds apiece as she climbed the stairs. She didn't believe she could be more tired or stressed out than she was, but then she reached the second floor. Muffled cries filtered through the bedroom door across the hall, the door to Christine's room. Vatonia hesitated so that she could listen. Indeed, Christine was crying.

She turned to make her way down the hallway to the stairs that led to her small suite.

She'd been through enough already.

She grabbed the doorknob of the door that led to the third floor.

There was nothing she could do for that poor girl.

Slowly, she opened the door.

She didn't want anything more to do with the situation.

She stepped through the door and closed it behind her.

She could no longer hear Christine's cries.

Good. It was none of her business anyway.

She managed to climb three steps before stopping. Perhaps the girl was hungry. Perhaps the girl was scared. Regardless of what the circumstances were, Vatonia found that she could not turn her back and ignore it. It simply wasn't in her.

She made her way down the few steps, through the door, and down the hall to Christine's room. After lifting her hand to knock on the door, she stilled, and then she opened the door to let herself inside and closed the door softly behind her. The bedroom was dimly lit. Only a small vanity lamp illuminated the far corner of it. Shadows fell across Christine, who was lying on the bed in the fetal position. Her face was flushed and wet with tears. Her hands were twisted tightly in the sheets. Vatonia sat on the bed next to her, gently brushing her hair away from her face.

"Easy, child. I know you're hurting. How can I help you?" she whispered.

Christine opened her haunted eyes, and then she threw her arms around Vatonia, hugging her tightly. "Hold me," she said, pleading with her. "Hold me… My head is pounding, and I deserve every bit of the pain. I can't believe what I did. How can Gina forgive me? How can I ever forgive myself?"

Vatonia's heart broke for her. She enveloped her in a warm embrace. "Sh, quiet now. Everything is gonna be okay. Everything is gonna be just fine."

"No, Vatonia. No, it won't. I did something horrible—something unthinkable. I'm going to jail, and then they're going to execute me." She buried her face in Vatonia's chest and wept.

"It wasn't your fault, child. That woman, that awful woman, gave you some medicine that made you do what you did to Gina. You had no control over yourself. You had no control over your thoughts or actions. I know…I was there, in the stairwell. I witnessed the whole thing."

Christine pulled back. "Medicine?"

"Yes, child. Don't you remember going down to the basement with August? He told you that Jingjing was gonna give you a shot that would help build your muscles."

Vatonia could see Christine searching her mind. Bits and pieces of the afternoon must've been sweeping through her memory. Her face was contorting. Vatonia surmised that it could have been any of the horrible experiences that Christine was recalling—her killing the rats, the flame's scorching her hand, her attacking Gina, August's screaming at Jingjing, or the blood on her clothing.

Finally, Christine said, "It's all a blur. I'm almost hopeful that I won't remember the details. I'm afraid of what happened."

"I think the medicine has worn off," Vatonia said. "That's a good thing. But…I'm not sure that we should let on to Jingjing that it has, or she'll give you more of the medicine. And who knows what effect it'll have? C'mon, we'll go to my suite and get you cleaned up, and then we'll have to figure out what we're gonna do to get ourselves out of this mess."

"You think I should pretend that I'm still under Jingjing's control?"

"If we want to get out of here alive, yes." Vatonia went to the bedroom door, opened it just a crack, and looked down the hallway. All appeared to be quiet. She motioned for Christine to follow her, and the two women hurried down the hallway. Just as they reached the door that led to the third floor, headlights flashed across the window at the end of the hall. They hesitated and saw a dark SUV roll down the driveway toward the back of the house—the service entrance. The men had arrived to take Gina away.

Vatonia grabbed Christine's hand. "Come, child. We have plans to make."

* * *

The rain began to fall steadily when they were about two miles from the ranch. When Tess and Dan pulled into the driveway on the Indian, they were soaked to their skin. It had been a full day of exploring back roads, walking trails, laughing, and yes, holding hands. They'd stopped at an awful, run-down mom-and-pop restaurant for one of the most wonderful burger-and-fries dinners she'd ever had—not to mention a tall glass of frothy beer.

Dan had watched her down the beer with wide eyes. "Not for one minute would've I pictured you as a beer-chuggin' kinda gal," he'd said with a chuckle in his voice.

Tess wiped her mouth with the back of her hand. "I haven't had a cold one in a very long time. Ballard considered beer to be too common, so we drank wine—only the very best vintages, of course. But I like to have a nice cold beer every once in a while—it reminds me of Monday night football in my parents' living room."

He raised a cocky eyebrow. "You and your *goldfish*?"

She tossed her head back, laughing. "Yeah, the goldfish and I would snuggle up on the couch and watch football with Mom and Dad."

To that, Dan raised his glass. "To Monday night football with the folks."

Tess clunked his glass with hers. "To goldfish."

He thought about it for a moment, and then with a lift of his shoulder, he said, "To goldfish everywhere."

No doubt about it—it had been a great day. Tess reviewed the list in her head: hot yoga first thing in the morning with a superhot cowboy, motorcycling all day with said cowboy, and artery-clogging food, and there was a hot tub waiting to warm them up after they'd been drenched in the spring rain. Yep, even though it had been devoid of chocolate bunnies and marshmallow chicks, it would definitely go down as the best Easter ever. Take that, Easter bunny!

The garage door lifted. Dan rolled the Indian inside and parked it next to Tess's rented Cadillac. In the corner was a wide, big-wheeled motorcycle-like vehicle. "What's that thing? A heavy-duty motorcycle?" Tess asked.

"In a way, yeah. It's an ATV—an all-terrain vehicle. I use it to get around the ranch when I'm in a hurry or when I just plain don't feel like walking—which is rare, I might add."

"Mm," she moaned, and then she teased him. "I'm rather surprised that we're not going to put the motorcycle away in its proper place. How will you ever sleep tonight?"

Taking his helmet off, Dan tossed her a sexy grin. "Oh, I don't think I'll have any trouble sleeping tonight." He helped her remove her helmet, and then he added, "Last one to the hot tub is a rotten egg!" With that, he dashed across the garage and through the door that led into the house. She could hear his hurried footsteps slamming up the stairs to the main floor.

"That's not fair!"

She heard another set of strange thumps and bumps, and then in a *whoosh*, his jeans landed on the floor at the bottom of the stairs. She cupped her hand over her smile. He was larger than life—a powerful seducer. How could she not allow herself to fall for this man?

* * *

The fire crackled. The water bubbled and glowed in gradually shifting hues of blue, green, and pink amid the underwater lighting. Rain gently patted the skylight directly above them. Dan had lit the candles that sat within the stones of the fireplace, and they lent a sensual radiance to the room.

"Time to warm up," Dan whispered into her hair. He left a hot trail of kisses down her neck. Closing her eyes, Tess leaned into them. He reached around her waist. Unerringly, he untied her silky robe. She could feel the length of his erection against her right butt cheek. She sucked in a gasp of desire when he slipped the robe from her shoulders, and it pooled at her feet. His fingers were not soft—rather, they were a bit abrasive—yet their coarseness added to the tingle and to the itching desire as he caressed her body, enticing every cell in her body to surrender to him. She felt the warm wetness between her legs as he turned her to face him. Only a white towel around his waist hid what she wanted to expose, to explore, and to experience once again.

With splayed fingers, she ran her hands over his chiseled chest and abs, and then she tugged the towel and let it fall to the floor, freeing his erection. He pressed his lips to hers and pulled her against his sex with passionate possession. He was strong yet giving as he let her know that he intended to please her while receiving pleasure himself.

"Are you cold?" he asked.

"Not anymore."

He smiled against her lips. "Well, we're gonna take the temperature up a notch or two. C'mon." He took her by the hand and led her into the tub. The warmth of the water and the anticipation of his lovemaking enveloped her, heating her senses almost to the boiling point.

Sitting on the underwater bench closest to the fire, Dan pulled her to him so that she was straddling him. Her breath hitched. He brushed an errant strand of hair from her eyes. He kissed the base of her neck. "I had a great time today. But to be honest, I couldn't wait to come home just to be alone like this with you."

Tess brushed her lips over his. "Mm, great minds think alike."

He snorted. "Seriously? After that dump I took you to for dinner?"

"That was one of the best burgers I've ever eaten, and the beer was so smooth."

Cocking his head to one side and narrowing his eyes, he asked, "You'd go back?"

"In a heartbeat. Not by myself, mind you, but yeah, I'd go if you took me."

Cupping her full breasts in his hands, he said, "It's a date." But he was done with talking. He didn't want to work at smooth conversation or wit. He wanted to feel. He wanted to taste, and he wanted to press inside her. Her fingers massaged his shoulders, digging in deeper and deeper as his tongue lapped over her pebble-like nipples. He took the right one into his mouth and sucked it until it fully peaked. She let out a soft groan at the pinch.

Arching her back, she offered up the other and moved her hips ever so slowly, feeling him grow harder and harder, she was rapt in the tingling sensation. His hand glided down her ribs and over her hips, and then he gripped her derriere to pull her against him.

"I want you now," he whispered as his lips found hers. He lifted her so that he could slide inside her, and then he lowered her until he was deep inside her heat.

She broke away from the kiss to hold his face in her hands. "Sit still," she said. "Let me do the work."

Dan lay back against the tub and opened his arms so that he could hold its edges. Closing his eyes, he whispered, "Have at it, sweetheart. I'm not one to argue with a good thing."

Never had she felt so empowered. Never had she felt so sexually free. Swirling around them, the water had turned a deep blue. She squeezed tightly around his erection, lifted herself to the very tip of it, and then dropped down until he was deep inside her. He watched her, which excited her all the more. She could see how much pleasure she was giving him with each rise and each drop.

As the water changed to pink, she leaned in closer to him, offering him her breasts, and he responded. Only this time he used just the very tip of his tongue to tease her. Without permission, he pumped inside her once and then twice. As if on cue, it sent a shiver of urgency through her. She felt that she would soon helplessly explode to the height of her pleasure. She moved her hips faster—harder. The water reacted, dancing and bubbling around them.

"Mm, yeah, baby." He pulled her closer. "C'mon, let's go there together," he said, pleading with her as he reached the crest of his longing. He hugged her tightly as he let it all out.

Tess took in a breath, allowing the climax to envelop her, and then she collapsed against him, feeling boneless and sated. These feelings were completely new for her. She'd never felt that way after making love with Ballard. Then again, had she ever really been made love to? The feeling was liberating and exhausting at the same time.

Closing her eyes, she surrendered to the contentment of the moment and fell asleep against her cowboy as the water transformed into a soothing emerald green.

* * *

What seemed like hours later, Tess felt a tickle under her chin. "Hey, wake up. You're gonna drown. Geez, I hope I wasn't such a boring lover that I made you totally pass out."

Dragging her eyes open, she chuckled. "How long have I been out?"

"About fifteen minutes." He kissed her. "Feeling okay?"

"I don't think I've ever felt better. How about you, Grumpy?"

He smiled in reply, and then he swam across the tub. He reached behind the pyramid of white towels, the place he'd retrieved a gun from just a few days before, but instead he pulled out two bottles of Sam Adam's Winter Lager.

"Thirsty?" he asked.

She feigned an affronted reaction. "What kind of girl do you think I am—drinking beer?"

"I'm finding out what kind of girl you are, and I—" He sucked the words back in. He licked his lips, or was he biting them? Either way, he seemed to be struggling to hold back something that he wanted to say—he just couldn't let the words tumble out. After screwing the top off of a bottle, he guzzled half of the lager down.

Tess twisted the cap from her bottle, took a swig, and then quietly said, "Dan."

She could see that he was still in the process of some sort of self-reprimand. He was haphazardly reading the label on the beer bottle, trying to avoid eye contact.

Slowly, he dragged his gaze to meet hers. "Yeah?"

"I want to start a new life...And I know that the only way I can do that is by freeing myself from Ballard—completely."

"I'm not following."

"Tomorrow, Talbot and Guseva will be arraigned. August will pay their bail, and they'll be free to go, and they'll come looking for me."

"You're scared."

She let out a breath. "I am. It's time to do what needs to be done. Tomorrow, I want to give Clark the serum."

He lowered his eyes back to the bottle of lager. "And then?"

"I dunno. I suppose we'll have to see what happens from there."

Ten

August's attorney, Tomas Murphy, was preparing to attempt to get the laundry list of charges against Leo Talbot and Vlad Guseva dismissed. As they entered the courthouse, August reminded him that they'd already lost three days waiting for the arraignment. Tess McMillan had a big lead, and she wasn't logging on to her damned computer.

August Crafton was sporting a sleek charcoal-gray Kiton Napoli suit that matched the color of his eyes. Tomas could see the agitation simmering deep in his gut as he sat in the back of the courtroom, tapping his fingers on the bench or rubbing the bags beneath his eyes. He looked as if he hadn't slept for days. August could be demanding, but on that day, his patience matched that of a mad bull. Yeah, something had August bugged—big time. After taking an early-morning flight and listening to August bitch, Tomas found that his patience was running on the thin side as well. At least they were the first case on Judge Brown's docket, at eight in the morning.

"Let me see here," Judge Brown said, looking over his bifocals at the defendants. "Eluding the police for three miles, speeding, reckless driving, reckless endangerment, endangering the public's safety, and leaving the scene of an accident. The list of charges goes on and on, Mr. Murphy, and you think that I should just wave my hand and dismiss it all away? I think not."

"But, Judge, the woman, Tessa Lee McMillan—"

"Yes, yes, yes, you've told me all about her, yet I have no real reason to forgive any of the charges—not one. Ms. McMillan broke no laws other than speeding to get away from two men whom she did not know. She was afraid for her own well-being, and I don't blame her." He nodded toward the Russian man standing before his bench. "Mr. Guseva, be thankful that your paper work is in good order. That being said, don't be surprised if the people move for deportation at your hearing."

A sullen Guseva nodded.

"I'm setting bail at one hundred thousand—each." With that, he slammed his gavel down. "Next case, please."

Well, that was that. Judge Brown wasn't pulling any punches. Tomas glanced down at his watch: it was eight fifteen. That had to have been some kind of record. Gathering up his paper work, Tomas quickly glanced at August, and then he was sorry that he had. His boss jerked from his seat to wait for him at the end of the aisle. Tomas could see the frustration in the man's expression and stance as he shifted his weight from one foot to the other. He wasn't sure whether August was angrier with him for failing to have the charges dropped—which the judge wasn't willing to do anyway—or with Talbot and Guseva for the hot mess they'd caused on the interstate and for letting McMillan get the upper hand.

The bottom line was simple. August had greatly underestimated his late brother's personal assistant. Yes, she was a beautiful blond bombshell. Yes, she had curves that appeared in every man's wet dream. And unfortunately for August, yes, she was smart as a whip. Ms. McMillan was more resourceful than August Crafton had ever imagined.

Tomas considered August foolhardy for thinking that Ballard would've hired an idiot to be his personal assistant—no matter how beautiful she was. The fact was that Ballard Crafton had surrounded himself with beautiful, talented, intelligent women. He'd kept Tess McMillan in his employ for many, many years. If she'd been incompetent, he would have left her behind long before his untimely demise.

In fact, when Ballard decided that a woman was no longer to his liking or that she no longer pleased him in the way that he required her to, he didn't just break off the relationship. Instead he broke the woman, hence Ballard's quickened departure for Russia, whose government had been waiting for the infamous serum that August was so eager to get his hands on.

As Tomas closed up his briefcase, his gut twisted with the anticipation of August's next move. Would he purge himself of Talbot and Guseva, or would he pay the bail and get more aggressive in his pursuit of Tess McMillan? Pushing through the gate into the aisle of the courtroom's gallery, he had a feeling that August would opt for door number two: a more aggressive hunt for Ballard's assistant, who he believed had the notes for the serum. No, August wasn't absolutely sure that she did. He merely believed that she did. Tomas considered his suspicion to be as foolhardy as his miscalculation of Tess's ingenuity.

"I think you should be absolutely certain that she has the information before you continue this quest," Tomas had said only hours ago, during the flight on August's private jet. It had been his sorry attempt to reason with a man who was not au fait with the concept of losing.

"She must have the serum. If not, why would she have worked so hard to escape? Why would she have been so vigilant?"

"You managed to frighten the hell out of her, August. Can you honestly blame her for running?" He snorted. "What would you have her do?"

"I would have her turn over my brother's notes, of course!"

"She told you months ago that she doesn't have them."

"She's lying. She has the serum, and she probably has some idea about selling it to the highest bidder."

"Like you do?" August glowered at him. After clearing his throat, Tomas said, "She's never asked you for a dime. Believe me, she knows just how wealthy you are. This could get really ugly, August. I'm advising you to back away from Tess McMillan."

"And I'm advising you to do as you're told," August said, backing the statement up with a hard poke into Tomas's chest.

He should have resigned from his position right then. He'd known that the situation was escalating to ugly, and then ugly had arrived in grand style.

As he moseyed up the aisle of the empty courtroom, Tomas took note of the flush on August's face. It started at his silk tie and then permeated his cheeks. Not really wanting to know the answer, Tomas asked what he was expected to ask. "Any luck tracking the woman?"

August's nostrils flared. His jaw tightened until the skin rippled over the bone, and his eyes looked as if they would explode right out of their sockets. Saying nothing, August pushed open the door that led into the hallway and marched through it. After letting go of a careworn breath, Tomas loosened his tie and then followed him.

The long corridor was abuzz with attorneys counseling their clients before a hearing, police officers waiting to be summoned into a hearing, and courtroom employees whisking by with armfuls of files. August kept his voice low as they made their way through the din.

"She hasn't used the computer since Friday at the filling station."

"She's a very smart woman. Perhaps she figured out that you're watching her through her computer. She might have ditched the damned thing," Tomas said. "I'll remind you again that what you're doing is against the law. It is an infringement of a person's privacy—"

"I'm not in the mood for your law-and-order bullshit, Murphy! Go pay Talbot's and Guseva's bails. Send them to my hotel suite immediately. We've got to find Tess McMillan. *Now!*"

* * *

Rolling over in the bed, Tess slowly opened her eyes. It was still raining. She could hear it tapping at the window. She snuggled deeper into the bed, pulling the blanket up to her chin. What a perfect day to sleep in.

Sleep?

She jerked to a sitting position. It was Monday! It was the day Talbot and Guseva would be set free to resume their hunt for her.

A rush of anxiety swept through her, and then just as quickly, she calmed down, remembering that she was under Dan Garrison's watch—that she was at his ranch. Dan wouldn't let anyone or anything harm her. She was safe.

As she ran her fingers through her long hair, her lips curled at the memory of their lovemaking the night before. Dan had insisted that the safest place in the house was toward the rear, so they'd slept in her room. Boo had slept at the foot of the bed. The dog had snored loudly, but somehow it hadn't bothered her. It certainly hadn't bothered Dan. He'd slept soundly with his arms wrapped around her. She wasn't accustomed to sleeping with a man in her bed. Ballard had had his room, and she'd had hers. It had been nice to snuggle in the warmth of a man next to her. She listened. The house was still. She glanced at the clock—it was nine. Dan and Boo were probably at the barn.

Jumping out of the bed, she decided to make a big breakfast. Dan would like that, and even though it was dreary out, she pinched back the curtain to look across the lake and over the field near the barn. Through the steady rain, she could see the bull in the corral. What was his name again? Amos—he was one big cow. She was still amazed by how Dan had named his animals based on their looks. Oh, sure, her goldfish had had a name: Goldie. Yeesh, how lame was that? Give that girl a huge pat on the back, and crown her Ms. Creativity!

As she hurried to pull on her jeans, the iPad lying on the nightstand next to the burn phone that Dan had given her for emergencies caught her eye—and she thought of her mom. Tess hadn't communicated with her parents since Friday morning, and even though she wasn't a young girl, she knew that she should at least touch base with them a few times a week so that they wouldn't worry themselves into comas.

She turned the device on and tapped out a quick e-mail to let her mother know that all was well.

Hi Mom,
I'm at a ranch in Harverton, Pennsylvania. I've met a wonderful man. His name is Dan.

I think you and Dad will really like him. I'm having a great time. Not sure when I'll be returning to Albany. I just wanted you to know that I'm okay.
Love,
Tess

She took note of the scads of unread e-mails crowding her inbox, but she didn't have time for them—she wanted to get breakfast started.

* * *

Well, at last! She's in Harverton, Pennsylvania," August said to the four men who'd gathered in his hotel suite, Leo Talbot, Vlad Guseva, and the two men he'd hired to assist in the capture of Tess McMillan, a man he knew only as "Ryder" and his partner, Stan Knox. He tapped at the computer and came up with a GPS location of the ranch where Tess had told her mother she was staying. He turned the computer toward his cohorts.

Ryder studied the coordinates, and Leo looked over his shoulder.

"That's a good six hours from here," Leo said.

"Why are you still here?" August asked.

"Let's go, boys," Ryder said. And then he added, "Don't worry, Mr. Crafton. She'll be at your home by morning."

They hurried toward the door, but Vlad hesitated. Meeting August's icy glare, he asked, "Where is Jingjing? Why did she not come?"

August's reply was clipped. "Your wife is committed to the success of this project. She is a busy woman, yet you're still standing here, Mr. Guseva."

"I will not fail this time," Vlad said.

"It's in your best interest to make sure that you don't."

* * *

Tess was rather surprised that Dan had never asked her about the whereabouts of the flash drive that contained the notes on Ballard's serum. He simply waited downstairs while she went into the drawer filled with his ties and retrieved the lipstick tube from the curl of the purple and gray striped tie. Her eyes glanced at the neat row of hats on the dresser. Taking in a cleansing breath, she ran the tip of her finger along the square rim of the black Stetson hat that belonged to her very strong, handsome, OCD-inflicted cowboy.

What now?

Once she surrendered the serum to Clark, would he whisk her away to some faraway place and give her a new identity? Would this be the last time she saw Dan's ranch? A tear dribbled down her cheek. Would this be the last time she saw Dan?

The sound of toenails on the floor caused her to turn, and she found Boo standing in the doorway of the room with his tail wagging and that friendly doggy smile stretched across his furry face. Instantly, she cupped her hand over her mouth to stifle a cry. Dammit, would this be the last time she saw Boo? She was impressed by how the thought of that broke her heart.

As if he knew she was fretting, Boo made his way to her. Tess knelt on the floor, and the dog cuddled up to her when she wrapped her arms around him. "I can't believe I'm saying this, but I'm going to miss you, Boo," she said through her tears. "You've kinda grown on me."

Boo licked her ear in reply. She hugged him tightly, and then she quickly got to her feet to hurry downstairs. Boo followed along at her heels.

Dan was waiting at the end of the stairs. "Are you ready?"

"I am." She reached for him. He pulled her tightly into his chest and caressed her long tresses.

"Everything's gonna work out okay," he whispered into her hair. "I won't let anything happen to you. I'd die before I'd let anything happen to you."

"Well, let's hope it never comes to that."

Tess's heart was in her throat during the twenty-minute drive to First Force Headquarters. They'd opted to take the Cadillac instead of a motorcycle since it was a dreary day and on the chilly side.

They drove along the winding roads in silence. Tess watched fat drops of water fall from the trees as they passed, and dark clouds moseyed across the ashen sky.

She glanced across the seat to take in Dan's intense stare out the windshield. His jaw was set. His fingers were wrapped around the steering wheel so tightly that it seemed like his knuckles would burst through the skin at any moment. His shoulders looked rigid with stress. The man could've used a yoga session right about then—a hot yoga session. How great would that have been, a hot yoga session instead of the task before them—instead of turning over the serum and then…And then what? Would she really have a say? She didn't want to think about it.

Finally Dan steered the car to the wrought-iron gate, placed his face to the iris-recognition screen, and, after the gate had slowly rolled open, drove the Cadillac along the driveway until they came to a stop in front of the mansion.

"Hope Clark's got those damned cats put away somewhere," Dan said as he opened the car door so that Tess could get out.

"Not in the mood to swell up and choke?"

He grew an ornery grin. "Well, I'm in the mood to swell up but not to choke," he said while giving her hand a gentle squeeze. She smiled to show her understanding. His little quip had put her at ease.

Clark met them in the foyer. "Hello, Ms. McMillan. Good to see you again. You've made a decision, I take it?"

"I have."

"Good. Let's go into the office to discuss your options and to take a look at what you brought. You brought the notes with you, right?"

She reached into her leather bag and produced the tube of lipstick. "Right here."

The right side of Clark's mouth lifted. "Very resourceful. Double O Seven would be proud."

"I suppose. So now what?"

Clark directed her into the office, and then he noticed that Dan was looking around the foyer. "Don't worry. I've been keeping the cats locked up in the pantry. I didn't realize how much trouble they could get into."

Dan let out a breath of relief and followed them into the office. He eased into the chair next to Tess.

She reached out to squeeze his hand. Clark didn't miss the gesture. He locked eyes with Dan and had no problem interpreting what he saw. It was validation that Dan had not only gained this woman's trust but also stepped over the line to a personal relationship—a way-too-personal relationship.

Clark raised a knowing eyebrow at Dan. He didn't flinch. Clark could see that Dan was invested in this woman and that he would have to tread carefully. "May I?" he asked, reaching his hand out for the lipstick.

Tess hesitated. She looked to Dan for reassurance. He nodded. Slowly, she handed the faux tube of lipstick to Clark. She watched as he twisted the lipstick up and up until the flash drive was revealed, and then he slipped it into his laptop.

Tess squeezed Dan's hand again while Clark studied what had appeared on the screen. After clearing his throat, Clark said, "I assume that you want to enter a witness-protection program, like we discussed the other day?"

"Yes."

"And you completely understand what that entails?"

She swallowed hard. "Yes, but I expect the serum to be destroyed so that it can never fall into the wrong hands."

"I'm not sure that there are right hands, Ms. McMillan, but yes, we will destroy the flash drive. This is the only copy of Mr. Crafton's notes?"

"Yes."

"You're absolutely sure?"

"Absolutely."

Clark's eyes flicked to Dan. He was waiting for him to say something, but he remained silent. Clark wasn't sure whether that was a good sign or a very bad one. What was Garrison thinking? He could see that the relationship between Garrison and McMillan had become intimate, yet she'd opted to go into the program. She would be given a new identity, a new life, and a new location. So was Garrison just going to let her ride off into the sunset without him, or did he have other intentions?

"Okay, I'll make all of the arrangements for you to get a new identity, and of course, you'll be moved to a new location. That will take a few hours, so you may want to go back to the ranch and gather your things. Meanwhile, I'll destroy the flash drive."

Dan stood, but Tess remained in her seat. "No," she said. "I don't want to leave the flash drive behind. I want to be certain that there won't be any copies made. No offense, Mr. Rhodes, but I don't know you."

"Again, let me remind you, Ms. McMillan, that you sought us out for help—"

"Hold on," Dan said. "Give her the flash drive." Clark's eyes snapped to Dan's in disbelief. "Let her hold on to it. We'll go to the ranch to get her stuff, and when we come back, you can destroy the flash drive so that she'll know it's been done."

"We can destroy it right here and now if you'd like, Ms. McMillan," Clark said.

Tess draped a tress of hair over her ear. "I've kept it safe up to this point. I can keep it safe for a couple more hours. I'm comfortable with Dan's idea. We'll destroy it when we come back."

Clark pulled the drive from his computer. "If that's the way you want it. I'll call you when the arrangements have been made."

He held the flash drive out to her. Tess looked at it as if it were a serpent, and then she took it. "I'm sorry if I seem untrusting or ungrateful, but I'll just feel better if I have possession of it until the last moment."

"No worries, Tess," Dan said. He held his hand out to her. "C'mon, let's get back to the ranch."

Eleven

Bored to tears, Tess turned the TV off. It had been several hours since they'd returned from First Force Headquarters, and she still hadn't heard anything from Clark. She'd spent the entire afternoon alone in the house. It hadn't taken long to pack her things. She didn't have much.

The rain had stopped and had been replaced by a blustery wind. Dan spent the day at the barn. Boo spent the day running back and forth between the barn and the house as if he wasn't sure whose company was more depressing.

When they returned from headquarters, they had a quick lunch, and then Dan made a quick exit for the barn. He had very little to say while they ate. There was no great confusion about what the problem was. Dan was feeling the way she was: uncertain, hesitant, worried, and, of course, afraid.

She had so many feelings ripping at her that she wasn't sure which anxiety to deal with first. She'd just reunited with her parents, and she would soon disappear into the mist. They would never know where she'd gone or what had happened to her. And then there were her feelings for Dan. How could she have allowed herself to fall so hard for him in four short days? She'd spent a lifetime with Ballard, yet she'd let this man, Dan Garrison, into her heart and into her bed in an instant. What had she been thinking?

It didn't matter anymore.

It was over.

She'd go her way, and he'd remain at his ranch.

She'd live her life—wherever and however she was told to.

He'd live his life at his ranch with Boo and his cows and Amos, and, of course, he'd go on ops with his team.

Running a harried hand through her hair, she had to wonder who would be lonelier. Just then she remembered that she'd heard a door slam downstairs about an hour ago. Perhaps Dan was in the basement doing something or other. She pushed herself up from the couch and made her way down the stairs. She found him in the garage wiping down the Indian while Boo lay a few feet away, supervising.

Leaning against the doorjamb, she said, "Why am I not surprised? That bad boy got caught in the rain. Of course it needs a full wax job."

"You're a quick study."

"That I am. Can I ask you something?"

"Shoot."

"Are you gonna miss me?" she whispered, regretting the words immediately.

Dan didn't look up from his chore. He didn't dither as he wiped a laser shine onto the motorcycle's chrome. He simply said, "Nope."

Tess's heart sank, her body straightened, and she pushed away from the wall. "Wow. Not exactly the answer I was expecting."

"You didn't let me finish. I'm not going to miss you, because I'm going with you."

"Excuse me?"

He straightened. "You heard me. I'm going with you. I'm not going to just let you disappear out of my life."

Her mouth was instantly dry. She didn't know what to say. After staring at him like he'd just grown another eye, she finally managed to say, "You can't just leave. You can't give up everything you have. You can't just leave this place."

"It's just a place, Tess. We'll get another place and start a new life together. Well, you, me, and Boo."

Her eyes immediately snapped to Boo, who wagged his tail when he was favored by her gaze. She felt panic crowding her chest. "But, Dan, you've only known me for four days—four very short days. How could you give everything up for someone you barely know?"

"Four days, four weeks, four years—what difference does it make? I know what I'm feeling, and I'm not going to let you go. I'm in love with you, Tess."

His words made her stagger back a step. She blinked and blinked again. "Four days and several sexual encounters are hardly the foundation of a solid relationship. What are you thinking? I can't let you give all this up for…for *me*. My God, Dan, I could be your biggest mistake!"

Using long strides, he closed the space between them and took her into his arms. "My biggest mistake would be letting you go. That's not going to happen. You got that?"

Pushing away, she grabbed her head. "This is all happening so fast. I'm so caught up in everything I'm losing because of the man I gave so much of my life to—a man who never truly loved me! I'm losing my parents all over again, only this time, it's forever, and I could possibly lose you—"

"You're not gonna lose me. I'm here for the long haul if you want me. Can you look at me and honestly tell me that you don't want me?"

Tears burst from her eyes. "This is all so fucked up! I don't know what I want right now!"

The cell phone in Dan's hip pocket rang. They stilled. Each ring seemed to suck more of the oxygen from the room. After pulling it from his jeans, he said, "It's Clark." He could feel the shiver that tickled her spine. Shaking her head to indicate no, she hurried up the stairs. Dan lifted the phone to his ear. "What's up, Clark?"

"Things aren't going as smoothly as usual. We won't be able to make it happen until tomorrow. She'll have to stay under your watch for another night," Clark said.

"She's pretty shaken up, so giving her a little more time for it to sink in might be a good thing. I'll talk to you in the morning," Dan said.

"Dan—"

"It's too late, Clark."

* * *

Ryder steered the black SUV down the winding road that the GPS said would lead to the ranch where Tess McMillan was staying. He was hoping that they hadn't been led astray. Based on the reports he'd received from August Crafton, this woman was good at getting Talbot and Guseva to chase their own tails. He glanced in the rearview mirror at the two men sitting in the back. Talbot looked pissed. His eyes were narrowed into thin lines of frustration, and Guseva was simply staring out the window with his big hands folded in his lap like he was in some kind of trance. He'd made several calls during the drive. Whoever he'd called hadn't picked up. Ryder noticed that Guseva's mood had darkened with each unsuccessful call.

He was surprised that Talbot hadn't been able to bring the woman in. Talbot had always been very competent. He knew nothing of Guseva. Mr. Crafton had said that he'd come in from Russia. Again, he'd been taken aback. Those security teams from Russia were usually damned capable. Evidently, Tess McMillan was just that much better. Not this time. This time she'd be captured and taken to Crafton's home. He would collect another cool ten grand and then leave Crafton to do whatever he wanted to do with the woman. Maybe McMillan would meet the same fate as the woman in the body bag that they'd collected from his basement in the wee hours of the morning. No one would ever find that young woman's body—ever.

"Comin' up on the right," Stan said.

Ryder slowed the vehicle. They came upon a huge stone entrance with a heavy wrought-iron gate across the drive. Through the gate they could see a large cedar home in the distance. As Ryder slowed the car almost to a stop, the four men eyed the landscape and the estate.

"Looks like they've got an eye-recognition system of some sort in the stonework," Stan said.

"The gate looks pretty heavy-duty. Not sure we can bust our way through unless we get a battering ram installed on the front of the SUV," Ryder said. Stan smiled. Ryder glanced at the clock and then added, "I know a guy who can attach one in a couple of hours. His garage isn't too far from here. We'll come back after midnight or so. They won't know what hit 'em."

* * *

The fire that Dan had built in the fireplace helped calm Tess's nerves a bit. The crackle of the dancing flames soothed her troubled mind. Tess sat on the couch and cuddled in a fleece blanket with a cup of coffee, watching the fire and using a few breathing techniques from her yoga exercises to ease her stress.

"Feeling better?" Dan asked, easing down on the couch next to her.

"Maybe a little. I'm at a loss, Dan. I feel all tangled up inside. I can't let you give up everything you've worked so hard to build to follow me who knows where. I can't let you make that kind of a commitment. Hell, I don't know if I can make that kind of a commitment."

He kissed her on the forehead. "You let me worry about what you think I'm giving up." He felt her shiver beneath the blanket. She wasn't cold. He could feel the warmth of her body next to his. She was nervous. "Are you worried that they'll find you?"

"I know that I'm safe. Really, I do. But yes, I'm afraid that they'll find us," she said. Dan pushed himself up from the couch. "Where are you going?"

"I've got a semisophisticated security system that can be easily breeched by gorgeous blondes," he said, and then he smirked at the snarky grin Tess was tossing him. "But I've also got a secret weapon that I unleash when I'm feeling uneasy. I'll be back in about fifteen."

Tess took another sip of her coffee while she watched Dan slip on his boots, and then he went downstairs. She heard the garage doors open and that ATV thing start up and drive toward the barn. She couldn't imagine what secret weapon he had hidden in the barn. Dan Garrison was full of surprises. She just wasn't sure she could handle many more.

* * *

Tossing and turning in the bed, Tess was glad that she hadn't allowed Dan to sleep with her that night. No one would've got any sleep. Well, nothing seemed to bother Boo—he would've slept and snored without any problems. She glanced at the clock; it was one thirty, and there was plenty of night left. Flipping onto her back, she closed her eyes, and then she took in deep belly breaths and slowly let out the air through her mouth. She breathed in. She breathed out.

Out of nowhere, her breathing exercise was interrupted by a crash, and then she heard the sound of an engine revving in the distance, and then there was another resounding crash and another. Alarms began screaming throughout the house. It sounded like a vehicle was racing up the driveway.

Tess sat up. Boo was barking. She could hear what she hoped were Dan's hurried footsteps in the hall coming toward her room. She was diving off of the bed to hide on the side away from the door when it flung open.

"Tess!" Dan said. "Where are you?"

She popped her head up. "Here!"

Growling and barking, Boo was dancing in circles in the hallway. Dan had pulled on jeans but no shirt, and he was clutching a gun in his right hand and holding out his left to her. "C'mon! Hurry!"

After catching a glimpse of the cell phone that Dan had given her and told her to keep on the nightstand at all times, she grabbed it, and then she ran to take his hand. With Boo leading the way, they rushed down the hallway and the staircase. Dan led her to the right side of the fireplace, but Boo kept going straight out the doggy door. Dan pressed a button, and a small brick door slid open.

"Get in there. You'll be safe. There's a tiny room that leads to a narrow hallway. The hallway leads to the basement, and there's a button on the wall that will open another secret door if you need to get out. But *do not* come out until I come to get you. Do you understand?"

"Dan—"

He shoved her through the small door into the panic room. "Do. You. Understand?"

"Yes, but—"

The door slid closed.

Twelve

fter the intruders' grand entrance, an eerie silence blanketed the ranch, but Boo's barking remained. *Damn, forgot to lock the doggy door last night,* Dan thought, scolding himself silently as he crawled across the kitchen floor to the door. There was nothing he could do about it. He wondered how many there were. After stuffing his Glock into his waistband, he reached into a tall wooden bin with the word "potatoes" carved down the front and retrieved his father's hunting rifle from it. Amanda had bought the bin at a craft show years ago and had used it to stockpile fresh potatoes from the garden, but it had become just another hiding place for weapons. He usually used the rifle to shoot coyotes, but he felt confident using it as a backup for the Glock.

Most of the time, paranoia was his nemesis—a vice that he tried to cure. But at that moment, it was his best bud. He unlocked the safety of the gun. Slowing his breathing and managing to stay completely still, Dan listened intently. Boo had stopped barking. Measured footsteps on the porch caught his attention. Lying on the floor, he eased the doggy door open. In the moonlight he could see the bottom half of the man who had hesitated on the top step. Carefully, he brought the barrel of the rifle to the small opening, cranked the bolt to release the bullet, took aim, and shot out the man's right kneecap. Letting out a shriek that was probably heard in the next county, the man fell backward, grunting with each bump and thump of the wooden stairs. His pistol hit the porch and exploded into the darkness.

One down.

He could stay in the house and hope that they would come to him, but that wasn't likely. It was more likely that they'd spread out—that they'd surrounded the house. Where the hell was Boo? Gunfire erupted from seemingly everywhere. The front window exploded out of its encasement. He could hear glass shattering over the floor. After jumping to his feet, he hurried to the front of the house, keeping close to the walls and keeping his gun close to his chest.

Dan knelt down at the corner of the window and let out several rounds into the front lawn. A dark shadow scampered from one tree to another. Dan shot at it, and the bullets stripped bark from the big, old oaks. He heard another shriek from behind the house.

"What the fuck!" someone yelled.

Dan's lips curled.

*   *   *

Once they had rammed through the wrought-iron gate, Leo and Stan took positions behind the house. They could see the moon glistening on the surface of the lake below them. Ryder had dropped Vlad off at the east side of the house and had taken position in the front. A dog had run from the house, barking, but they'd lost sight of him. They weren't sure what kind of dog it was or how big of a dog it was, but one thing was for sure—if he showed his face, they would shoot to kill.

The house was still. No lights, but they were certain that their entrance had alerted the resident to their arrival. The alarms that had been screeching were then silent.

They held their position behind a cluster of bushes, waiting for Ryder to attack the house from the front. And then with rapid gunfire, they would make their move. They had heard two shots, and they wondered if Vlad was okay. Even though his wife was playing a huge role August's project, Vlad didn't seem to have his head in the game. Perhaps they'd overestimated his experience, or perhaps for some reason, he simply wasn't as committed to the objective as everyone else was.

"I'm thinkin' Vlad got shot," Leo whispered while swiping the back of his neck.

"Didja hear that scream? You might be right. What's takin' Ryder so damned long?" Stan wondered out loud. He loosened his collar. "It's gettin' hot out here. Are you hot?"

Rapid gunfire sliced through the silence, and then more gunfire replied to it. It was time to move, but just as Stan lifted his weapon and prepared to abandon the bushes, he was rammed to the ground. Pain shot through his spine as he was pressed violently against the ground as though he were a cigarette that the Hulk was crushing with all his might. He couldn't breathe. He heard something in his body go *crack*!

"What the fuck!" Leo screamed.

Planting his fingers deep in the soil, he tried to crawl out from under whatever was crushing him. He heard it grunting. He heard Leo's footsteps running away. He was leaving him behind! Why wasn't he shooting whatever it was? Dirty bastard! With what breath he could manage, he said in a rasping voice, "Leo! Don't leave me! No!"

Suddenly the pressure let up. Barely conscience, he could hear that whatever had crushed him was running. It sounded heavy. It sounded mighty, and then there was…no…sound…at…all.

* * *

R yder looked up and saw the shadow of a man running toward him. He raised his weapon, but he realized it was Leo Talbot. What the hell? He was supposed to attack the house from the back as soon as he launched his own assault on the front. Screw-ups!

Shots from the house forced him down, but he could see something rounding the bend behind Leo. What was it? More shots from the house. He ducked.

"Get to the car! Get to the car!" Leo shrieked at the top of his voice.

Slowly, Ryder climbed to his feet behind the tree. Then the dark figure came into full view—it was a bull! There was a freaking bull chasing Leo!

Shit!

Another round of fire from the house.

That bastard knew that they'd have to run from the bull.

He was going to have some clear shots as they hurried to the SUV.

Leo was almost to the car.

That bastard in the house was shooting at him, and the bull was gaining ground.

Taking aim, Ryder took a shot at the bull, who came to a sliding stop just as Leo slammed the passenger door closed. The bull turned. It was as if he knew where the shot had come from. It was if he knew who had tried to take him out, and he came charging straight at Ryder.

Shit!

Ryder's breath caught in his throat. His mouth instantly went dry. Dropping his weapon, he veered right, making a wide circle around a cluster of trees and trying to get to the driver's side of the SUV before the bull got through the tight group of trees. Bullets coming from the house bounced off of the trees. Bark landed in his hair as he ran faster than he'd ever thought he could to get to the SUV!

He was within ten feet of the vehicle when the bull finally made his way through the trees. Damn, that SOB could run fast. Arriving at the driver's side door, Ryder grabbed for the door latch—but it was locked.

"Leo! Unlock the damned door!" He heard a *click*—it was like his fingers wouldn't work. They fumbled with the latch until finally, the door opened. He jumped in just as the bull smashed into the door with his head, not only slamming the door closed but also caving it in almost to his Ryder's hip.

Ryder started the SUV and pressed the accelerator, causing the car to fishtail out of the front yard toward the driveway. Clumps of grass flew into the air, and bullets pinged off of the sides of the vehicle.

* * *

Tess felt her way along the walls. It was dark. She couldn't believe that Dan hadn't provided the space with a light source. Surely he had—she just hadn't found it yet. With her fingers splayed out wide, she ran her hands over the walls, trying to find a switch, a Coleman lantern, or anything that would give off light. Finally her fingers found a switch. She prayed that it wasn't a detonator of some sort. She didn't want the house to go up in smoke—she just wanted some light. With a sigh, she flipped the switch. A dim lightbulb illuminated the narrow passageway.

There were no surprises—weapons of all kinds hung on the walls just above her head. She was certain that Dan didn't need weapons—God bless him, he had arsenals hidden throughout the house. No, Dan needed help. She turned on the burn phone that he'd given her—no service. She was too deep underground, or the walls were too thick. The reason didn't matter—the fact was that she had no cell service. Not helpful.

Continuing down the corridor, she came to a short row of metal shelving units filled with canned goods and basic medical supplies. She kept an eye on the cell phone as she traveled, hoping it would come to life as she made her way. No luck. She came to the door that Dan had said led out of the space. There was a button on the wall next to it that slid it open.

"Do not come out until I come to get you. Do you understand?"

"Dan—"

He shoved her through the small door into the panic room. "Do. You. Understand?"

"Yes, but—"

Their rushed conversation before he closed the door and locked her away in this secret hideaway played in her mind. She laid her head against the door. What was going on upstairs? Her head jerked up at the sound of gunfire and then more gunfire. Her spine stiffened. She stood statuesquely and listened—nothing. She cupped her hand over her mouth as she tried not to push the button and not to imagine the worst scenarios that were molesting her mind.

Silence.

She listened.

Suddenly the merciless silence was broken by a volley of rapid gunfire. It went on and on and on for what seemed like hours until it finally stopped. Trepidation crawled over her skin. She waited. She listened. Nothing.

"Do not come out until I come to get you. Do you understand?"

Tess pressed her forehead to the door again. "Yes, but," she whispered as her shaking fingers crawled up the wall, edging toward the button. Her hand hovered over the button as she contemplated whether to push it, and then her finger caressed it. She considered doing it…decided to do it…and pressed the button. The door slipped open. She almost fell through it and into the dark basement.

Covering her mouth with both hands, she made her way through the basement with measured steps. There were no windows. The only light to guide her was the dim light seeping into the huge area from the passageway. She could see a door on the other end of the open room.

How much time had passed since she'd heard the last set of gunfire? One minute? Five minutes? She dug down deep to find the courage to unlock the dead bolt, to pull the door open a crack, and to peek into the night air. Again, she listened. Only the sound of a heavy breeze greeted her. The cool air swept over her face. Through the slight gap, she eased outside, listening and searching the moonlit landscape for movement, for Dan, for Boo, and for August's henchmen, who'd managed to track her once again.

The breeze lifted her hair from her sweaty neck as she inched her way around the house until the lake came into view. She continued her deliberate comb of the yard, and then she stilled, unable to move and unable to swallow or breathe. It was as if her heart had stopped—and so had the world.

The wind whipped across the yard, causing the damp green grass to ripple over Boo's fur in the moonlight. He was lying still and was unmoving. Panic consumed her. Tess hurried toward him. As she drew closer, she slowed, taking tentative steps. Sorrow crowded her heart; fear for what she knew she was about to discover gripped her soul.

Before she reached him, she saw the dark shadow that stained the grass—blood. Finally she stood over the dog, Dan's best buddy, the one who'd been to hell and back with the man. It was just as she'd feared. Boo lay dead on the ground.

Tess swallowed back hard.

She couldn't afford to speculate.

He was too important.

She had to be sure.

Slowly, she fell to her knees next to him and placed her hand over the area where she believed his heart to be, even though she knew that Boo had more than merely a beating heart—Boo had a soul. But his heart had indeed stopped beating. There was nothing she could do.

Boo was dead.

Tess had never known the power of a pet's love, but somehow, in the short time she'd known him, Boo had showed her that power. Somehow the damned dog had made his way into her heart, captured it, and come to own it. Burying her face in her hands, Tess wept. Her tears flowed down her cheeks, and droplets of her remorse spilled on Boo's long, thick hair.

She didn't move when she heard the footsteps approaching from behind, brushing swiftly through the grass. She didn't have to look. She knew they were Dan's. The footsteps stilled. She glanced upward. Dan's face was twisted in angst. His eyes were filled with torment.

He knelt beside her next to Boo, placed his hand near hers on Boo's chest, and bowed his head. Tess didn't know what to do. She didn't know what to say. There were no words for a moment such as this. Her heart was broken for Dan. She wished that he would say something—anything. She wished that if nothing else, he would let out a bellowing cry of ache—but he did nothing. He left it all unspoken. It was almost as if he weren't even breathing.

He scooped the dog up from the bloody ground. Hugging him to his face, Dan whispered in a watery voice, "C'mon, Boo."

Tess watched Dan carry his friend away over the hillside and toward the lake.

Thirteen

er head bowed against her clasped hands, Tess sat at the kitchen bar waiting for Dan to come into the house. She had been greeted by Vlad Guseva's dead body when she'd approached the kitchen door. She had only seen him momentarily at the police station after the chase on the interstate Friday morning, but she remembered him—tall and muscular with a scowl that seemed to be permanently affixed to his hard-bitten face. His body was sprawled out on the short set of steps, and he was facedown in the pool of blood dripping over the paint.

For the hundredth time, Tess dragged her gaze to the clock. It was six thirty. Where was he? Her head snapped toward the door when she heard Dan struggling to push through it. He was carrying a large piece of plywood. She rushed to hold the door open for him. As he stepped through it, she looked outside—Vlad

Guseva's body was gone. A cold shiver skittered down her spine. She grabbed one end of the plywood to assist Dan in carrying it into the living room, where a window had been shot out.

"Careful of the glass on the floor," Dan said in a quiet voice as he hoisted the wood over the broken window. She helped him steady it as he nailed it against the opening. As he worked, he said, "I secured the property. Amos is back in the corral. There were two fatalities. I put the bodies in the barn and covered them with tarps."

When he stepped back from his work, she could see the anger smoldering in his eyes. His set jaw said one thing—he was a man set on revenge. Her heart beat like a frantic fist inside her chest as he marched past her toward the hidden door behind the fireplace—the one he'd shoved her through not long before.

After hitting the button, he went inside. She could hear him yanking weapons from the wall. With hesitant steps, Tess made her way across the living room and into the concealed passageway.

"What are you going to do?" she asked, but she knew the answer before he turned toward her.

"I'm going after them. No one comes onto my ranch and shoots it up without paying a price."

He was stoic. It was as if Dan Garrison weren't inhabiting the body before her. He was someone else—the OCD was all but gone. He was in soldier mode. She no longer recognized the man before her. "But... You don't know where they went. You don't know where to look."

"I know exactly where to look—Stamford, Connecticut," he said, continuing to load ammo into a duffel bag.

He was right. There was no question about who'd sent those men. "You can't go alone, Dan. They'll kill you."

"Not if I kill them first." He turned to her. "That's what I do, Tess. That's what I am—a paid killer, A mercenary."

"That's not true. You help people. You protect them."

"I kill the people who are after the people who need protecting, Tess. Isn't that why you came looking for First Force? Isn't that what you were looking for—someone to eliminate the threat against you?" His eyes were as icy as a January blizzard as he shrugged into a Kevlar vest.

"First Force! You need to call them in—you need your team!"

Without warning, he grabbed her roughly by the arm and dragged her through the tunnel toward the door that led into the basement. He was moving so quickly that she didn't have time to negotiate with him. They were almost at a jog as he dragged her through the basement and into the garage. Stumbling and tripping along, she could barely keep up with his powerful pace.

Upon entering the garage, he yanked the driver's side door of the Cadillac open and shoved her into the seat. He pointed his finger in her face. "Listen to me, and listen good this time. You drive to First Force Headquarters—no detours, and don't try to follow me. You go to headquarters, where you'll be safe. Don't break in—that's not necessary. Just press the buzzer and announce yourself, and Clark will let you in. Tell him what happened. He'll assemble the team. He'll put together a plan—maybe they'll need one, and maybe they won't. You got that?"

"But, Dan—"

"I said go! Go *now*, Tess!"

Tears welled up in her eyes so quickly that she could barely see him. He reached over her to start the car as the garage door opened. Her hands trembling, she pushed the gearshift into reverse. There would be no reasoning with him. She had no choice but to do as he'd told her to do, and she would—as fast as the Cadillac would go, she would drive to First Force Headquarters to get this man help.

*   *   *

As he jerked from the pillow up to a sitting position, Clark's eyes snapped open. He grabbed his glasses from the nightstand next to the bed and quickly plopped them on his face as the buzzer from the security gate sounded throughout the house. Rubbing his eyes, he tried to focus on the security screen stationed above the bedroom door. Finally, it came into clear view. He could see a panicked Tess McMillan pressing the buzzer over and over again. His hand slid up and down the wall next to the bed, looking for the button for the speaker.

Pressing the button, he said in a groggy voice, "What's wrong, Tess?"

"Please let me in! The ranch was attacked! Dan has gone after them!"

He tapped another button on the wall to open the gate and jumped out of the bed. "Get in here quick! I'll meet you at the front door!" He pulled on a T-shirt, yanking it down over his lounging pants, and then made haste down the hallway and down the staircase to the door just as Tess leaped from the car. After swinging the door wide open, he ran down the front steps to meet her and took her by the hand to escort her into the house. "Tell me exactly what happened and where Dan is now."

Tess was trying to catch her breath. She felt like she'd been pressing the buzzer for an hour, but it had only been a few moments. Clark led her into the office, flicked on the lights, and directed her to a chair, but she couldn't sit—her body was too full of adrenaline. She was running on sheer panic.

"About an hour or so ago, the men who were chasing me broke through the gate at Dan's ranch. They attacked the house, but Dan was able to chase then off—except for Vlad Guseva and one other. They're dead."

"Is Dan okay? Where's he now?"

"He went after them. He's headed for Stamford—where August lives. We've got to get the team! He can't go after them alone!"

"What the hell prompted him to go after them without backup? He knows better."

"They attacked his home—and they killed Boo."

"That would do it." He scratched his forehead and then scrubbed his fingers over his whiskers. He checked the time on the wall clock—it was 4:50 a.m. He turned on his laptop, his fingers raced over the keys, and then he let out a careworn sigh. "It takes about four hours to get to Stamford from here by car. I'll get the team together. We've got to get a plan in place fast, and…I'll have to call Walt. He's got to know that Garrison's gone rogue." After letting out a beleaguered breath, he grabbed his cell phone.

* * *

Vatonia carried a breakfast tray into the dining room, where August was sitting at one end of the table, and Jingjing, at the other. She usually served breakfast at eight o'clock sharp, but she was serving an early breakfast at six thirty, as August was going out of town to attend a charitable dinner for the Wounded Warriors Project.

She set the tray on the server and proceeded to place the breakfast entree in front of August, who she noticed was out of sorts. He yanked his napkin from the table and slapped it across his lap in disgust.

"I don't know what you're so upset about, August," Jingjing said. "The project is a success. Christine is doing as she is told at every turn. We couldn't be in a better position. Now if your *friends* can find Ms. McMillan, everything will fall right into place. If we had called Ballard's man in, McMillan would be ours right now."

August glared at her from across the length of the table as he forked a piece of sausage into his mouth. Vatonia continued around the table to set a glass of orange juice and an English muffin in front of Jingjing.

Sneering, Jingjing said, "Don't worry about it. I'm sure you can find other bimbos to move in and to be at your beck and call."

Slamming his fork down on the table, August yelled, "Stop calling them bimbos!" He shoved his plate at Vatonia as she hurried past them toward the kitchen. "I can't eat! Take this away, and call my driver to take me to airport."

Barely grabbing the plate before it slipped to the floor, Vatonia said, "Of course, Mr. Crafton."

As she rushed into the kitchen, she heard Jingjing say, "What's the hurry? Your flight doesn't leave until eight."

August snarled. "I'd rather sit in the airport than here with you." With that, she heard his heavy footsteps stamp out of the dining room.

Happy to be in another part of the house, Vatonia sent a quick text to August's driver and then leaned against the wall, letting out the breath that she felt she'd been holding in for days. She was relieved that Christine had been successful in convincing Jingjing that she was still under the control of the injection that had forced her to kill her good friend, Gina. Unthinkable.

Christine was also doing a remarkable job of holding her emotions at bay. Vatonia wasn't sure how much longer the young woman would be able to do that. She was just thankful that Jingjing's demands over the past several days had concerned simple tasks instead of self-inflicted wounds or pain. Maybe August had put a stop to the torture after day one.

So what next?

How long could they hold out?

Who would rescue them, and how would they get out of this mess?

What would Jingjing do if she discovered that Christine was not under the influence of the drug?

She swallowed hard—she knew the answer to that question. She just didn't want to think about it.

Swiping an errant hair from her cheek with the back of her hand, she decided that she would stay in the kitchen until Jingjing went downstairs or to her room. There was coffee in the carafe on the table. She'd let the little witch serve herself. Just as she poured herself a cup of coffee and sank into a chair at the small table, she heard August calling for her from the foyer.

"Vatonia! Where is my suitcase?"

Her shoulders slumped. She lifted her chin to the ceiling and rolled her eyes, squeezing them closed as she tried not to scream the words that she so wanted to scream. Screaming them just wouldn't have been a Christian thing to do, but Lord, her patience for those good-for-nothings was wearing way too thin.

She pushed up from the table to make her way into the foyer, where August was pacing and waiting for the driver to carry his suitcase to the car for him.

"Your case is right there, Mr. Crafton," she sweetly said. "I'm so sorry that you're having such a bad morning. Is there something I can do for you?"

"Ah, Vatonia, they just don't make them like you anymore. I wish there were something you could do, but I'm afraid not—"

There was a knock at the door, yet Vatonia could see through the glass that it wasn't the driver. She glanced at August, whose eyes had narrowed, and his face was pallid—she could see that he knew who was at the door. She opened the door to find two tough-looking men standing on the other side. The men looked exhausted and disheveled. Just then August's limo pulled up behind their dark SUV, which was parked in front of the house.

"The driver is here," Vatonia said.

His eyes locking with those of the men at the door, August said, "Tell him to wait, and then please go into the kitchen, Vatonia."

She waved to the driver, indicating that he should hold up. The men stepped into the foyer. Vatonia hurried toward the kitchen, passing Jingjing in the hallway. She was almost certain that one of the men was the individual she'd seen coming to pick up Gina's body, and she'd seen the other man, whose name she believed was Leo, in the house meeting with August on several occasions. She kept the kitchen door open just a crack so that she could hear their conversation.

"What are you doing here?" August asked. "Have you got Tess McMillan with you?"

"No, sir, we don't. I'm sorry to say that she's escaped again," the man with a deep, hard voice said. She heard a loud sigh of disgust that she knew belonged to August.

"How could you lose her again?" Jingjing asked.

There was a long pause, and then the same deep voice replied to her. "We went to the ranch. Whoever she was with was very skilled in weapons and security, but he had something that no one...I mean...that *we* never expected."

"What? What did he have?" Jingjing practically screamed at them.

Again, there was a long silence before the man said, "He had a bull loose on the property."

"A what? What are you talking about?" Jingjing yelled.

"A bull...a large male cow—very large and very mean."

"Why didn't you just shoot it? It was a cow! Just shoot it! Idiots! Can't you do anything right?" she shrieked, pounding her feet on the floor with every syllable as though she were a spoiled child in a candy store.

"Wait a minute," August said. "There are only two of you. Where's Stan? Where's Jingjing's husband, Vlad?"

The foyer fell completely quiet. It seemed that no one wanted to talk about the absent men. Finally, the same man said, "To be honest, I have no idea what happened to Stan. I think the bull got him. As for... Vlad...um...He was killed. He was shot. We had to leave them both behind. I'm sorry, Mrs. Guseva."

"Idiots! If I want something done right, I must do it myself! Get out! I can't stand the sight of you! Get out! Get out!" Jingjing said, screeching.

"Okay, okay, c'mon Leo. Let's blow this one-horse town," the man who'd done all the talking said.

Vatonia cupped her hand over her mouth. She heard shuffling feet, and someone slammed the door. The house was quiet for several moments. And then

Jingjing said, "It's time to hire someone who can bring this woman in!"

"No, Jingjing, *you* must hire someone. That's what you've wanted all along anyway. I have a dinner to attend," August said.

"Hypocrite! You go to a dinner for wounded Americans, yet you're involved in a project that could destroy your military if it's not the highest bidder for the serum!"

"No one sees the hypocrisy more than I, Jingjing."

"So you're just going to go to your little dinner and leave me to deal with this situation alone?"

"Somehow I think you won't have any problem at all." Vatonia heard the door open, and August said, "Driver! You may come in now for my suitcase."

"You are not only a hypocrite but also a coward."

"Call me anything you'd like. I know you're more than capable of handling this. That said, I think Vlad is probably better off dead."

The front door slammed.

From her vantage point, Vatonia saw Jingjing jog up the staircase while pulling her cell phone from her hip pocket. "It's me…I should have called you weeks ago. I need you now," Vatonia heard her say before her voice faded away.

Feeling defeated, she shrunk back into the kitchen and carefully closed the door. She sighed. It was time to clean up breakfast and run the dishwasher—at least the hum of the washer would drown out the sound of Jingjing's voice.

* * *

Orlando, Florida,

It was a beautiful sunny morning. Walt and Jack were lounging by the pool in their swimming trunks, drinking mimosas, and soaking up the warmth of the sunshine.

"Too bad we're so used to getting up early," Walt said. "It would be so nice to be like the girls and sleep till nine."

"Well, they're pretty exhausted by the end of the day—all that walking through the park beats them up. Lil drops into bed, and since Rayne is pregnant, she does too. What do you want to do while the women go to the princess tea this afternoon? How about a round of golf?"

"Sounds good, although I think you know you'll be able to kick my ass—I haven't played golf in about a hundred years."

Jack chuckled. "C'mon, how often do you get to kick the boss's ass at golf and not get fired?"

"True—"

Just then Walt's cell phone, which was lying on the table between them, started to ring and vibrate. The screen announced that it was Clark Rhodes. Jack and Walt exchanged wary glances.

"*Great*…the bat phone." Jack groaned.

"Not necessarily. They could be just checking in."

Jack looked at his watch. "At eight forty-five in the morning?"

"Pessimist," Walt said, bringing the phone to his ear. "Wabash."

"Hey, Walt, having a good time?" Clark asked as he and the team eyed Tess, who was busy braiding the all-important flash drive deep into her thick blond mane.

"See? He's just checking in," Walt whispered to Jack, who shot him a baleful look over his sunglasses. "We're having a blast. What's up?"

"We've got a blast from the past up here. Remember Tess McMillan? Ballard Crafton's wife?"

"Yeah…She had some kind of superhuman serum known as the XM, I believe. We thought it had been destroyed in the explosion at the lab, but she had the notes and promised to destroy them, as I recall. What about her?"

"Well, seems she didn't." Knowing that Walt was clinging to his every word, Clark went on to brief his boss on every detail that he'd been provided with. In conclusion, he said, "Well, now Dan's gone rogue."

Walt sat straight up. "Casualties?"

"Two dead. I sent Little and Smitty out to the ranch to clean up. Dan had things pretty well in hand. The team's sitting here in the office with Ms. McMillan and listening in on the call. We've got a plan in place, but we felt you needed to be apprised of the situation. We're going in after him and them."

"Where?"

"August Crafton has a home in Stamford, Connecticut. According to Tess McMillan, that's where Dan was headed. So that's where we're going."

"What the hell would possess Dan to go rogue?"

Clark cleared his throat. "They shot the ranch up pretty good…and…They killed Boo."

"Yeah…That would do it. I'll meet the team at Bradley International," Walt said. He looked to Jack.

"I'm in," Jack said.

"I'm not sure that's necessary, Walt. I think we've got it," Clark said.

"One of my men is out there on his own. No way will I be sitting in Florida, basking in the sun—I'm on my way to the airport immediately. I'll get a charter. Keep me in the loop."

"Will do. And Walt, I told Ms. McMillan that we would personally destroy all information about the serum this time."

"Noted." Walt disconnected the call. Setting the phone aside, he turned to Jack. "Text Grant. Tell him that we're going. I want him to stay behind to keep an eye on the girls. He'll want to come, I know he will, but I'll feel better knowing that one operative is keeping watch."

"Agreed," Jack said. Walt picked the cell back up and began to dial. "Who're you calling now?"

"The XM has resurfaced, as I suspected it would. I'm obligated to inform a former colleague."

* * *

As Clark disconnected the call with Walt, he looked around the room at team First Force—Will Smith, otherwise known as Smitty—the team's field medic, and a former medic in the US Army Special Forces. Clark's twin sister, Casey Rhodes, the team's sniper; Stewart Little, a First Force pilot and a former airman; and, even though she wasn't part of the team, Tess McMillan were ready to play an important role in thwarting August and Jingjing's plans and making sure that Dan Garrison came home safely. They all sat rigidly in their seats, waiting for his cue.

Clark's eyes met those of Little, who said, "Chopper's ready and waiting."

Clark turned to Tess. "You've got the flash drive all secure?"

Flipping her long tresses over her shoulder, she said, "I do."

"Good. Casey…Grab Kevlar vests, weapons, and ammo for Jack and Walt." She nodded to show her compliance and quickly exited the room. Clark continued. "It's nine in the morning. They've got a big head start on us. Let's move."

Fourteen

Hunkered down behind the groomed boxwood hedging at the edge of the Crafton estate, Dan watched. He had to chuckle slightly to himself. Tess would've been disappointed. For a multimillionaire, August Crafton had a pitiful excuse for a security system. *Snip, snip,* and he had disengaged it within a nanosecond. Maybe he didn't have as much to hide as his older brother had, or perhaps he wasn't as paranoid. Either way, August had made it most convenient to get onto the estate. The reason didn't really matter—he was in.

He checked his watch again: it was 9:40 a.m.

All was quiet.

No cars came in.

No cars went out.

No one was working on the lawn.

No one seemed to be around at all.

Didn't matter. He was going in anyway.

Someone had to be caring for the house, and he would get August Crafton's location from him or her—whatever it took.

Crawling on his belly, he was making his way along the hedging toward the back of the house, looking for a good and quiet point of entry, when a door on the east side of the house opened. He stilled and slowed his breathing as an older black woman carrying a broom stepped out onto a small porch. Dan pulled a pair of binoculars from his vest and pressed them to his eyes.

The woman glanced around the grounds and swiped her forehead with her hand, and then she took to sweeping the slight space while furtively looking over her shoulder at the door. He noted that she seemed uneasy. Suddenly, she stopped sweeping. Someone had come to the door. They spoke through a small gap. The conversation appeared rather apprehensive. After another cautious glance, she slipped inside the house.

Through the binoculars, he continued to watch. The door had a window, and through the sheer curtains, he could see the older woman talking with a younger redheaded woman. He could tell by their actions, body language, and facial expressions that their tête-à-tête was not casual—at all.

Furthermore, the old woman had failed to close the door completely. With any luck, he'd just found an easy access into the house. His lips curled. Tess would've been in a full belly-rolling laugh by then.

Tess—he was feeling bad about the rough way he'd treated her back at the ranch. He had to protect her. Walt was going to be pissed as hell that he'd gone rouge. He let out a breath. He'd been willing to wait for instructions. He'd been willing to go with the team, but then Crafton had made this personal—he'd attacked his ranch. Yeah, maybe he'd lost his cool. But it was too late. He was going to take care of business—on his terms.

* * *

After August's car had pulled out of the driveway and Jingjing had retired upstairs, the house became quiet. Relieved to hear only the hypnotizing hum of the dishwasher, Vatonia sank into a seat at a small table to take a sip of her coffee—which was cold. She hated cold coffee.

She usually loved quiet mornings, but this silence threatened to explode into something that she wasn't sure she was prepared for. She could feel the tension permeating all around her like a dark, deadly phantom waiting to pounce.

She picked up the mug from the table, took it to the sink, and poured the undrinkable coffee down the drain. Her nerves were getting the best of her, and she was beginning to think that a serious dose of seasickness would've been a far better problem than what was looming over her at that moment. She would've much rather died at the hands of the God she had faith in, the God she understood, than at the hands of these greedy, self-absorbed heathens.

All at once she became aware that she was standing at the scarred butcher-block prep table, wringing her hands. She grabbed the meat cleaver from one of the knife blocks and slammed it into the wood. Better to take out her aggression on the old table than on a human being. Still...How was that helping anything or anybody? Fresh air...That was what she needed. Some fresh spring air. Knowing that the small stoop off of the kitchen door could use a good sweeping, she grabbed the broom from the pantry and headed out the door to keep her hands busy doing a small, mindless chore and to breathe in some air to calm her frazzled nerves.

Once on the porch, she took in the sweet air of the April morning. The sky was blue, and the grass was turning greener by the day. Soon the leaves on the trees would bravely burst into full splendor, celebrating summer's return. Wiping a bead of sweat from her forehead, she thought, *I only hope that Christine and I will still be around to see summer.* With that, she set to sweeping the small space, and then she heard the door creak open behind her. She turned to find Christine peeking out at her.

"What's going on? I heard Jingjing having one of her tantrums," Christine said, anxiety filling her tone.

"I'm not exactly sure, but you shouldn't be here. We can't afford to be caught talking to each other. What're you thinking, girl? Now get back in that house this minute," Vatonia said in a loud whisper. Setting the broom aside, she shooed Christine inside and then slipped into the kitchen behind her.

"I can't take this much longer, Vatonia. Let's just go. Let's just get the hell outta here. August's gone. It's just that little bitchy scientist here. What's she gonna do to stop us? " She spoke quickly, wringing her hands and fussing with the bandage that covered her burned palm.

Christine was right. There really wasn't any reason to sit around waiting for something horrible to happen. But what would happen when August returned? What would happen when they realized that Christine was no longer under their spell? Would they send those men to hunt them down? There was no way that she or Christine was as stealthy as this Tess McMillan they'd been so unsuccessful in apprehending.

Where would they go?

Where would they hide?

How would they stay ahead of August's headhunters?

Christine's hands squeezing her arms broke through her deliberation. "Vatonia…We can do this. By the time they realize we're gone, we'll be miles away."

"How? To where? Where will we go, Christine? They'll send those men after us."

"We'll go to the police. They killed Gina. We'll report it to the police."

"Honey, do you honestly believe that the police will help us? They might check out Gina's death, but August is a wealthy, influential man in this area. I'm not sure they'd even believe us."

"We've got to try, Vatonia, or we're dead for sure. Now I want you to get a few things together, and then we're getting in my car, and we're getting the hell out of here *together*."

"You're out of your mind, girl."

"Better out of my mind than dead." She tried to stifle a cry but failed. "Like Gina."

* * *

Something was up. There was some kind of distress in the household. That wasn't Dan's concern. He had two objectives: The first was to find August Crafton and his cronies. The second was to kill them. Period. Stuffing the binoculars away and staying low, he jogged across the yard toward the door that the old woman had left ajar.

After sidling up to the wall right next to the door, Dan peered into the kitchen. It appeared to be empty. He slipped to the other side. Yes, the room was unoccupied. He could hear the soft hum of a motor running. Pulling his Glock from his shoulder holster, he slid through the door and swiftly crossed the room to lean his body flat against the far wall. He found the source of the motor sound—the dishwasher was running, making it difficult for him to hear noises throughout the house.

He eased the door open to creep into the formal dining room. With measured steps and his gun at the ready, he found his way into the foyer. He was forced to blink his eyes several times, as they were beginning to water. Sniffing back a sudden surge of congestion, he eased toward the stairs. The sound of cautious footsteps descending the stairs accompanied by frantic whispers filled his ears—he was most likely hearing the two women he'd seen moments ago.

He could feel the choke of a cough pushing through the stuffiness and the swelling in his tearing eyes. He swallowed hard to stifle the cough and wiped his nose with his forearm. His eyes searched the floor for a cat, the only thing that could've caused his sudden discomfort.

"Who are you, and what are you doing here?" a woman's voice asked. The cold steel of her gun caressed the back of his neck.

Dan tensed.

"Give me your gun," the woman said.

Fuck.

Slowly, he lowered the gun toward the person behind him, but when she reached for it, he swiftly twisted, flipping his arm over hers and pulling her forward to the floor before pointing her own weapon at her.

The Chinese woman did not show any fear. "Who are you?" Just then the two women stepped into the foyer, duffel bags in hand. When their eyes fell upon him and the woman, they froze. Her piercing gaze never left his, yet she seemed to sense that the women were behind her. "Where do you think you're going? Is this man here for you?" The older woman couldn't speak. Her mouth opened, but no words tumbled from her lips. The very attractive young redhead swallowed hard. "Christine…What is going on?"

The redhead stared at him, unable to move and unable to answer her. The old woman had the wherewithal to set the duffel bags out of sight.

Dan's eyes were swelling and tearing all the more, but through the haze, he had a pretty good idea of who the Chinese woman was—Jingjing Choo.

"Get off the floor slowly," Dan said to the woman.

Before she could make a move, a man in the door that Dan had just passed through spoke. "Don't move, Mr. Garrison. Drop your weapon to the floor, put your hands on your head, and drop to your knees— you know the position I'm talking about."

Dan was without options. Whoever the man was, he was too far away for Dan to make any quick moves without being shot. Slowly, he complied with the man's demands.

"You okay, Jingjing?" the man asked.

The Chinese woman had no reaction of relief or pleasure at being rescued; nor did she acknowledge the man's question. Instead she picked herself up, retrieved her gun from the floor, stuffed it into the tiny waistband of her jeans, and grabbed Dan's gun too. Before he dropped to his knees, she stepped up close to him.

Dan's six-foot-three physique dwarfed Jingjing's small five-foot frame, but she didn't shrink away from him. "I'm going to ask you again: who are you, and what are you doing here?"

His eyes locked with hers. Dan didn't move. He offered her nothing. He could see the agitation boiling beneath her skin. He lowered to his knees.

"Meet Dan Garrison, former US marshal, now a member of First Force," the man said in a deep, growling voice as he stepped into the foyer. Dan locked eyes with the hard-bitten stranger. He was big and muscled. He'd been in the military. He had the look, but it was plain to see that he was not using his military training to work against the bad guys—instead he worked right alongside them. "It's his ranch that Tess McMillan has been hiding out at. He killed your husband. Give me a little time with him. I'll get the woman's location."

"I'm glad that I called you when I did, Cashton," Jingjing said. He stepped forward, eager to carry out his promise, but Jingjing put her hand up to stop him. "First Force…Was that the group that attacked Ballard's lab in Russia?"

"It was."

"And you know how to contact them?"

"I have my ways, yes."

"Just as I had hoped," Jingjing said, finally allowing herself to smile. The curl of her thin lips was poisonous. She reached into her pocket to pull out a cell phone and tossed it to Christine, hitting her in the chest. The girl fumbled to catch the phone, and after failing to do so, she plucked it from the floor. "Call August, and tell him to come immediately. Tell him that I found the subject whom Ballard and I were searching for all along. Tell him that we have the means to get Tess McMillan and the serum to come to us." She turned to her new ally. "In the meantime, Cashton, please take Mr. Garrison downstairs to my laboratory—the first door on the right after the staircase."

"Yes, ma'am."

* * *

Two and a half hours later, the team arrived at Bradley International. The chopper landed on the pad, and they made their way into the executive-plus hangar, where charter flights and private aircraft landed and departed. The hangar was a miniature version of the main terminal with a smaller staff.

The uncertainty of how long it would take Walt and Jack to join them had the team members on edge. They weren't absolutely sure that time was of the essence, but it usually was in these cases. Because he was the field medic, Smitty was perhaps feeling the burn more than Casey or Little. Not knowing where or what Dan Garrison was up against and not knowing whether there would be injuries had him stressing. Tess tried to hold it all at bay, but anxiety was creeping up her spine, and despite her best efforts, her stomach was tossing like a rowboat on rough waters. Upon entering the hangar, they each found a place to put their gear and sit and wait.

"I saw an open-air café on our way in. I'm going to grab a coffee," Casey said.

"I'll come along," Little said. "Need to stretch my legs a bit. You got this, Smitty?" he asked, indicating the gear sitting all around the small space and the woman they needed to protect, Tess McMillan. Smitty nodded, and with that, Casey and Little set off down the terminal.

Smitty looked up at Tess, who had sunk into a chair and was holding her head. "You okay?"

"I'm not sure."

* * *

Glancing around the empty café, Ryder leaned back against the chair. He checked his text messages for the hundredth time. "The plane should be here soon to pick us up, but they still haven't confirmed who we're meeting on the other end in Seattle," he said, stuffing the phone back into his jacket.

"Thanks for letting me in on your next job. Still, pisses me off, that girl gettin' away. Crafton ain't gonna pay us now," Leo said.

"He'll pay us. Maybe not what we agreed on, but he'll pay us some. Fact is, neither of us delivered the goods, so we don't deserve the whole bank. I'm just glad I didn't get slammed by that bull. Now it's on to the next customer, next job." Ryder peeked up from his phone to see a tall, shapely brunette dressed in camo pants and a black T-shirt approaching the café with a huge man who looked like he'd just as soon step on your head as look at you. "C'mon, Leo," he said, urging his friend away from the table. They meandered down the terminal.

* * *

I'll get the coffee. Black?" Casey asked.

"Yeah," Little said, taking a seat at the closest table and covertly keeping an eye on the two strangers leaving the open-air café in a little bit too much of a hurry for his comfort. Somewhat satisfied that they were leaving without looking back, he glanced down and found an abandoned half eaten blueberry muffin on the table.

"Slow day—fast service," Casey said a few minutes later as she slipped into the chair across from Little and set a steaming cup of coffee down in front of him.

"Yeah, I'm glad we don't fly commercial," he said around a mouthful of muffin.

"Where did you get that?"

"This?" he asked, pointing at his mouth. "Found it on the table." Clearly appalled, her eyes widened. "What? I tore off the part that had been chewed on."

Snatching her mug off of the table, Casey pushed up from her seat. "I *cannot* sit with you."

The right corner of Little's lip curled.

* * *

"**A**re you gonna be okay, honey?" Smitty asked, concerned about Tess's complexion, which was turning pastier by the second.

Choking, she cupped her hand over her mouth. "No…I…I…I'm gonna to be sick—" She gasped and jumped from her seat to run toward the restrooms. With Smitty on her heels, she burst through the ladies' room door after almost plowing down two men on her way there.

Tess dashed into a stall. Smitty stood outside it, holding the door closed and listening to her dry heave over the toilet. She was quiet for a short time, and then she emerged from the stall, flushed. "I guess that's all there is. Sorry."

He placed the back of his fingers across her forehead. "You're warm but not feverish."

"I think it was the ride in the chopper. It was rather…choppy. Not to mention the fact that I've been under a lot of stress for several w…w…ee—" She couldn't hold it back. There was no longer a threat that bile would spew from her mouth. Instead, it had arrived—down the front of Smitty's black T-shirt and camo pants and over his boots.

Tess was no longer flushed—she was beet red with embarrassment.

Rigid, Smitty winced.

"I'm so sorry!"

"No…It's okay. I just need to…clean up." He stiffly made his way toward the line of sinks on the nearby wall.

Immediately, Tess was ripping paper towels from the dispenser and wiping down his chest and arms, but it only seemed to make things worse. Smitty turned on the faucet to begin washing off what he could.

"I'm so sorry. I can't believe I did *that*."

"Do you feel better?"

She stilled. Her eyebrows rose. "I do."

"Well, that's good, then."

She continued to try to help him, but she could see that it was an exercise in yuck. "Do you have a change of clothes?"

"In my duffel, yes."

"I'll get it!"

Continuing to wash, he did not look up. "No. Stay here. I'm—" He looked up, only to find that the door had closed. She was already gone. "Dammit!" He attempted to follow her, but he slipped in a puddle of vomit on the floor.

Horrified by what her body had just done without her permission, Tess rushed from the ladies' room to attempt to right what seemed so unbelievably wrong. Honestly, through the wall of embarrassment, she had to chuckle to herself. She simply couldn't imagine how Mr. OCD, everything-has-to-be-spotless Dan Garrison, would have reacted if she'd barfed all over his clothes and, God forbid, his boots. Her momentary amusement was cut short when she suddenly felt a powerful grip around her arm almost yank her off her feet.

"Hey there, Tess. Boy, are we glad to see you," the hard-looking man said while dragging her down the terminal. Another man grabbed her left arm. Their grasp was so forceful that she feared her bones would break. They were walking at such a pace that she could barely keep up. This was not good. She twisted her arms to no avail. They squeezed them that much harder. "C'mon, sweetie, you can walk faster than this," the man said, picking up speed and almost jogging toward the exit where taxis were lined up at the curb, waiting for passengers.

She tried to dig her heels into the floor, but the floor was so slick that it was almost as if she were skating along with them. She looked over her shoulder— no one from First Force was in sight. Finally, they had reached the exit. The man to her right shoved the glass door open, and before she could resist, he was pushing her into a cab. One man slid in next to her while the other jogged around the cab and jammed in against her on the other side.

"Let's go, buddy! Stamford—move it!" the man said, pulling his cell phone from his pocket. He dialed it. "Mr. Crafton…Ryder here. Seems we bumped into your friend Tess McMillan. If you're interested in renegotiating the original deal, we can bring her straight over." Smiling, he listened. "No…No, I was thinking triple the price. After all, you fired us, but we kept on pluggin' away until we got exactly what you asked for—Tess McMillan on a gold platter. So what's it gonna be, Mr. Crafton? Triple or nothin'?" His smile never wavered. He nodded. "Sounds like a deal. We'll have her there directly."

Disgusted, frustrated, defeated, and squished between August's henchmen, Tess let out an exhausted sigh and stared at the back of the cabdriver's turban.

* * *

When Tess didn't return with his duffel bag within a few minutes, Smitty rushed from the restroom. Not finding Tess in the seating area where the team's equipment remained undisturbed, he snapped his head from right to left and back, looking up and down the terminal. She was nowhere to be seen.

Not. Good.

At a dead run, Smitty made his way toward the café where Casey and Little had said they were getting coffee. He slid to a stop next to Little, who looked at him with his usual scowl, and then he grimaced. "What the hell happened to you? You stink to high heaven, dude."

"Tess is gone."

Casey and Little jerked to their feet. Casey hurried from her table. "What happened?" Getting a whiff of him, she took a step back. "You do stink!"

"Tess got sick—all over me. That doesn't matter. She's gone, and we've gotta find her. Fan out—move!" Just then the burn phone in his pocket buzzed. He yanked it out. "Smitty."

"We're landing now on runway five. Hope things are going better on your end—just got a call from Clark. They want to exchange Dan for Tess and her serum," Walt said.

Shit. Could things get any worse?

The entire situation had just gone from bad to FUBAR—fucked up beyond all recognition.

Fifteen

August slammed his cell phone on the seat next to him as his private plane's landing gear hit the landing strip. He should've been relieved. He should've been ecstatic. Ryder had Tess McMillan in his custody—and Jingjing hadn't had a chance to send Ballard's man out. It was all coming together—although he had been surprised when Christine had called to tell him to return home. No matter. They were supposedly on the same team, and this was the moment that they'd been anticipating. Tess had the formula for the XM-11 serum. Soon he and Jingjing would own said formula—she was administering the mind-control formula to the intruder who'd broke into the house at that very moment. She felt sure that he would not only be a perfect test subject but also the key to finding Tess. Why? Was there evidence that Tess and the man were lovers? Again, no matter. Soon they would hold the world's militaries hostage like no one ever had before.

He would be worth millions.

No…He would be worth billions.

He would be worth more than Ballard could have ever imagined himself to be.

He sighed.

Still…He was feeling unsettled. Why?

Maybe it was because he was stuck with Jingjing. He scrubbed his fingers over his jaw. He could handle that little bitch. Most likely, she would take her share of the fortune, collect her lousy little cat, and head home for China. Maybe she wouldn't, but he had no doubt that she wouldn't want to continue living in his house.

He looked down at the cell phone lying next to his leg. He thought that he should probably call the little bitch to let her know that his men had captured Tess and that she would be at the house shortly—and then he thought better of it. He would rather gloat in her face when he arrived home.

He looked out the window. He could see the hangar in the near distance. He sighed. What he needed was a woman at his side who was worthy of his name and his fortune. A woman who understood what it meant to be influential. Over the years, he'd had his fun with many college girls. They'd been fun, and the sex had been wild and wonderful and carefree, and yes, he truly felt bad about Gina. He hated to think of her as collateral damage, but what else could he do? What was done was done.

He didn't want to think about that.

The woman who would share his name and his fortune would have to be not only intelligent, elegant, and charming but also beautiful. He stared out the window as the plane taxied toward JetStar private hangar at Bradley. He knew whom he wanted. He'd been watching her awhile—Tess.

Not only was Tess McMillan intelligent, elegant, charming, and oh-so beautiful, but she was also a survivor, and he would offer her an opportunity to survive. She would accept it, and in time, she would learn to care for him as she had Ballard. He was sure of it.

"You can exit the aircraft, and your car is waiting just outside, Mr. Crafton," the attendant said, bringing him out of his funk.

"Thank you."

August gathered his cell and rose from his seat. His future was mere miles away. He would have it all. Everything his brother had strived to have. But he had failed—epically. He'd have money beyond belief and respect—no, admiration…no, fear—from world leaders and a beautiful woman at his side. Better yet, his brother's woman.

Ah, that unsettled feeling was starting to fade.

* * *

With Shan on her shoulder, Jingjing stood over the gurney on which Dan Garrison lay, strapped down and unconscious. She checked his vital signs once again. She was most unhappy with his reaction to the injection. His eyes were teary and swollen, and his breathing, shallow. Christine had not had that kind of reaction to the serum.

"How long will he be out?" Cashton asked.

"I can't be sure. Everyone reacts to the sedatives differently."

"Is he supposed to be so red and swollen?"

Jingjing's eyes roamed over Dan's body from his head to his feet. "Not usually. Have you had a response from First Force yet?"

He glanced down at his cell. "No. I'm sure they're mulling the situation over. Don't worry. They're not gonna leave one of their own in harm's way. We'll hear from them soon, I'm sure." He lifted from his seat, stretching his lower back. "I'm going outside for a smoke."

"Tell Christine to hurry up with those cool compresses."

Cashton's lips curled. "I like redheads best. She's got a nice body too. Didn't you say she's been injected with that mind-control stuff?" Hesitating and looking up from her chore, Jingjing dragged her gaze to meet his. "Hey, I could use a little downtime. She'd do it if you told her to, and I'd be willing to knock a couple hundred bucks off my services if you provided me with a little *service*."

Removing the gauze from the injection site on Dan's arm so that she could examine it, Jingjing said, "Smoking is bad for your health, Cashton."

"So is—"

"I'm a scientist, not a madam. Just hurry Christine along with those compresses." The buzzer that rang throughout the house when someone was at the front door sounded. Without moving another muscle in her body, Jingjing rotated her eyes from Cashton to Vatonia. "Once again you are required to do your job, Vatonia. Someone is at the door. Send him or her away. Cashton, go with her to make sure that she does."

Making eye contact with the housekeeper, Cashton hitched his chin toward the stairs. Vatonia followed him up the stairs and into the foyer, where they found Christine holding a basket of compresses and looking out the long narrow window beside the door. She turned when she heard Vatonia and Cashton approaching.

"Two men and a blonde," she said.

"Step aside, and let the old lady answer," Cashton said. He took Christine by the arm and stepped off to the side, out of sight.

The buzzer sounded again. Vatonia opened the door and found the same two surly-looking men from that morning and a blonde. She pretended not to remember them. "May I help you?"

"August Crafton will be expecting us." He nodded toward the blonde in his grip. "This is Tess McMillan."

Vatonia could see the trepidation in Tess's eyes. She attempted to close the door. "Mr. Crafton is not home—"

Ryder caught the door with his hand, and Cashton, with his gun drawn, grabbed ahold of it to jerk it open. Vatonia was almost knocked to the floor during the quick moves. Christine was able to steady her. The two women backed into August's study to get out of the way of any trouble.

"What's up, boys?" Cashton said, sticking his Glock in Ryder's face.

"Who the hell are you?"

"I'm the one holding the gun. Who the hell are *you*?"

"I'm Ryder, and this here's Leo. We were hired by Crafton to find Tess McMillan and to deliver her here. So what's the deal?"

"There ain't no deal," Cashton said as he lifted his gun to the man's forehead. "Kindly step on inside, Ms. McMillan." Wiggling from Ryder's and Leo's grasps, Tess complied, only to find herself in another man's grip.

"Wait just a damned minute!" Ryder said.

"I don't think you should wait that long, dude, 'cause you've got less time than that to clear out before I start shootin'."

Leo began backing away from the door, but Ryder wasn't ready to give it all up so easily. "What about our money?"

Cashton pressed the gun harder into Ryder's forehead. "What about it?"

"C'mon, Ryder, let's go," Leo said, pleading with him and gingerly tapping him on the shoulder.

Ryder pushed his hand away in disgust. "We'll go. You have Crafton give us a call. Tell him we want our money.

"Let's go!" Leo said.

Finally Ryder turned to return to the taxicab waiting in the driveway. Dragging Tess along, Cashton stepped out on the front porch and waited until the cab pulled out of the drive. Once the cab was out of sight, he yanked her into the house and then dragged her into the study so that he could collect the other women. "Tess…Meet Christine and Vatonia. Now let's go back to the lab." He smiled at Tess. "Jingjing's been waitin' on you."

Cashton followed the three women down into the basement laboratory, and when Tess stepped away from the wooden staircase and into the open space, her eyes immediately went to the still figure of Dan Garrison, who was strapped to the gurney. She tensed. What had Jingjing done to him? And then her eyes found Jingjing at her worktable, tapping at her laptop with a cat perched on her shoulder.

"Christine, put those compresses on Mr. Garrison's face—now," Jingjing said over her shoulder. Christine rushed to the man on the gurney. Tess followed her, horrified to find him in such a bad state. She ran her fingers over his forehead and down his plump red cheek.

"He's allergic to cats. That's probably what all this swelling is about," Tess whispered to Christine.

Jingjing spun on her heels at the sound of a familiar voice that had not been present before. Her venomous eyes narrowed all the more. "Tess, when did you arrive? I can't believe they gave you up so easily."

"They didn't," Cashton said. "She was delivered here by Mr. Crafton's men. We've got what we need now. You'll be able to start the second phase of your testing before Crafton comes home."

"It's too late for that. I'm here," August said, his voice booming through the room. Everyone turned to find him stepping into the room with a gun in his hand. "What the hell is going on here, Jingjing? A mutiny of sorts?"

"Put that away, August," Jingjing said. "Cashton took it upon himself to collect Tess from your men, inadequate as they are. As for our test subject, if I'd waited for you, we would be years away from our objective." She made her way toward Tess. "Now, Tess, you will give us the formula."

"I'm sorry. I don't have the formula," Tess said.

Cashton grabbed her by the shoulder, spun her around, and backhanded her, knocking her to the floor. "Give Jingjing the formula, bitch!"

Wiping the blood from her nose with the back of her hand, Tess said, "I can't give her something that I don't have."

He was lifting his leg to boot her when a shot was fired. The room froze. Everyone's eyes flicked around the lab to see who'd been eliminated, yet everyone was accounted for. August lowered his gun from over his head and pointed it at Cashton. "You will not strike her again. I will take Ms. McMillan upstairs, and we will have a conversation. I'm sure we will come to an agreement quickly. Now help the lady off of the floor." He looked at Jingjing. She was glowering at him. August smiled. "You may continue with your tests, Jingjing. I won't disturb you. Vatonia, please get something to clean Ms. McMillan's face with, and get some of my finest Cognac. The lady looks like she could use a drink— a good stiff one."

"Of course, Mr. Crafton. Do you want it warmed?" Vatonia asked. She scurried as quickly as she could past everyone and to the stairs.

"Not today. And Vatonia…Deliver it to my room."

"Of course, Mr. Crafton."

August glanced at Christine, who was standing near the gurney. Her complexion was sallow. She looked gaunt from stress. When this was over, he would see to it that she was properly compensated and sent on her way in exchange for her silence. As soon as Cashton had Tess on her feet, August reached his hand out to her. Hesitating, she studied him. He offered his hand to her again, this time with its palm up, and she realized that it was in her and Dan's best interest to take it.

Once Tess's hand was in his, August led her up the stairs, pausing to take a glimpse at Jingjing, whose grimace was as deadly as a toxic dart to the jugular.

* * *

Team First Force, including Walt and Jack, gathered near the ladies' room where Smitty had last seen Tess. "She's not in the terminal," Little said. "I'm thinkin' those two guys we saw at the café have everything to do with this. They're not in the terminal either."

"Gear up," Walt said. "Clark's got an SUV waiting for us, and he's sending us GPS coordinates of the location of Crafton's estate and information on the best way in. He thinks we're about ten miles away. Because it's a residential area, we'll have to park the vehicle about a mile or so out, so get ready for a brisk jog."

Casey looked around. "Where's Ketchum?"

"We left him in Florida with the girls," Walt said.

"Ouch. I'll bet he was mad," Casey said.

"I've seen his wife in a bikini. He'll get over it," Walt said.

* * *

From the moment August escorted her into his bedroom, Tess was calculating an escape. August wasn't as strong as his older sibling. She was impressed by how weak his touch was. When she held his hand, it was almost like holding the hand of a child—but maybe she wasn't giving children enough credit. His grip was flimsy. His skin, as smooth as a hand model's—or at least she imagined it was. Ballard's skin had been silky smooth, but his grip had been firm and dominating.

As she meandered deeper into the room, her eyes were drawn to the taffeta drapes that framed the huge window and the beautiful Regency desk and... Ballard's Ming vase. She ran her fingers around the rim of the fine porcelain piece, recalling how Ballard had loved his vases—how he'd loved his things and his possessions and how he'd considered women to be possessions too. Pulling her fingers away from the vase, she shook her head. Why did she still allow Ballard into her thoughts?

"I see you've found Ballard's vase. It's beautiful, and I appreciate your sending it to me."

"You're welcome. I'm glad you're enjoying it," she said while eyeballing the items on the desk and hoping to find something sharp, like a sterling-silver letter opener or a metal nail file that he used on his delicate hands. No such luck. There was nothing but his laptop, a few letters, envelopes, and a folded *New York Times*.

Without warning, his hands caressed her shoulders. His touch sent a shiver of derision throughout her body. His face drew closer to her hair. He breathed in deep. "I have so much to offer a woman like you, Tess. I want you to consider that for a moment." Her stomach coiled. There was a soft knock on the door. "Come in," he said, moving away from her.

Keeping her gaze to the floor, Vatonia carried in a tray holding two wobble snifters filled with Cognac, a bottle of antiseptic liquid, and an ornate crystal cup filled with cotton balls. She set the snifters on the desk, and then she brought the medicine to Tess.

"You can use the bathroom right through that door, Ms. McMillan. I'm sure you'd like to clean up a bit."

Tess took the antiseptic and several cotton balls from the tray. "Thank you."

She glanced askance at August, who was pouring a glass of Cognac, as she stepped into the bathroom. She closed the door and leaned against it, pressing her eyes closed, thankful to be alone.

"Please return to the lab, and keep an eye on Christine, will you, Vatonia? Make sure she's okay," he said.

"Of course, Mr. Crafton," the maid replied, and then Tess heard the bedroom door close. When she opened her eyes, she saw the ornate bathroom for the first time. The walls were marble, as were the floor and the vanity tops. Deep, wide veins of rose and amber curled through the rich stone. Glorious white-marble sculptures of women bathing stood in the corner of the large garden tub and on the vanity between each of the three gilded mirrors. The room was beautiful, but it wasn't anything that she hadn't seen before—in many of Ballard's homes. She didn't need a fancy toilet—she needed an escape route or, at the very least, a weapon. No windows—there wasn't a single window. Who didn't have a window in their overly ornate bathroom?

Under the watchful eyes of the stone maidens delighting in their bathing, Tess rifled through drawers, looking for something, anything, only to come up with toothpaste and a variety of toiletries. The door clicked. She turned to find August peeking in.

"I'm waiting for you, Tess. We have much to discuss but only a short amount of time."

The maidens seemed to be mocking her as she followed him into the bedroom. She had the urge to run through the bathroom, knocking all of them to the floor just to hear the stone crashing and breaking and to see their heads rolling over the floor. Instead, she asked, "What do you want to discuss, August?"

He sank down on the edge of the bed, patting the space next to him. "Sit." Reluctantly, she did so. He caressed her bruised cheek with his soft, weak little hands. "You are a survivor, Tess. I've admired your resourcefulness and intelligence over these past weeks. I was watching you when you had no idea that you were being observed."

She batted his hand away. "What are you talking about? When?"

He pointed to his laptop. "I can't believe that you don't know. I can see you through the camera on your computer if you leave the lid open."

She was aghast. "I don't use a computer. I use a tablet."

"It's the same concept." He raked his fingers through her hair to push it away from her shoulders. She stiffened. The last thing Tess wanted was for anyone to touch her hair. As for August—she didn't want him to touch any part of her body. "You were a part of my brother's life for a long time. I know that, and his death must have been devastating for you. I understand. But you can move on from all that. I would like to offer you sanctuary. A life of wealth and luxury that will far surpass what Ballard could've provided you with. When we blend the mind-control formula that Jingjing has created with my brother's XM-11, which you possess, we'll be able to market it for billions to world leaders clamoring for their military to be the most powerful. I will be the wealthiest man alive—powerful and feared. And with you at my side, I will be the happiest as well." Nuzzling her cheek, he ran his fingertips down her spine. "We don't have much time, Tess. I won't be able to protect you unless you agree. I know that that's not the best foundation to build a relationship on, yet many great leaders of past times built relationships on less. What do you say?"

He was touching her with those sissy, girly hands. She wanted to retch—the man fancied himself a leader. He was nothing more than a weak little man who happened to have a lot of money. "What do you say?" What the hell else could she say but yes? *Suck it up, McMillan. It's go time.*

"My relationship with Ballard wasn't built on much more than what you're offering, August. I'll count my blessings and join the team."

Taking her face into his hands, he pulled her to him and kissed her lips with primal possession. His right hand caressed her throat and moved down her chest until his fingers found the three tiny buttons at the neckline of her T-shirt. Unerringly, he plucked the buttons open and slipped his hand inside her shirt and her bra, finding one of her stiff, pebble-like nipples. He moaned at the touch. His breath quickened as he eased her down onto the bed and lifted her breast from the bra so that he could savor the taste and see a small sampling of what was then his.

"I want you, Tess. I've been waiting for this moment, and I want to enjoy it, but as I said, we don't have much time. So give me the formula. I'll send it down to Jingjing, and you and I can spend as much time as we wish celebrating our new partnership, which will no doubt grow into the kind of relationship that Ballard never could've given you."

Tess lay on the bed, allowing him to circle his thumb round and round over her nipple as the thick column of his erection pressed into her thigh, "I told you, August. I don't have the formula with me. I have it hidden away."

"Where?"

She favored him with a demure smile. "I'll take you to it. On your jet, and while we're flying high in the sky, we'll celebrate like you've never celebrated before."

His lips curled. "I'm not a fool, Tess."

"I can't imagine that you are. You're a Crafton. Princeton didn't raise fools—he raised intelligent, handsome opportunists. You'll have to trust me, August. Isn't that the relationship that you want to build with me—a relationship of trust?" She pulled him down on top of her and smashed her lips to his, making sure that his hard-on was against her pelvis as she moved her hips to entice him that much more. The sensation was made up of nothing more than friction—clothing against clothing—but he was getting the main idea. His sex was hardening and growing by the second.

"What the fuck, August?" Jingjing said, slicing through the interlude.

August jumped up to find himself in the direct line of fire of Jingjing's gun. He held his hands up in surrender. "What are you doing in here?"

"I came to see what was taking so long, and I found exactly what I thought I would find—a traitor making plans to cut me out of our carefully detailed objectives. You bastard!"

"No, Jingjing, it isn't like that at all. Tess will join our team. She has the formula that will allow us to achieve our objective, and she'll take me to it. We'll leave immediately and return with the XM."

"You're such a fool! Falling for the desires of a beautiful woman. I will get the XM from her *immediately!*"

"You will do as I say—"

"I am so done with that." The gun went off. August's body flipped off of the bed. A nanosecond later, Jingjing made haste for the bed. She grabbed Tess by the arm to yank her to the floor, but when she hit the carpet, Tess punched her in the knee. It buckled quite nicely. Jingjing screeched. Tess grabbed Jingjing's wrist, trying to reach the hand that held the gun, and twisted it downward as she managed to climb to her knees and then to her feet. When Tess fiercely wrenched her wrist, Jingjing was forced to release the gun, but Tess missed the opportunity to seize it before it fell out of reach.

An upper cut rife with a sense of rage-filled vengeance smacked Tess in the chin, flinging her backward onto the bed. Jingjing dived on top of her, trying to pin her to the bed as she screamed, "Cashton! Cashton! I need help!"

Wiggling and squirming under Jingjing's slight weight but surprising strength, Tess managed to slide her legs up under Jingjing's stomach. She pushed with her knees and her shins to lift Jingjing upward, trying to fling her off of her body, but Jingjing had a death grip on Tess's shoulders. Determined to succeed, she began rocking from side to side, using Jingjing's weight in her favor. Finally, she tossed Jingjing to the mattress and rolled on top of her. She pinned her down, but Jingjing reached up to claw Tess's hair, and then she wrapped her tiny fingers around the braid that was securing the coveted flash drive in Tess's thick blond tresses.

Jingjing's eyes widened at the discovery. She knew exactly what she'd found, and it only increased her resolve to win the wrestling match. Using the braid, she yanked Tess's head back hard as she splayed out her hand on her chest, trying to push her off.

This was it. Tess had to get away. Jingjing knew that the flash drive was on her person—there would be no lying about another location. There would be no opportunity to leave the house and to then make a daring escape—she was trapped once again.

"Cashton! Cashton!" Jingjing screamed.

Tess punched her in the face to quiet her, and then she stretched her arm toward the crystal lamp on the nightstand next to the bed. She would smack the wicked scientist over the head. It didn't matter whether she killed her—she just had to get away. Her arm reached for it. Her fingers strained to grow just a few more inches so that she could grab the shade and tilt it—and then it would be in her grasp. Wincing, she wiggled her fingers, willing them to extend…a…little…bit… farther.

Large hands gripped her shoulders, dragging her from atop Jingjing and to the floor. Cashton's boot made hard, swift contact with her ribs. Crying out, she curled up on the floor.

"You okay, Jingjing?"

Wiping the blood from her nose, Jingjing said, "What took you so long?"

"I had to secure the two women. I couldn't leave them without making sure that they'd still be there when we got back and that they wouldn't make a phone call, could I?"

He roughly dragged a dazed Tess to her feet. "What do you want me to do with her?"

"Bring her to the lab. All that stands between that formula and me is a pair of scissors," she said as she scooped her gun up from the carpet.

"Where's August?"

"He has no need for the formula anymore. Come, we don't have much time."

Tess's ribs were on fire. Her head was spinning. Where was First Force? She'd thought they were good. Surely they'd discovered by then that she was missing, and surely they had to know where she'd been taken.

Sixteen

Jack rolled the black SUV onto a dirt road lined with tall weeds. It looked like it led back into a wooded area. Maybe it led to the back entrance of a farm or to a wildlife preserve of some kind. Regardless, the path looked as though it didn't see much traffic, if any, and he was able to pull in far enough that the SUV wouldn't be detected by cars driving along the main road. As usual, Clark had done an excellent job locating good camouflage for the team.

Shrugging into their Kevlar vests, the members of the team poured out of the vehicle and gathered around the hatch to collect and prep weapons.

While studying a tablet, Walt briefed his team. "According to Clark's coordinates, we follow this dirt path about a half mile and then head east through the woods for another half mile or so. Crafton's property butts up against this area. Everyone got their assignments? Jack, Smitty, and Casey will enter the home, and Little and

I will flank the house for cover. Ears on. Let's go." Walt stuffed the tablet into his vest and then led the team down the winding, weedy, rutty path at a jog. The midmorning sun glimmered through the canopy of trees above, casting away the chilly morning air and bringing forth a warm spring afternoon.

It wasn't long before Walt held his hand up for the team to hesitate as he checked their location on the tablet, and then with a hitch of his chin, he indicated that they should make their way through the trees and thickets toward the Crafton estate.

Their forward progress was slowed as they broke branches and stomped down underbrush to make their way through the dense, undisturbed woods until at last, the large stone house came into sight. They were facing the east side of the house. The driveway was split—part of it curved gracefully to the left, to the main entrance, and another section continued along the east side past the kitchen and to a service entrance around the back. Four other large homes were in view. They were well spaced with expansive yards and long driveways. A dog was barking insessantly at one of the homes.

Jack moved twenty feet ahead of the team and dropped to his knees. He pulled out a pair of binoculars to scout out the easiest access to the house. Walt knelt next to him.

"What've ya got?" he asked.

Jack's lips curled. "The kitchen door is hanging wide open. I'm thinking that that's the way Dan entered and that he left it open as a signal for us. We could make our way around back and try to get in through the service entrance, but this seems more viable. Thoughts?"

"The place looks pretty dead. It's almost too easy. We don't know how many are in the house. The man who called Clark didn't indicate whether he had a team or was working on his own, but Clark did say that he kept saying 'I,' so he may be a lone mercenary. That doesn't mean we should underestimate his resources or ability. I'll provide cover from here. Little's going around back," Walt said.

"Exterior security has been cut," Little said through the earbud.

"Good deal. We've got a plan," Jack said, handing Walt the binoculars. He waved to Smitty and Casey, and Little took the cue to head for his post. He turned back to Walt and saw him dialing his cell. "Are you calling Clark?"

"No, I'm calling my former colleague from the CIA. Like I told you before, obligations, Jack. Obligations." With that, Walt watched Jack turn to stealthily move into position with his team. "We're on site, and mission is underway," Walt said into his cell.

* * *

Removing the protective goggles from her face, Jingjing smiled at the liquid that she'd concocted using the formula she'd gleaned from Tess's flash drive. She felt some regret that she hadn't had the proper amount of time to fully test the formula, but Dan Garrison would provide her with the information she'd require to move forward with modifications to the serum. After filling the syringe, she made her way toward the gurney on which Dan lay quietly, no longer tied down.

She held the syringe up high so that Tess could see it from her perch on a stool in a corner near the gurney. She was handcuffed to a long drainpipe.

"Success, thanks to you, Ms. McMillan." Tess scowled at her. "Be patient. My test subject will be with you soon—most likely not in the way you would desire him to be, but he'll be paying attention to you very soon." Jingjing nodded at Christine, who obediently pushed up from her stool to join her at Dan's side. As smoothly as a mother speaking to her new baby, Jingjing asked, "How are you feeling, Dan?"

Slowly, Dan rolled his head and acknowledged her. "I'm feeling good."

Jingjing noted that he was still swollen and red and that his eyes were still weepy, but he'd been cooperative and alert since he'd come to consciousness shortly after they'd returned to the lab. Good. Her mind-control serum was working very well, although it was quite obvious that Christine was no longer affected by it. She was playing along, and that was okay. She had an assistant, and Cashton was keeping watch over the estate for possible intruders.

"I'm pleased. Soon you will feel even better. You will be stronger than ever before, and you will bow to my every request. Do you understand?"

"I do."

"Good—very good." She turned to Christine. "We used his right arm for the mind-control serum. I want you to place the tourniquet on his left arm, dab his arm with the alcohol, and find me a good vein, and I want it done in a quick manner. Do *you* understand, Christine?"

Keeping her chin high, Christine looked at her askance. "I do."

"How nice. Everyone understands what I need." She turned to Christine, wearing a baleful expression. "Even you, Christine."

Christine bit her lip and then made her way to the other side of the gurney. She picked up the tourniquet from a metal tray and wrapped it tautly around Dan's left arm. As she poured the alcohol onto a cotton ball, the veins in Dan's arms began to bulge and throb. He lay patiently, staring at the drainpipes and the duct-work that ran along the ceiling.

"This Crafton dude sure could've used better security—or any at all. What was up with this guy?" Cashton said as he descended the wooden stairs.

"I have no idea. He wasn't as serious about life as his older brother was. Perhaps that's why Ballard never spoke of him. He was ashamed. I don't blame him," Jingjing said.

"Well, good news—just got a message from First Force. Seems they're willing to make a trade."

"Took them long enough to respond. It's too late. I now have what I want. But tell them that we're willing to make a deal. I don't want them to think that I have the serum. I don't want them deploying a team, so we must make them believe that there's still time to bargain." Seeing a juicy vein ready to accept the injection, she hurried around the gurney and then pushed Christine out of the way with a swing of her hip. Pressing the needle into Dan's vein, she said, "Tell them that we'll meet them with Dan Garrison in two hours."

"Where?"

"A place of your choosing will be fine. They will get more than they bargained for. They will get a Dan Garrison they've never seen before." Cashton typed out the message. Glancing over at him, she said, "Tell me that they can't trace that phone!"

"C'mon, Jingjing, what do you take me for? An amateur? It's a burn phone—they'll have no idea where the signal is coming from. Besides, I've changed phones several times since I got here."

Satisfied with his answer, Jingjing eased the empty syringe from Dan's arm. The serum leached out into his vein as she slowly loosened the tourniquet. In wide-eyed wonder, Cashton rushed to the gurney to witness the transformation that promised to be nothing short of amazing. Discarding the syringe, Jingjing took a guarded step back. Christine had already moved away, and Tess tensed her body, horrified by the thought of what would happen in the coming moments.

Dan's fists clenched.

His body trembled, and his back arched up from the gurney.

His eyes bulged, and his red-hot cheeks shook.

The wheels of the gurney squeaked as it rocked and shook from the violent movement of the patient on it.

Dan's mouth opened wide. His head tilted back. He let out a sound that was somewhere between a

groan and a scream, and then he fell completely silent—completely still.

Everyone in the laboratory was statuesque—afraid
to move and afraid to breathe. They were waiting for
something to happen, but they weren't sure what—
weren't sure whether they should stick around to find
out. Still, no one moved.

* * *

Using as much stealth as possible, Stewart Little
crept through the brush, pushing branches out of
his way and keeping the house in his view. As he
drew closer to it, the incessant barking became louder.
He came to a halt when he heard a branch snap nearby,
followed by the rustle of leaves and undergrowth. His
eyes flicked from right to left. He knelt down for cover,
keeping his weapon at the ready, and then he discovered
the source of the sound—two unidentified men not
far ahead were making their way through the woods.
They too were carrying guns, yet they weren't dressed
like hunters, and it wasn't hunting season. Their interest appeared to match his own—the Crafton mansion.

Slowing his breathing, he waited and watched,
and then his lips curled in recognition. Those two
were the same men he'd seen in the café at the hangar.

His instincts had been correct. They did indeed have something to do with Tess McMillan's disappearance. Perhaps they'd abducted her, and perhaps someone had taken their prize away. Too bad.

More branches crunched and snapped and crackled under their heavy footsteps. Good scouts, they were not. "We've got company," he whispered into his mic.

"How many?" Walt asked.

"Two. Don't worry. I've got this." He waited a little longer, keeping silent, still, and vigilant until they settled on a spot in which to make their plans. They didn't seem very organized, and again, his mouth turned upward in satisfaction. Ever so slowly, Little rose and circled around behind them, measuring each step so as to not break twigs beneath his boots until he was directly behind the two.

"If we go in that service door, we should be in the basement. We'll have to find our way to the main floor and then figure out where they're at in the house," one man said to the other. He appeared to be in charge.

"You think there's more than just that one guy inside?" the shorter of the two asked. He seemed nervous and unsure of the plan. Little didn't blame him. Figuring that the shorter one was definitely the weaker of the two, Little whacked Mr. In Charge on the back of the head with the butt of his rifle. He fell facedown into the brush.

Taken aback and panicking about his boss's sudden un-consciousness, the weakling whirled around and found himself nose to nose with the business end of Little's gun. He dropped his weapon and flipped his hands in the air.

"Hey, man, don't shoot."

"Do you know Mr. Crafton?" Little asked in a gruff, official voice.

"Yeah…well, not personally. I mean…We work for him," the weakling said, stuttering.

"Really? You work for him? Why are you sneakin' around with guns if you work for him? Looks to me like you're fixin' to break in and rob him, or maybe you're planning to kidnap him." He bumped the weakling in the chest with the barrel of his gun. "What about it?"

"No…No, he owes us some money. We just want our money—that's all."

Just then a white poodle trotted onto Crafton's lawn. The dog's pink-rhinestone collar winked in the sunshine. Little gestured for the weakling to be quiet as an older woman wearing a floral muumuu hurried after the dog. "Mimi! Mimi! You come back here right this instant! You've been such a good girl, and now you're back to your naughty ways." Glancing furtively around the Crafton estate, she gathered the poodle in her arms and marched back toward a stone mansion next door.

Once the woman and her poodle were out of sight, Little said, "Who's in the house?" The weakling's eyes popped. Little kicked him in the chest, pitching him onto his back next to his boss, who was still unconscious. He pressed his knee into the weakling's chest and the rifle to his head. "I asked you a question. Who's in the house?" The man tried to speak, but nothing tumbled from his lips. Little decided to help him along. With a loud click, he turned off the safety of his gun, and he smiled.

After gasping for air so that he could answer, the weakling said, "There was a guy. A big guy. Don't know who he is, but he wouldn't let us in the house to see Mr. Crafton."

"Was Crafton there?"

"Don't know—didn't see him. Just the big guy and an old lady…the maid, I guess. She answered the door, anyway."

"Anyone else?"

"Nobody."

"You're sure?"

"Look, that's all I saw."

"What about Tess McMillan? Did you see her?"

The weakling swallowed hard. Little speculated that he was gauging his answer. The weakling finally mad a decision to answer. "No. Only the man and the old woman."

Little made a big show of tickling the trigger. "So you're tellin' me that you know this Tess McMillan, but you haven't seen her. Hmm, not even at the hangar at Bradley? You didn't see her there?"

Recognition suddenly flooded his face. Yeah, it became clear to him that he'd seen Little before, and he knew where. The weakling cleared his throat. Little smiled. "Say good night."

"What?"

In one swift move, Little turned on the safety and swung the gun to crack him across the head with its stock.

"I'm securing the prisoners now," Little whispered into his mic. "They saw two in the house, a large man, prob'ly our friend who's been contacting Clark, and a maid. Not much, I'm afraid."

"Roger that," Walt said.

* * *

It had been only moments, but it seemed like hours had passed. Finally, in a quivering voice, Tess asked the question whose answer she was terrified of. "Is he okay? Is he alive?"

"He's breathing," Cashton said.

Jingjing stepped forward. "Dan...Can you hear me?"

Dan's eyes fluttered open. "I can."

Tess dropped her head against the pipe that she was handcuffed to, letting out the breath she'd been holding. Christine slowly made her way back to where Vatonia was seated with her hands clenched at her chest.

"Good…Raise your right arm," Jingjing said. Dan did as he'd been told to do. "Good. Now sit up." As Dan pulled himself up to a sitting position, Jingjing scanned the room like she was looking for something to have him break or destroy so that he could demonstrate the strength that the XM-11 was supposed to provide. Would the uberpower be immediate, or would it come on slow and steady as the days and weeks ticked by? She needed to begin the testing to know what she was dealing with.

Her eyes met Cashton's. If she didn't need him for protection, she would seriously consider allowing Dan to fight him—possibly to Cashton's death. Unfortunately, that was not a viable option—not at that time, anyway. Her attention was drawn to Vatonia and Christine, who were sitting across the room. While neither was of any particular use to her, they seemed too easy a mark—it would've been like feeding a Chihuahua to a pit bull. Only one other remained. Tess's strength would certainly be no more of a match for Dan's than the others would be, but it would be far more gratifying to watch him kill her.

"Remove Tess's handcuffs, and bring her to me," she said to Cashton.

His face brightened at her command. He knew what she intended to do, and it was clear that he was keen on the idea. After pulling the key from his belt loop, he roughly grabbed Tess, unleashing her from the pipe. He let the handcuffs slide down the metal, and they hit the floor with a clang. He hauled her off the stool to drag her to the gurney, tossed Vatonia and Christine a "you're next" look, and reveled in their petrified expressions as they huddled close together.

"Stand, Dan," Jingjing said. He slipped from the gurney to stand in front of his master. Seemingly out of nowhere, Shan jumped up on the gurney on which he'd been lying. Jingjing took a moment to run her tiny hand over the cat's fur. "Pets are truly the only loyal friends one can count on. The Chinese believe that cats bring a household great luck. Don't they, Shan?" Her slow, wicked eyes dragged to meet Tess's gaze. Her lips curled in derision. "How lucky am I to now possess the most powerful serum the world has ever known? How unlucky, or perhaps stupid, was August to think that he could betray me by making a pact with a beautiful woman? He paid, and so will you." Jingjing hesitated. Her eyes snapped to meet Cashton's when they heard a creak on the floor above and then another and another. Footsteps—footsteps gingerly making their way through the main floor over their heads.

Stone still, they listened as the sound moved in measured progression overhead. "Someone is in the house," Jingjing said, hissing.

Watching the ceiling above as if he could see through it, Cashton inched his way toward the stairs, slowly climbed them, listened at the door, and then, realizing what he feared, he hurried back down.

"If you want to get out of here with your notes, we've gotta go now, Jingjing! I'm not gonna be able to hold First Force off by myself. I can get you out, but we've gotta go out the service doors—now!" Cashton said from the stairs.

He was right. She would've preferred to do extensive testing on Dan Garrison, but she would have to accept a different subject at a different location and time. She certainly didn't need Tess McMillan. Not then. She had the serum. It was all hers. Dan was poised to do her bidding. She locked eyes with Tess, who watched her intently as she scrambled to the table to gather her notes, and then she returned to her subject and her hostage.

"Jingjing," Cashton said.

She laid her hand on Dan's muscled arm. "I'm leaving now, Dan. But I need you to take care of some things for me while I'm gone. Listen carefully. You will strangle Tess McMillan until she is dead, and then when a team of men enter this room, you will kill every one of them. You will leave no one alive—*no one*. Do you understand?"

Dan's swollen, bloodshot eyes never left Tess's. Instantly, his hand moved to her throat. In a raspy voice, he said, "Yes."

Christine and Vatonia exchanged horrified glances. Vatonia grabbed Christine's hand.

"That's my good boy," Jingjing said. She turned to pitch Vatonia and Christine a venomous grin, but before she could take a step toward the stairs leading from the laboratory, a gun exploded. Cashton's body jerked backward, slamming against the wall with a hard thud. His body slid down the wall, leaving a wide blood smear over the block work.

Jingjing dived under her worktable to hide from the sound of heavy footsteps rapidly funneling down the wooden stairs. The stairs vibrated as they descended them.

Suddenly the footsteps came to a complete halt. From her vantage point, she could see three sets of legs draped in camo. Their stance was very rigid—they were unsure. She could tell that they had their weapons drawn.

"Garrison!" a man's voice called out. "What the hell are you doing?"

When Dan did not respond but rather continued to carry out his task—strangling Tess McMillan—the men hurried across the room. She heard a woman's voice call to Christine and Vatonia. "Stay where you are, ladies!" the voice said.

From under the table, Jingjing saw an opportunity to escape. They hadn't detected her presence—they'd been too focused on Dan. Clutching her notebook and laptop to her chest, she pushed up from the floor to scurry for the stairs. She glanced over her shoulder and saw that two men and a woman were preoccupied with Dan. The two men set their weapons aside and laid their hands on him, trying to pull him away from Tess.

Good luck with that, gentlemen, she thought, and then she stepped over Cashton's body to rush up the stairs, careful not to clomp.

Christine jumped up from her seat. Vatonia grabbed her by the shoulder. "No."

"She's not going to get away! Over my dead body is that little bitch gonna get away!" With that, Christine slithered along the wall to follow Jingjing up the stairs with similarly quick yet light footsteps. Vatonia furtively trailed behind her, doing her best to keep up.

* * *

Tears streamed down Dan's flushed, swollen face. He squeezed Tess's throat, but his grip would loosen slightly after a short time when he used his shoulder to wipe his eyes. He had an objective, but it was clear that his OCD was still in charge. Dan needed to see what he was doing—most likely to be sure that he was doing it correctly.

Tess took advantage of those precious moments to grab a breath, jimmy her fingers under his, and try to peel them from her throat. It was no use. He was too strong. Soon she couldn't breathe. Her head felt as though it would explode under the pressure. She gasped and coughed. He would let up, and she would catch another quick breath, but it wasn't enough. She was fading. He was winning. He was going to choke her to death, and he wanted to. It wasn't Dan—not the Dan she'd fallen in love with at the big, beautiful ranch in Harverton. Not the man who was neat and organized to a fault. No. It was someone else. Someone who'd been created by the serum that she'd failed to destroy. The look in his eyes was haunting. He was focused on his task as if he knew not whom he had in his grip but knew only that he had to destroy her, as he'd been instructed to do.

Gasping and trying to hold on to the last bit of consciousness she had, she decided that she almost deserved what she was getting—almost. It was ironic—Ballard would have the last word. Ballard would own her to the very end.

She couldn't hang on for another moment.

The room was blurring.

Darkness was taking hold.

* * *

Jack and Smitty pulled and yanked on Dan's shoulders, but they couldn't move him. He had ten times the strength of Superman. He couldn't possibly have been choking Tess because he wanted to—no, he must have been injected with that damn serum. He was so freaking strong! No matter how they tried, they couldn't force him to deviate from his task.

Suddenly he became aware that someone was pulling at him. Dan let go of Tess's throat with one hand to shove Jack away—but he did more than just shove him. Jack flew backward ten feet across the room like a rag doll and crashed onto the worktable, collapsing it. Beakers, burners, and flasks of all types smashed to the floor around him. Smitty hesitated, shocked by Dan's action against his own teammate and his unbelievable strength. Writhing under his fierce grip, Tess gasped in a short bit of air.

They had to stop him. And then Smitty looked over his shoulder. From across the room, he saw a sight that he'd never thought he'd see. It was a horrifying sight. Casey was standing in the far corner with her rifle pointed at Dan. When had she moved to that spot? She was the team sniper—her job was stealth. She was accustomed to taking out the bad guys in her sites from the shadows, but he was one of their own.

He could see the sweat dripping down her temples and over her cheeks and then dribbling from her jaw. He could see the agony in her face as she carefully got Dan in her cross hairs and slowed her breathing. It was almost as if she were ticking off a checklist in her brain. Her hands were shaking— Casey's hands were usually as steady as steel. He'd never once seen them shake. He'd never once seen her rattled.

It seemed that the room had stopped. Time was literally standing still, but, oh, how he wished that it would move—that it would somehow move past this horrible moment. Again he looked to where Jack had fallen and saw him push himself to his feet. Jack's eyes trained on exactly what he'd been looking at—Casey.

Glass crushed and snapped beneath Jack's boots as he slowly made his way across the room to where Casey was standing, aiming, deliberating, sobbing, and sweating. And still, Tess gasped, struggling for her life.

Finally, Jack stood beside the sniper. Tears welling in the big man's eyes, he whispered in her ear. "I know it's hard, but it has to be done, Case. You've got to do it."

Lifting her shoulder to wipe away the sweat and the tears that were streaming down her face, she tried to steady her hands and her nerves. "I don't know if I can, Jack. How could I shoot one of our own?"

Dread coiling through every cell in his body, Smitty stepped back, giving her a clear shot. Tess let out a loud gurgle. He wasn't sure if she was giving Casey permission or if she was begging for Dan's life. Moving backward, he leaned against the wall, pressed his eyes closed, and waited for the sound of a single shot—a shot that would forever change them all.

Pallid, Jack swallowed hard. His voice soft and steady, he whispered, "You have to. Don't think...Just do it. Just do it, Case. Just do it."

Taking a deep breath, careworn, beleaguered, and tortured, Casey pulled the trigger.

The gun spit.

Dan's head jerked backward.

His fingers released Tess's neck.

Desperately gulping in air, Tess collapsed to her knees in one direction while Dan fell to the floor in the other, blood spewing from the side of his head.

Instantly everyone in the room went from moving in slow motion to a rush of hustle. Smitty pushed away from the wall to get to Tess, who was holding her throat, taking in air, and trying to crawl across the floor to where Dan was lying motionless.

Grabbing her by the shoulder, Smitty said, "I need to examine you."

Tess pushed his hands away. She was shaking her head feverishly and barely able to speak, and her words were hoarse and raspy. "No...Dan first!"

"Can you breathe?" She nodded her head to indicate yes. "Can you swallow?" Again Tess nodded her head, confirming that she could. Contusions were already appearing on her throat, and her eyes were already showing evidence of subconjunctival hemor-rhaging, but she seemed to be holding her own for the moment. So he turned to his comrade who was lying stock-still on the floor, the comrade they'd been forced to subdue.

Trepidation filled Smitty's very soul as he reached to place his fingers on Dan's throat, terrified that it would only confirm what he and his fellow teammates feared—that Dan Garrison was dead. Smitty was a trained military medic. He had to check—regardless of the outcome, he had to check for a pulse. Closing his eyes and saying a quick prayer, he placed his fingers on Dan's neck. His eyes snapped open. His head jerked to the far corner, where Jack was holding a grief-stricken Casey in his arms and trying to console her.

"He's alive!" Smitty shouted, and then as Jack and Casey rushed toward him, he proceeded to do a hasty preliminary examination. He turned Dan's head to take a closer look at the wound. Tess buried her face in her hands, and Casey and Jack stood over Smitty, waiting. "Wow, that was a great shot, Case. It's deep, but it's more or less just a graze." Casey let out a breath that she seemed to have been holding for hours. Smitty continued. "We've got to get him stabilized, and I think we'd better tie him up. If he comes to, he's gonna be mad as hell, and we've seen what he's capable of."

Ninja quick, Casey yanked a pair of handcuffs from a pocket in her vest. "Good old-fashioned handcuffs should do the trick. I've got a pair of flex-cuffs, but I know that Dan's an expert in getting out of those."

"Let's just hope Hulk boy can't break the cuffs as if they're licorice ropes," Jack said.

Smitty tore off his vest to get to the medic go-bag that he kept strapped to his back. He retrieved a package of gauze squares and a syringe. "If he's violent when he wakes up, which is a good bet, I'll zap him with some haloperidol. It can be given intramuscularly, so I won't need to take the time to set up an IV."

"I wonder how long the effect of the serum holds on. You don't think it's permanent, do you?" Casey asked as she looked around the room.

"We didn't have the answer to that question in Russia, and that was before they added the mind-control formula, and who knows how that changed the mix. Here, help me move him around and get the cuffs on." Jack helped him roll Dan onto his side. Smitty pulled his arms together. Casey attached the cuffs to his wrists. Smitty turned to Casey. "Jack and I will carry him out. I need you to stay with Tess in case she starts experiencing breathing issues. Let's move."

"Wait a minute," Casey said. "What happened to the women who were against the wall when we came in?" Smitty and Jack looked around the lab. "We've got to find them and Jingjing Choo."

Seventeen

Christine cautiously stepped onto the main floor. Looking up and down the hall, she realized that Jingjing was nowhere in sight. She couldn't let her escape.

Huffing and puffing, Vatonia came up behind her. Shan scurried up the stairs to slither through their legs and trot into the dining room. "What now?" Vatonia asked between breaths.

"Follow that cat," Christine said.

Shan led them through the dining room. He scratched and mewed at the swinging door that led into the kitchen. Carefully, Christine eased the door open and peeked inside. Jingjing was standing next to the window, pinching back the eyelet curtains and scanning the grounds. Shan trotted to his mistress to rub his body against her legs. The sound of a loud crash from downstairs caused Jingjing to spin around, and Christine and Vatonia flinched. Jingjing's and

Christine's eyes locked only momentarily before the scientist made a dash for the kitchen door, almost tripping over her cat.

"I don't think so, bitch!" Christine yelled as she shortened the space between them with long, fast strides. She managed to grab Jingjing by the hair before she made it out the door, but Shan made his escape into the yard.

Christine whirled Jingjing around to punch her in the face. The tiny woman fell back against a chair, but pure rage yanked her to her feet. Still clasping her precious notebook and laptop to her chest, Jingjing spun in a tight circle and kicked Christine in the chest. The air knocked out of her, Christine flew backward to the floor.

Jingjing turned to make haste out the door, but Christine wasn't done just yet. She lunged forward onto her knees and grabbed Jingjing by the ankles, pulling her to the floor. Jingjing let out a painful grunt. Christine scrambled to get on top of her. Desperation setting in, Jingjing was willing to use her transcripts as a weapon. She swung the laptop, smacking Christine across the face with it and knocking her back to the floor. As Christine pushed up, Jingjing whacked her again across the back of the head.

"Jingjing!" Vatonia yelled.

Jingjing looked up. She heard Vatonia's voice and the sound of a gun exploding somewhere in the house, but the gunfire melded with the sting and the loud, echoing ring of an iron skillet smacking her in the face. The room spun.

Vatonia stepped back. She dropped the skillet, astounded by her own actions. Jingjing appeared to be down for the count. She knew that the gunshot from downstairs could only mean one thing: they needed to get out—immediately! After dropping the skillet, she hurried to where Christine lay, attempting to push herself to her feet for another round.

Vatonia looped her arm through Christine's. "C'mon, child. We need to get out while we still can."

Christine shook the daze from her head and searched the room for Jingjing, only to find the scientist staggering toward the door with her notebook dangling from her fingers. She'd abandoned the laptop on the floor next to an iron skillet. Jingjing leaned on the partially open door, obviously trying to gather her bearings.

Christine shimmied out of Vatonia's hold.

She rushed to the prep table, where the old housekeeper kept several blocks of knives.

Jingjing managed to step through the doorway and onto the small stoop outside.

A meat cleaver was stuck in the table next to one of the blocks as though it had been set there for this moment.

She yanked it from the wood.

"Hey, Jingjing!" Christine yelled.

Still dazed, the scientist turned.

"This is for Gina!"

"No!" Vatonia screamed. But there was no stopping the passion, the anger, and the pure adrenaline rush of revenge that made Christine's hand throw the cleaver athwart the room, where it sank deep into Jingjing's forehead.

Vatonia gasped, turning away.

Jingjing stood stock-still as if she were confused by what had just happened.

Blood oozed from the slice down her face.

The notebook slipped from her fingers onto the stoop with a *thud*.

She plunged to her knees, and then her body fell facedown and sprawled out over the short set of steps, blood pooling and dripping over the painted surface.

"Don't move," a woman behind them said. "Put your hands on your heads, get down on your knees, and don't move a muscle."

Vatonia and Christine turned to see a woman dressed in camo pointing the business end of a very serious-looking rifle at them. Immediately, they placed their hands on their heads. Christine went to her knees, but Vatonia stood, trying to figure out how she was going to manage it.

Tess stepped into the room behind the woman. "It's okay, Casey," she said in such a low tone that her words were barely audible. She swallowed hard before continuing, never taking her hand from her abraded throat. "These women were hostages just like Dan and I were. This is Christine and, I believe, August's housekeeper, Vatonia."

The woman eyed them cautiously, and then, with her weapon still at the ready, she made her way along the trail of blood that led to the body on the stoop just outside the door. With the toe of her boot, she repositioned the deceased so that she could see her face and the cleaver protruding from her forehead. She hitched her chin, indicating that Tess should take a look.

Peering over Casey's shoulder, Tess winced at the gruesome sight. "That's Jingjing Choo."

Casey lowered the rifle to turn and face the two women. "Anyone want to tell me what happened or who the ax murderer was?"

"Th...That's a meat cleaver," Vatonia said.

"I stand corrected. So who put the *meat cleaver* into Ms. Choo's forehead?"

"I did," Christine said. "But I'm not an ax murderer. It was self-defense, and I have no regrets. She murdered my friend Gina." Christine choked on the words. Her eyes filled with tears, and she fought to hold them back, but she'd been holding them back for so long that she was now defenseless. "Or should I say that…I murdered Gina?" It was out. She'd said the words, and the admission overwhelmed her. Christine collapsed to her knees and buried her face in her hands, weeping uncontrollably

Vatonia's heart broke for the young woman whose life would be forever damaged by the events that had taken place in Augustine Crafton's home. And while kneeling was usually not an option for the aged woman, she sank to her knees beside her to cradle her in her arms, brush back locks of her red hair, and whisper, "It's all right, child. It's time to ask for the help we all desperately need." Pressing her forehead to Christine's, she began to pray: "Dear God in Heaven…"

* * *

Vatonia jumped and almost spilled the hot tea that she was handing to Christine when they heard the loud thump in the next room. Both women looked to Walt for reassurance. He favored them with a comforting smile and a nod from his seat at August's desk. Wearing a pair of latex gloves and talking to Clark on his cell phone, he was searching August's files for any information about the serum. Luckily, the only files that he found were on Jingjing's laptop, on the flash drive, and in her notebook.

Little leaned into the study. "The prisoners have been secured and are taking a nap in the foyer."

"Thanks, Clark. I think we've got it. See you soon." Walt disconnected his call. Satisfied with what he hadn't found on August's computer, he pushed away from the desk. "Thanks. Has Garrison been secured in the SUV?"

"He's stable. Smitty sedated him to keep him quiet and comfortable for the duration of the trip. They're waiting in the driveway. We're ready when you are." With that, he nodded to the women and left.

"Will that young man be all right?" Vatonia asked.

Walt took a seat next to Christine on the sofa. "Our medic believes that he will be."

"That's a relief. I wish I could tell you more about my experience. I only remember bits and pieces. What I do remember are the terrible headaches that would hit me out of the blue. They were massive. I hardly remember anything about killing Gina. That's probably a blessing," Christine said.

"How long do you think the mind-control formula lasted before you came out of it?" Walt asked.

She shook her head. "I'm thinking eight, maybe ten hours—at the most, twelve. I don't remember every moment of what went on." She lifted her bandaged hand. "But Jingjing left me with a mark that will force me to remember what happened forever." Narrowing his eyes, Walt cocked his head to the side. "It was a test, I suppose, to make sure that I was completely under the serum's control. She...She made me hold my hand over a Bunsen burner's flame until she said that I could remove it." Christine unwrapped the bandage to reveal the healing burn that would definitely leave a scar.

Walt scrubbed his fingers over his jaw and then down the nape of his neck. "I'm so sorry that you had to go through all that. I'm just glad that we stopped her and Crafton from carrying out their plans. That being said, are you ladies sure that you understand the plan? After we leave, a small team of agents will arrive—former colleagues of mine. I trained them, and I trust them. They will take your statements, take some samples from the lab, dismantle it, and take care of the bodies. Do not under any circumstances untie the two men in the foyer."

"You don't have to worry about that, honey," Vatonia indignantly said.

He patted Christine's hand. "I know you've been through a horrible ordeal, both of you, but you understand the importance of never repeating what happened here and never identifying us?"

Christine nodded. "We understand. We're just so grateful that you helped us. They would have killed us for sure." A stress-filled whimper climbed up her throat before she could suppress it.

"It's all over now, Christine. I want you to seek out help. You're going to need a support system," Walt said.

Vatonia put her arm around Christine. "I've decided to retire. I think I've cleaned up after wealthy people long enough. I'm going to get a condo near my daughter and her family. Christine is going to come stay with me awhile. She's gonna be just fine."

Walt smiled. "That sounds like a great idea. You can give each other support."

"I only hope that they'll be able to locate Gina's body so that she can have a proper burial," Christine said.

"I know they will. Although I understand that neither you nor Gina have family. You came out of the foster-care system. The lab looked very pristine. Do you have any evidence that a murder was committed? Otherwise, they may consider her to be a missing person or an adult who's left the area and doesn't have to answer for her disappearance."

"I have evidence," Vatonia said. "Christine's shirt covered in Gina's blood. I have it in the kitchen."

"Good. I'll get in touch with you in a couple of weeks to make sure they're doing everything possible to find her. If not, we'll be back."

"How will you contact us?" Vatonia asked.

"Don't worry. I'll be in touch. Thank you, ladies. I wish you all the best."

Just then Casey stepped into the room with a Siamese cat tucked under her arm. "Is this your cat? It was crying at the door." She held the cat out to Vatonia and Christine, who replied with dismay washing over their faces.

"That's Jingjing's cat, Shan. What are we going to do with the horrible little animal? I can't even look at it," Christine said, burying her face in her hands.

Walt and Casey exchanged regret-filled glances. Vatonia slowly lifted from her seat to make her way across the room. Apprehensively, she reached out to the cat. "I understand how you feel, Christine. I can't say that I don't feel the same, but Shan is one of God's creatures." She scratched the cat's ears. Shan leaned into the caress, purring. "He cannot be held responsible for his owner's actions." She took the cat from Casey's arms. "I don't know whether I can keep him as my own, but if not, I'll surely find a proper home for him." Taking Shan into her arms, she did her best to cuddle him.

"Take care, ladies," Walt said, and then he and Casey made their exit.

*   *   *

Smitty, Tess, and Casey kept close vigil over Dan during the ride to the hangar where the First Force Black Hawk was waiting. Jack rolled the SUV to a stop to let Little out of the vehicle so that he could file a flight report. Then he drove directly to the chopper to load Dan onto a gurney and to make sure that he was settled before takeoff. Smitty also exited the vehicle to obtain a gurney.

Just as Jack was about to slip out of the SUV, his cell phone rang. He looked at the screen—it was Rayne. Smiling out of relief that the mission was over, that Dan was likely safe, and that he was about to talk to his pregnant wife, he lifted the phone to his ear. "Hey, baby, miss me?"

She chuckled. "Yes, but I won't for long. I'm at headquarters waiting for Dan's arrival."

"What? You left Disney? How did Lil feel about that?"

"Jack, when Clark told me what happened with Dan, I had to come back. I had a talk with Lil, and she agreed. Grant and Silja moved into our suite to care for her and to continue her Disney vacation. Dale wasn't happy about it either. While it's not perfect, it's what I felt I had to do."

Jack understood how she felt. Rayne had a great sense of loyalty to the team. After all, each man had risked his life more than once to pluck Rayne from the ashes of hell. He got that. Yet he felt bad that Lil had had to watch not only her father abandon the vacation but also the stepmother she adored. Sure, Lil understood. She was a little trooper. Still, his heart ached for her. He would make it up to her. Yeah, how? He feared that he would spend the rest of his father-hood making that promise to himself—and to his daughter and to his son, who would be born in the coming months. It was unavoidable. It was part of the job description. It was unacceptable, but it was his and his family's reality.

"Jack…Are you still there?"

He sighed as the SUV rocked with the movement of people getting out. The hatch opened. He looked up into the rearview mirror. Smitty, Walt, and Casey were carefully unloading Dan from the back onto a gurney. He rotated the mirror to locate Tess. His eyes narrowed. She was standing off to the side, looking lost. Her arms were tightly wrapped around her torso in a protective stance.

"Jack?"

"Yeah…I'm still here, but I've gotta go. See you in a bit." He shoved the cell into his pocket and jumped out of the vehicle to make his way to the back end. The team was already rolling the gurney toward the Black Hawk. He slammed the hatch closed, which caused Tess to flinch. "You okay, Tess?"

She dragged her gaze to meet his. "I don't know."

"Talk to me."

Shrugging, she let out a long, burdened sigh. "I didn't want to fall in love with him."

"Dan?"

She looked toward the Black Hawk. "Yeah, Grumpy. Ever since I was seventeen, I've almost always been with a man. I'd never been on my own until recently—after Ballard's death. I had no intentions of getting involved with a man for a very long time. Maybe never." She stopped, raked her fingers through her hair, and came up with a clump that had been chopped off but somehow hadn't fallen from her head. She scowled, tossing it to the pavement.

Hugging herself tightly again, she rolled her eyes. Whether she was disgusted with herself or with the situation, Jack couldn't be sure. "And now?"

"I don't know. I love him. I do, but I'm afraid. I'm terrified. Of what, I just can't say, but my stomach is in knots. I don't know what to do."

"Are you thinking about leaving?"

Her eyes snapped to meet his. "No…Not now. I can't. I have to make sure he's going to be okay. I have to make sure he's going to make it. But afterward? I can't be sure. I have to think this through, and I have to think it through on my own. In my own way. Whatever the hell that turns out to be."

Jack glanced up to see Little hurrying from the hangar toward the chopper. "I agree. You need to think it all through. How about we get back to headquarters, where Dan can get the help he needs and you can get the rest you need? You might just work it all out in the interim."

Eighteen

Saying that Tess was exhausted when they finally arrived at the Georgian mansion would've been an understatement. A lovely dark-haired woman dressed in green scrubs and a long white lab coat met the Black Hawk at the landing pad, which was about five hundred feet beyond the house. She immediately hooked up with Smitty, who gave her an in-depth briefing on Dan's condition. During very quick introductions, Tess learned that her name was Rayne—and that she was Jack Haliday's wife—and then, with the team jogging alongside the gurney, Dan was whisked away from the chopper and into the house. Tess hurried along behind the team and into the medical unit, where she'd first become acquainted with the big, masculine, OCD-obsessed ex–US marshal. The memories of that first encounter echoed through the pristine white hallway, sending waves of emotions, including guilt, through her very core.

Yep—her fault.

This was all her fault.

If she'd destroyed the serum or if she'd allowed August to catch up with her or if she'd—

Too weary to handle the flood of feelings, she pressed her head against the wall and let the tears spill from her eyes and down her face, which made her throat and her head and her ribs hurt all the more. And then a strong hand clasped her shoulder.

"This isn't you fault, Tess," Clark said. "I know you think it is, and it probably feels like it is, but it isn't."

Gingerly dabbing the tears away with the palms of her hands, she turned to face him. "I should've—"

"Probably, yeah, you should've destroyed that flash drive. But do you honestly think that August Crafton would've believed that you had? Do you think Jingjing Choo would've taken your word for it and believed that the serum was gone? No way. They would've hunted you down and killed you when you couldn't give them what they wanted."

"At least Dan wouldn't be in this condition—"

"Dan knows the score. Every member of the team knows the score. You go out on a mission, and you may not come back in the same shape you were in when you left. Hell, you may not come back at all. They know that. They accept it. That's what they do."

Suddenly, Tess realized that the hallway was empty. The team was gone. "Where'd everyone go?"

"Well, Doc Haliday sent Smitty upstairs to take a shower and change his clothes—she couldn't stand the smell of him. Smelled like puke when I passed him on the stairs. Anyway, she took Dan into the surgery to work on him. The team's not permitted in there. They went upstairs to chill out, get something to eat, and wait. I think you should do the same. We have no idea how long it'll take them to figure out what they're dealing with and what to do about it."

"But he's going to make it, right?"

"From all indications, yes. They're trying to assess whether there's been any permanent damage and, if there has, the extent of that damage."

"Brain damage?"

Clark favored her with a svelte smile. "C'mon, let's go upstairs and get something to eat, and then you should lie down awhile. We have very comfortable guest rooms. I know Doc is gonna want to take a close look at you after they get Dan settled. Your throat is looking very sore, and that's a nasty bruise on your cheek."

She flinched when he touched it. She'd almost forgotten that it was there, but her ribs were still screaming and aching from the kick Jingjing's goon had given her.

When they stepped onto the main floor, they could hear voices wafting down the hallway from the kitchen, and as they approached the room, she could hear the concern in those voices for Dan, the injured comrade.

Jack, Walt, and Little were sitting at the breakfast bar. They munched on sandwiches and drank beer. They looked worn and sweaty and dirty but glad to be out of harm's way. Casey was sitting at the kitchen table with a mug sitting in front of her. Unconsciously, she dipped a tea bag in and out of the steaming water as she she stared out the window.

"When this is over, Dan's going to have to go through some retraining. You can't just go out half-cocked. Going rogue isn't an option," Walt said.

"It was over that woman—that would be my guess," Little said, slapping his beer bottle down on the counter. And then his eyes met Tess's.

Her throat was sore and her voice was weak and raspy, but she forced the words out. "They attacked his home. They killed Boo." Swallowing hard, she couldn't believe that the words had come out of her mouth—her mouth. Just four days before, Boo had been nothing more than a dirty old dog who got in her space. But he'd come to mean so much more.

What the hell?

How had Dan Garrison and his dog wiggled their way into her heart in four days?

It was scary.

She wasn't sure that she was ready for this—for all of…this.

It was obvious that the big man regretted his words but that more, he regretted that she'd been standing within earshot. He dropped his gaze to the counter. "Sorry," he said around a sigh of self-reprimand.

"Tess?"

She blinked back into the moment, realizing that Walt had been trying to get her attention for a few seconds. "I'm sorry. Yes?"

"Would you like something to eat?" Walt asked.

"No, I don't think I could eat. Maybe later. Is there somewhere I could lie down for a while?"

"Of course. I'll show you to a guest room. You look like you could use some rest," Walt said.

"Thank you. You'll wake me when they know about Dan?"

"Don't worry. I'm sure you're next in line. My niece is going to want to examine your face and your throat. I'll send her up as soon as she's through with Dan."

Tess followed Walt into the foyer, up the winding staircase, and down a long hallway until they came to a bedroom. "Did you destroy the flash drive?"

"Yes. It's gone, and so is Jingjing Choo's notebook—I tossed it into the incinerator before coming upstairs. Someone somewhere may be working on a superhuman-strength formula, but he won't get any assistance from Crafton Labs or Jingjing Choo. All of the information that she had to offer is burning up as we speak. I saw to that personally. I hope you believe me," Walt said.

She favored him with a withered smile. "I do."

Turning on the light, he nodded toward the bedroom. "Use the bathroom on the far side of this room if you'd like to shower or just wash up. I'm sure Rayne will be in to see you within an hour or so."

She stepped into the room as Walt retreated, closing the door softly. The room was dressed in a simple, elegant Victorian decor—it wasn't nearly as ornate as the bedrooms found in the Craftons' households. She was glad. She'd grown quite tired of that life—whether she'd realized it or not. The room had a welcoming charm about it, yet she didn't find it as alluring as Dan's rustic log house steeped in rich wood tones. She ran her finger over the curly brass footboard and then lay across the light-green chenille comforter, trying to calm her frazzled nerves. They were safe. They were at First Force Headquarters. Everyone who'd threatened them had been eliminated, but it wasn't over. It was far from over. Dan wasn't out of the woods yet, and she wasn't sure that he ever would be. How could she forgive herself if he had permanent brain damage?

She didn't want to think about that. She had to think positively. Dan would be okay. Dan would pull through and return to his normal, overly neat, organized, OCD self—the man she loved. Wait! Hold the phone. Dan was a man she'd known for four days—that wasn't nearly enough time to form a relationship, and certainly not enough time to fall in love. Right?

She needed to clear her head.

She needed to think it all through in a neutral environment.

She didn't need another man messing with her life and telling her what she could do and when she could do it. She'd been there. She'd done that—for seventeen freaking years. She was so done with all of that.

Hey, the sex was great. Sex with Dan was about pleasure for both of them—not just about pleasure and domination for him. The ranch was great—safe and comforting. Boo was great—well, he had been.

Shaking her head, Tess took in a deep, cleansing breath. The decision was made. She would stay until Dan was stable and she knew that he was going to be okay, but then she would leave before he or any of his friends could guilt her into a relationship that she wasn't absolutely sure was right for her—but mainly for Dan. Somewhere between the relief, the guilt, the decision, and the pure exhaustion, Tess fell asleep.

* * *

Somewhere in the house, a grandfather clock chimed the hour, waking Tess with a start. She jerked to her elbows, and just as quickly, she fell back to the bed, wincing at the pain from her ribs, her throat, and her face. Consciousness offered her nothing more than the realization that very few parts of her body didn't ache. She pushed up to a sitting position more slowly. The room was dark. The pearly light from the moon sifted through a slight gap in the drapes, which someone had closed during her sleep. Her eyes immediately looked for a clock and found one on the nightstand—it was four in the morning.

Dan!

The drawn drapes and the glass of water on the nightstand were evidence that someone had in fact been in the room but had failed to wake her to tell her how he was doing. *Dammit!*

As quickly as the pain would allow her to, she dragged her stiff body from the bed to make her way to the bathroom. The flood of bright light when she flicked the switch knocked her back a step or two. Her eyes adjusted, and she splashed her face with some cool water, and then she made the mistake of looking in the mirror. "Death warmed over" would've been a compliment to the reflection that was staring back at her. Her right cheek was swollen and badly bruised, as was her throat. Purple, red, and pink abrasions molested her face and neck. She didn't want to know what her rib area looked like, and it didn't matter much—she needed to get downstairs to the medical unit to see how Dan was faring.

The big house was quiet. Lovely mosaic table lamps with low-wattage bulbs were stationed here and there on antique stands along the hallways, providing a soft glow. As she descended the staircase, she could see moonlight casting sinewy shadows across the marble floor below and glinting subtly off the tall Chinese palace vases that lined the perimeter of the foyer. Upon stepping from the staircase, she noticed that the door to the office where she and Dan had conferred with Clark Rhodes was closed. She could tell that no one was in the room—she couldn't see any light under the door.

When she reached the door that led downstairs to the medical unit, she took in a breath and braced herself, mentally preparing herself for what might lie ahead. The stairs and the corridor through the unit were well lit. Perhaps Smitty and Dr. Haliday were still in the unit, yet as she inched her way toward the room where they'd taken Dan, no one appeared to be about. The unit had an abandoned atmosphere—silent and motionless. Slowly, she eased the door to Dan's room open. The lights had been dimmed. She could see the silhouette of Dan lying in the bed hooked up to an IV. A heart monitor blinked and beeped on the far side of his bed. He looked to be resting peacefully, so she approached him with measured steps, only to notice another person in the room—Casey.

The team's sniper was slouched over and fast asleep in a chair next to Dan's hospital bed. Someone had thrown a blanket over her. Tess understood why Casey was there—she felt responsible. Evidently, she was feeling some guilt for shooting Dan. She needn't have felt any—Tess was bearing enough guilt for the two of them. Still, she was glad to see that Dan had such a strong support system.

She ran the pads of her fingers over his forehead. He didn't stir. Her voice raspier than before her nap, she whispered, "Hi, Grumpy, it's me, Tess. You re-member—the smarty-pants. C'mon, big guy, you can pull through this. You're tough enough. I'm going to wait right here until you wake up—"

"That might be a while," Casey said. Tess jumped. "Sorry, didn't mean to scare you."

"No…I thought you were sleeping. Hope I didn't wake you."

"I heard you come in. I'm a light sleeper—part of the job, I'm afraid. Anyway, Rayne is keeping him sedated in an attempt to keep him calm. Christine said that the serum that she was injected with only lasted about eight to twelve hours, so Rayne's hoping that this one will be comparable. Of course, she can't be sure, so she's doing what she can. The IV is just fluids—standard stuff, I guess."

"Where's the doctor?"

"She's pregnant. She needed some rest. He's stable. I said I'd stay with him."

"It's good of you."

"I shot him. I have to see him through this. Rayne thinks he's going to be okay. I hope she's right." Her voice was filled with regret. Tess's heart broke for her. "Mind if I ask you a question?"

Trepidation crowded Tess's chest. "Sure. What?"

"What's your relationship to Dan?"

"I came to him for help. He protected me. I'm grateful." Tess could see the doubt in Casey's eyes. She didn't believe a word of it.

"You're sure?" Casey asked.

No, she wasn't sure. She was sure that she was in love with the man, but she was also sure that she was the last woman Dan Garrison needed. "Why don't you go get some rest? I'll stay with him."

Tossing the blanket aside, Casey stood, studying her with narrow eyes. "I'm sure Rayne won't mind if I lie down in the next room. That's where I'll be if you need me."

Before Casey stepped out of the room, Tess asked, "How long does she plan to keep him sedated?"

"At least forty-eight hours, I think. Is there a problem?"

"No…No problem. No problem at all."

* * *

Ms. McMillan…Ms. McMillan."
The voice seemed far away—as though it were hidden somewhere in a mist. Then Tess realized that the woman's voice was right next to her. A gentle hand caressed her shoulder in an attempt to wake her calmly. She lifted her head from the mattress next to Dan's arm, wiping the drool from her mouth. "I'm sorry. I fell asleep. Is he okay?" she said, her voice croaking.

"He's doing as well as expected. It's you I'm concerned with," the woman known as Dr. Haliday said. Her hair was pulled back in a loose braid. She was sporting a pair of blue scrubs covered by a long white lab coat. Ah, there it was—a baby bump that she hadn't noticed yesterday was poking out from the coat. Dr. Haliday smiled. "I didn't have a chance to examine you yesterday. When I came to your room, you were sound asleep, so I checked your vital signs and left you to rest. You were absolutely exhausted. You didn't stir at all. I'd like to have a look today. Could you follow me into the examination room?"

Tess glanced at Dan. He hadn't moved from the position she'd found him in the night before. "Is Dan going to be okay?"

"As far as I can tell, yes. I just want to keep him quiet until I think—or at least hope and suspect—that the serum he was injected with has worn off. The young lady who was injected reported suffering from severe headaches afterward, so I may be doing him a big favor." She favored him with a svelte smile. "I hope so. C'mon, we won't be long."

Tess stood a little too quickly. The doctor grabbed her by the arm. "Easy does it. Maybe I should put you in a room and give you some fluids as well."

"No, that won't be necessary. I want to stay with Dan."

The doctor studied her for a moment. "Okay, I won't for now, but if you continue to be light-headed, I'm going to have to insist."

"I'll be fine, Dr. Haliday."

"Please, call me Rayne. Any friend of Dan's is a friend of mine." As they were stepping out of the room, Casey was coming in. "I'm taking Tess into the examination room."

"I'll stay with Dan while you're gone," Casey said.

"It's really not necessary—"

"Yes, it is."

Tess watched as Rayne and Casey locked eyes. Something passed between them, but she couldn't quite identify what it was. Finally, Rayne dropped her gaze. It was as if she were submitting to Casey's need to watch over the man she'd harmed in the hope that some kind of healing would soon take place.

When they arrived in the exam room, Rayne directed Tess to the exam table, where she then performed a complete examination. They hadn't been in the room for more than twenty minutes or so when there was a pounding on the door.

"Rayne! Come quickly! I think he's waking up!" Casey said through the door.

Rayne's eyebrows rose.

"Oh my God! Is that a bad thing?" Tess asked, panicked.

"I guess we're going to find out," Rayne said, calmly tugging off her latex gloves before hurrying from the room.

This was it.

He was gaining consciousness.

Was it too soon?

Would he be violent?

Would he be the man she'd met five days before?

Finally, would she have the courage to uphold the decision that she'd made? She sat on the table, unable to move and unable to breathe. Tess felt crippled by her fear as she stared at the open door leading into the pristine white hallway. She could hear voices wafting down the corridor. She found a small sense of relief in the fact that they didn't sound panicked.

She eased off of the table to make her way out of the room and down the hall. The door to Dan's room was open. When she stepped in, Rayne was hovering over him, holding up his eyelid, and looking into his eye with an ophthalmoscope, and Casey was standing in the corner, worrying a cuticle, and waiting for a prognosis. Tess took a place next to

Casey. Her heart was pounding inside her chest so hard that she was certain that they could hear it.

Finally, Rayne straightened, smiling. "His eyes look good. His vitals are great. All of his scans have come out clean. I truly believe that he's going to make a full recovery."

Casey let out a long breath right along with Tess. They'd both been holding their breath for a long time. "Thank God," Casey said.

Tess needed to see for herself. She needed to touch him. Rayne stepped out of the way to give her access to him. "You're sure he's going to be okay?"

"I don't see any reason that he shouldn't be. I'm going to let him come to consciousness. He seems ready. I don't know if he'll be spared the headaches, but I'm going to move forward."

Tess's heart ached. She'd made a decision, but she didn't want to put Dan through her leaving. "I should go now," she said, brushing her lips over his forehead. "I don't want to be here when he wakes. I don't want to deal with the good-byes." Before she could change her mind, she pushed away from the bed and headed for the door.

As Casey blinked, her jaw dropped.

Peeking at Tess askance, Rayne adjusted the flow of fluids draining from the IV into Dan's vein and then gently pressed her fingers to Dan's shoulder.

Stirring, he whispered, "Don't go."

Taken aback by her comrade's desperate plea in his less than conscious state, Rayne hurried toward Tess with Casey on her heels. "Look, Tess, I understand. Good-byes are tough, especially when you're saying them to someone you love," Rayne said.

Tess hesitated and turned back. Rayne could see that she was torn between leaving and staying to somehow work out her feelings for Dan. Rayne could also feel the agitation coming from her friend behind her, Casey. Trying to keep Casey at bay, she laid her open hand on Casey's arm.

Okay…Perhaps Tess was confused by her feelings, or maybe she was terrified of them. Rayne barely knew the woman. She really didn't know the circumstances of Tess McMillan's relationship with Dan Garrison, but she'd just heard him beg her to stay. That held power, and so did the struggle that was going on in Tess's posture and hesitance but mostly in her eyes.

"I can see it in your eyes, Tess. You have feelings for Dan. Why don't you stick around and see what happens?" Rayne said.

"I can't. I just can't."

"He's a good man—a *damned* good man," Casey said.

"I know," she said as she turned back toward the door.

"You're a coward, Tess McMillan," Casey said.

Tightening her grip, Rayne said, "Never mind, Casey. She's not good enough for him."

Tess's feet stilled at the doorway. Her jaw clenched. Her emotions betrayed her as tears sloshed over the rims of her eyes to her lashes. She couldn't bear to turn around. She couldn't afford to turn around.

"You're right…I'm not, Dr. Haliday." With that, she hurried down the corridor and out the door. Holding her ribs as tightly as she could, Tess broke into a dead run for her car, yanked the door open, and plunked down inside to press the ignition button. Fists of frustration beat inside her chest as she threw the Cadillac into reverse and whirled around to speed up the driveway. But the wrought-iron gate was closed.

Tears rippled down her cheeks. She wiped them away with the palms of her hands. The last thing she needed was a man screwing up her life. That was right. The last thing she needed was an obsessive-compulsive total badass with one hell of a gorgeous, muscled body keeping her fulfilled and replete night after night. The last thing she needed was a man who wanted her for her, a man who was eager to make her happy, and a man who she needed more than she—

To hell with that.

The fact was that she needed to go home to Albany, New York. To go back to her beautiful town house. She could think there. She could think without any- one telling her what to think, how to feel, or what she should do.

Her fingers tapped against the steering wheel. When were they going to open the freaking gate? They had to know that she was sitting there, waiting for it to open. She'd seen the security system. She'd seen the se- curity screens that monitored every movement around the mansion and were stationed in all of the rooms. In any case, Dr. Haliday damned well knew that she was there, waiting for the gate to open. What? Did the doctor think that if they kept the gate closed, she'd change her mind and go running back? Oh, God, she might've been right!

She revved the engine.

Open the gate.

Clenching her jaw, she revved it again more aggressively.

Open. The. Gate.

She laid on the horn.

Open the freaking gate!

There was a click, and then ever so slowly, the gate rolled open as if to say, "There you go. Leave. Go ahead, Tess, get the hell outta here." Taking a breath, she pressed down on the accelerator. Fishtailing, the Cadillac passed through the gate and peeled out onto the gravel road. In the rearview mirror, she watched the gate swing closed. *Click.*

Epilogue

One Week Later

The fire crackled and danced and sparked inside the fireplace. It really wasn't cold enough for a fire that night, but Dan felt like sitting in front of one. He felt like staring into the flames and letting them consume his dark mood. At least the freakin' headaches had diminished from a nasty throb to a dull ache.

The big room felt empty without old Boo curled up at his feet shamelessly snoring louder than the crack of the logs' burning. Yeah, it was different without him—lots of things felt different those days.

As he took a sip of the coffee that he'd forgotten he was holding, Tess brushed through his thoughts. He realized that it wasn't just Boo whom he was missing. He was missing the warmth of that woman's soft, smooth body sliding beneath his in a sensual rhythm. The sound of her heated breathing and the way her sex tightened around his as they climbed to the apex of their desire…And then he felt the hot, hot, *hot* sensation of coffee spilling onto his thigh!

Scowling down at the wet brown stain on his jeans, Dan jerked the mug to an upright position and silently reprimanded himself for letting her into his thoughts—for letting Tess McMillan break down his carefully built walls. Yeah, she'd torn through them as though they'd been made of Lincoln Logs.

Why had he let that happen?

What had he been thinking?

"The last thing I need is a woman screwin' up my life," Dan said out loud for no one to hear.

That's right. The last thing he needed was a beautiful blond woman with one hell of a sexy body bringing him to his knees on a nightly basis. The last thing he needed was that blue-eyed bombshell waiting for him when he came home from a mission or making him want to give her anything that made her happy, because he wanted to make her happy and because he wanted—

To hell with that.

Fact was that he didn't need a damned cup of coffee. He needed a beer—a tall, ice-cold beer. After pushing himself from the chair, he padded across the room to the kitchen, dumped the coffee down the drain, rinsed out the cup, and placed it carefully in the dishwasher. He was going to the fridge to get the beer when there was a knock on the door.

He stilled midreach into the fridge. What the hell? The buzzer hadn't sounded to announce that some-one had driven through the gate. His eyes snapped upward. The security screens were dark. His jaw tight-ened. Had someone breached his system? Seriously, his brand-new retina-recognition security system had just been installed not three days ago, and already there was a hitch?

Then again, since when do unwelcome intrud-ers knock? Paranoia crept up his spine. Hell, it crept through his freakin' life. For a brief moment, he won-dered how it would feel to be a person with a normal occupation and a life devoid of constant paranoia and the need to watch his back.

What would that have been like?

He opened the pantry door to retrieve the loaded Glock 19 that he kept hidden behind a can of coffee, four cans of soup, a jar of spaghetti sauce, a jar of pea-nut butter, and two jars of strawberry jelly. He checked the safety as the next set of knocks sounded.

After stuffing the gun into the waistband of his jeans near the small of his back, he buttoned his tan-gerine shirt and made his way to the door. It was probably just one of the guys from the team stopping by to check on him. They came around quite often with a deck of cards or just to watch the game, as did Casey. He'd tried to convince her that she'd done what was necessary, but the woman watched over his recovery like an old mother hen would have. He had good colleagues—no, good friends.

Still, it was bugging him that the security was down. He'd have to check into that right away. He'd call the security company that had installed it later and give them a piece of his mind—what was left of it, anyway.

He opened the door only to find himself looking into those blue eyes—the ones that belonged to that blond bombshell with one hell of a sexy body. And what did she have the audacity to do? She used those plump, juicy, pink-glossed lips to smile up at him and to say, "I could really use a beer right about now. How about you, Grumpy?"

The mystery of his breached security system was solved, and this was his chance. Yes, sirree, this was the moment when he could slam the door in her face after informing her in no uncertain terms that he had reconstructed his walls and firmly reconciled with common sense—and that no women were allowed!

But there she was, leaning against the jamb, her blond tresses spilling over her sexy little shoulders as a black and white border collie puppy squirmed in her arms. And then he noticed the slight bruising that remained around her throat. Sorrow filled his heart. She must've been horrified when his big hands had attempted to squeeze the life out of her. He didn't remember the moment—not really—but it had been described to him by Walt. Yeah, how could he have blamed her for running?

He tried to speak. His jaw was working, but nothing seemed to be coming out. He was just so damned glad to see her. He couldn't believe it, but yeah, he was thrilled, relieved, and happy that Tess McMillan was standing on his doorstep. His eyes flicked to the sleek silver Mercedes Coupe sitting in the driveway.

"Nice ride," he managed to say, hitching his chin toward the car.

"Yeah, it's mine, actually. If it makes you feel any better, he peed in it," she said.

The right side of his mouth lifted. "It does make me feel better."

Tess cleared her throat. "Well…I thought you might be missing Boo, so I stopped by a farm that was advertising that they had one little border collie puppy left—the runt, no less."

Dan tickled the little guy's ears—and as a thank-you-very-much gesture, he latched onto Dan's finger with his razor-sharp puppy teeth. "He's an ornery little cuss, isn't he?" He chuckled as the pup growled and chewed and tugged on his finger.

Tess swallowed hard. "He reminded me of Boo and you and here and us. I was...um...hoping that you might be missing me too."

There was nothing to say. He couldn't find any words anyway. So he simply grabbed her by the shoulders and pulled her mouth to his. His lips sank into hers as though she'd been gone for twenty years.

She tasted so good.

She tasted like forever.

The puppy squirmed and moaned and then let out a frustrated bark. He was a little indignant at being squished between two full-grown humans. Patting the pup's head, Dan pulled back from the kiss. He could feel the remnants of her lip gloss on his lips. He licked it, and it was almost like tasting the kiss over again—almost.

"So you're staying?" he asked.

"If you'll have me," she said.

He arched his right brow. "Can I have you right now?"

Shaking back her hair, she laughed and looked toward the ceiling. It sounded good, and he realized that he'd been missing the sound of her laughter too. Hell, he was in the midst of realizing that he'd missed everything about the woman.

"So what should we name the ornery little cuss?" Tess asked.

Dan took him from her arms so that he could hold him up and look into the pup's face. Without much pause, he shrugged. "He looks like a Jake to me."

Her eyes narrow, Tess leaned in. He could tell that she was trying to distinguish what he was seeing in the little guy's face that screamed, "Hey! My name's Jake!"

"I still don't get what makes you say that," she said.

He shifted the pup so that she could have a full view of the squirming bundle of fluff. "His personality. Look at him—he's as ornery as the day is long. The most ornery person I know is Jack, but we wouldn't want to confuse anyone from First Force by having Jack the man and Jack the dog, so we'll settle for Jake."

Again, the blonde laughed, and again, it was music for his soul. Suddenly he realized that his headache was completely gone. Well, how about that?

He set the pup's paws to the floor to let him scamper into the house. Jake ran and jumped, hitting the polished wood floor, which sent him sliding and spinning across the room in a spread-eagle position on his tummy. The pup's panicked expression was fodder for a belly-rolling laugh as Dan pulled Tess under his arm, and she wrapped her arms around his waist. That's when Dan realized that he was standing with his back to an open door. All of the alarms in his head went off. He wanted to spin around and to slam it shut, but just as quickly, he thought, *This is it. This must be how it feels to let paranoia fall away and to just let life happen.* Good God, it was liberating. Without looking to see if anyone was charging the door with an AK-47 at the ready, he reached back to close it with a flick of his hand, and that's when he decided that he had some life decisions to make. Maybe it was time for a new start. For a new life apart from missions and rapid gunfire and the alarms of paranoia, *stay down! Watch your teammate's six!*

Maybe it was time for a new life with Tess—a life devoid of missions and devoid of First Force. And yet the powerful hold of paranoia poked him one more time.

"Uh-oh, Jake just christened his new home," Tess said, bringing Dan back from his funk. "I'll get a paper towel." Just as she attempted to pull away from his body, he swept her up into his arms, carried her across the room to the sofa, dropped her and her big zebra-print purse, and then planted his body on top of hers to hold her firmly in place.

Grabbing her wrists, he held them over her head against the smooth, cool leather. Her breathing quickened. Her eyes transformed from darn right beautiful to darn right sultry when she licked those plump pink-glossed lips. The light from the flickering fire glimmered over her golden hair, which was splayed out over the chocolate-colored cushions. Regardless of the goddess aura swirling around her, Dan's tone was concise and direct. "*Why* did you come back?"

Tess's breath caught. He wasn't seducing her. He was interrogating her. She tried to free her hands, but it was an exercise in *seriously*? He had a strong hold on her, and he wasn't letting up. The only saving grace was that she could feel the column of his erection against her thigh. Still, the look on his face screamed, "This is a grilling, baby, and the coals are just gonna get hotter." She was just thankful that it wasn't quite the same look he'd had when he'd strangled her. That had been the look of a killer—this was the look of a man desperate for answers.

Bearing down to keep her absolutely immobile, Dan repeated his question. "Tell me, Tess, why did you come back here? I thought you were gone for good."

"I told you…I missed you."

"Why?"

"What do you mean, why? I…I missed you. What more do you want me to—" Dan's lips crashed against hers. His mouth was hot with primal passion and possession. He pushed his tongue through her lips to taste the very essence of her mouth.

Then she got it.

She knew what he was searching for.

When he released her from the kiss, she answered him with uncompromised fervor. "Because I made a terrible mistake. I never should've left, because I love you. Because I want to be with you, and if you don't get off me right now, I'm going to suffocate, you big galoot."

He dropped his forehead against hers. She didn't need to see it. She could feel his smile. She could feel the throb of his erection pressing through his jeans and into her leg. She could sense the love that he'd been holding back until he'd received the confirmation of her feelings. It was so Dan. He'd wanted to be right—no mistakes or misunderstandings. For the badass, obsessive-compulsive operative Dan Garrison, it had to be spot-on implicit. She would have to work on loosening the man up—it might take a lifetime, and she was okay with that.

"Breathing is way overrated, and I have no intention of letting you catch your breath for the next several hours," he whispered. With that, he released her hands and dragged his fingers down her arms to unbutton her dainty plaid sleeveless blouse. When he reached the last button, he meticulously opened each side of the blouse to expose her pink lace bra. He took a moment to admire the alluring up-and-down pumping of her breasts with each anticipating breath. Ever so lightly, he ran the tip of his tongue along the edge of the lace—and then over the top of her right breast, through the crowded valley, and up over her left.

"Yeah," he said, moaning. "You won't be breathing for a while." He pushed up from her body to scoop her up into his arms and carry her toward his bedroom.

"Wait a minute."

He stilled. "What?"

"I've got one more thing that I need to bring into this relationship."

"You're scarin' me, Tess. What is it?"

Letting out a giggle, she reached down to the couch, snatched up her purse, and pulled out a plastic bag full of water with two tiny goldfish swimming frantically around in it. She held it up with a teasing smirk and pumped her eyebrows up and down.

Taking the bag from her hand, Dan had to put her down. He was laughing so hard that he feared he would drop her. After he caught his breath, he said, "Guess we'll be getting an aquarium."

"Damned straight," Tess said, a grin stretching across her face.

Placing the bag of fish on the coffee table, Dan wrapped his arms around her to lead her toward the bedroom. Jake let out a bark.

"What about Jake?" Tess asked with a wary glance over her shoulder.

"Let him get his own girl," Dan said, even though he was well aware that the pup was chomping on the bearskin rug in front of the fireplace. He didn't care. Tess was home, and he wanted nothing more than to hold her in his arms forever—goldfish and all!

END

T hank you for reading *To the Brink*. I hope that you'll read the next installment from the First Force series, *Into the Dawn*, coming in 2017. Below is a short synopsis to entice you to check it out.

INTO THE DAWN
Rocky Mountain Retribution!

While on a camping trip in the Rocky Mountains, First Force operative Casey Rhodes and Hawke International operative Peyton Mattock were having the time of their lives. Normally separated by an ocean, the two operatives rarely saw or heard from each other, but on the short vacation, the sparks ignited the flames of passion that they believed to be real before their trip—the sparks that they could no longer deny. Before departing on the lovers' holiday, Peyton insisted that they leave all weaponry behind—after all, what would they need them for? Casey reluctantly agreed, and it seemed like a wonderful idea. But then Peyton went missing.

Trapped in the middle of ever-lovin' nowhere, Casey must find the man she yearns for and fight with primitive weapons alongside an unlikely ally to gain his freedom from those who want him dead!

Sign up for Cindy's newsletter on her website, www.cindymcwriter.com, and you will receive the first chapter of her latest book delivered directly to your inbox as a thank-you!

No worries!
*Cindy *does not* share e-mail addresses, and she *never* spams.*

About Cindy McDonald

For twenty-six years Cindy's life whirled around a song and a dance. She was a professional dancer/choreographer for most of her adult life and never gave much thought to a writing career until 2005. She often notes: Don't ask me what happened, but suddenly I felt drawn to my computer to write about things that I have experienced with my husband's Thoroughbreds and happenings at the racetrack—she muses: they are greatly exaggerated upon of course—I've never been murdered. Viola! Cindy's first book series, *Unbridled*, was born. Currently there are five books in the series.

Cindy is a huge fan of romantic suspense series', especially with a military ops theme. Although she isn't one to make New Year's resolutions, on New Year's Day 2013 she made a commitment to write one. At this time, there are four books in her black ops series, *First Force*: *Into the Crossfire*, *To the Breaking Pointe*, *Into the Dark.*, and *To the Brink*. Book number five *Into the Dawn* is scheduled to release in September of 2017.

People are always asking Cindy: Do you miss dance? With a bitter sweet smile on her lips she tells them: Sometimes I do. I miss my students. I miss choreographing musicals, but I love writing my books, and I love sharing them with my readers.

Cindy resides on her forty-five acre Thoroughbred farm with her husband, Bill and her Cocker Spaniel, Allister near Pittsburgh, Pennsylvania.

Into The Crossfire

BOOK #1 of the FIRST FORCE SERIES

A notorious killer leaves Jack Haliday's world in shambles.

It had been four years since ex-Navy SEAL, Jack Haliday, had an explosive run-in with a biker gang wounding their leader, Gunner. During those years Jack had acquired everything he ever wanted: a beautiful wife, an adorable daughter, and a lovely home in the suburbs—everything was as perfect as it could get, until Gunner returned to twist Jack's world inside-out with a vengeance that he could never have prepared for. Critically injured, he found himself surrounded in the security of First Force International and in the care of their head medic, Dr. Rayne Lee, a beautiful and compassionate woman who knows firsthand the sharp slice of loss and grief.

Now Jack has a score to settle and he's got some new friends to help him, but in the end, can Rayne help to ease his grief and encourage him to start a new life with team First Force?

Reviewers and readers love
INTO THE CROSSFIRE!

"This was a suspense-filled read that had me on the edge of my seat, I read it in one sitting as I just needed to know what happened." **~Scandolous Book Blog**

"*Into the Crossfire* is one heck of a read! It is filled with many emotions- anger, pain, agonizing heartbreak and beautiful love." **~Cat's Reviews**

"I couldn't put this book down, its fast paced, its chalk full of great story and characters. Wow what a powerful story." **~My Family's Heart Blog**

To The Breaking Pointe

Book #2 of the FIRST FORCE SERIES

Pushed to the breaking pointe!

Five years ago, First Force operative Grant Ketchum let the ballerina of his dreams dance out of his life. Silja Ramsay traveled to Russia to take the position of the principal dancer for the Novikov Ballet Company. She was living her dreams, and although they had very little contact, Grant was proud of her.

The owner of the ballet company, Natalia Novikov, has a dark secret: the ballet company is broke. Natalia has become so desperate for funds to keep the company afloat that she's forced her dancers to prostitute themselves to financial contributors at exclusive after-show parties.

Silja has been exempt and kept in the dark about the parties, until a big-time American financier, who is obsessed with Silja, offers to bail the failing ballet company out. His prerequisite: Silja must become his personal companion, live in his home, and fulfill his every desire.

Against her will, Silja is taken to the American's mansion, but before she goes she manages to send a text to the only man who can save her—Grant: HELP!

Now Grant Ketchum is on a mission to find his lost ballerina and rescue her from this powerful man's subjugation. He will do anything to get her out alive. If they survive, will he let her dance out of his life again?

Reviewers and readers love
To the Breaking Pointe!

"Love this series...This is an author to watch!"
~GA Bixler Reviews

"Cindy McDonald has created the perfect series with lots of wonderful characters." **~ Girl with Pen Blog**

"Cindy McDonald has given her readers a book worth reading more than once!" **~Stormy Nights Reviews**

Into The Dark

Book #3 from the FIRST FORCE SERIES

Ghosts from the past are chasing her!

our years ago, Dr. Rayne Lee lost her husband and her four-year-old daughter, Sierra, to a group of hostile guerrillas in the Amazonian Valley of Peru. It had taken every bit of her constitution to rebuild her life and to join her uncle's international security firm, First Force, as the team's head medic. She still desperately missed her husband and her daughter, but all-in-all everything was back on track—until the phone calls started.

A young girl was calling claiming to be Sierra. The tiny trembling voice claimed that the guerrillas were holding her captive, and there was only way for them to be reunited: Rayne must travel to Peru and give them something that she has. Moreover, the guerrillas have another stipulation: Rayne must come alone.

Suddenly the ghosts from Rayne's past are chasing her down a dark road.

What could they possibly want from her? Could she return to the place where her family was murdered and she was brutalized for seven horrid months? Was it really Sierra calling? Rayne knew she had to take the risk—she had to find out.

Reviewers and readers love
INTO THE DARK!

"Kudos to McDonald... I love how she is handling and developing this series! Really enjoyed this one and recommend it highly!" **~GA Bixler Reviews**

"If you are a fan of romance, military romance, and characters who are complex but written well, you will really enjoy this book." **~Stranded in Choas Book Blog**

"I love Cindy McDonald's writing and her way of telling a story. This is a must read." **~Girl with Pen Blog**